Trencher's Bloom

Trencher's Bunker Trilogy - Book III

Trencher's Breakout - Book II

Trencher's Bunker - Book I

Shane Noble

SHANE NOBLE

Cover Design by Elijah Hollis
Instagram: elijah_hollis

First paperback edition November 2024

ISBN: 978-1-7360486-4-1 (paperback)
ISBN: 978-1-7360486-5-8 (ebook)

10 9 8 7 6 5 4 3 2 1

To my hometown, Sullivan, Indiana.

Trencher's Bunker

Side View

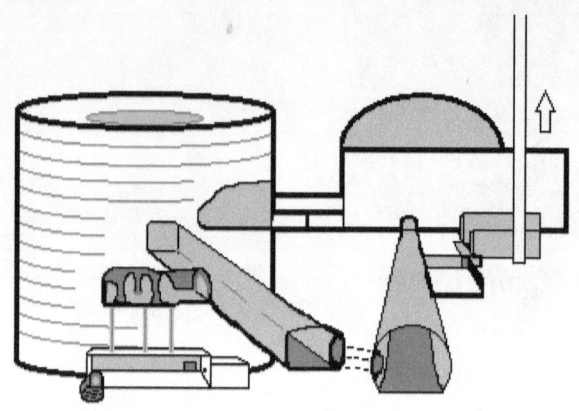

Top-Down

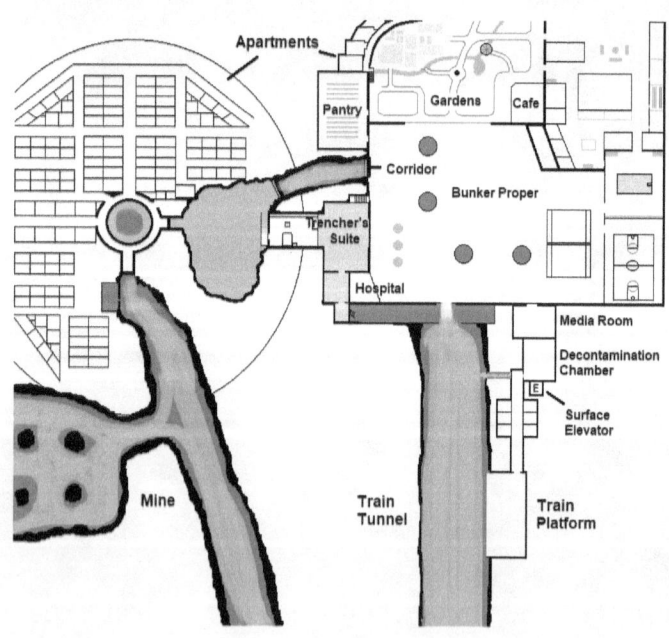

Bunker Network

Prologue

A matte-gray monstrosity landed softly on a remote countryside vertiport once reserved for Ag-Drones. Cleated skids clicked into the platform's grooves, and the transfer of power commenced.

This craft was no Ag-Drone. It was no big city air taxi, either. They never saw much of those in Sherman County, Indiana, even before the apocalypse.

Two men waited in a dug-out deer blind eighty yards out. A slab of corrugated steel and packed dirt hid their heat signature.

"Dougie, wake up! We got company."

The slumbering scout awoke with a start, kicking empty beer cans at his feet. He looked across the field at the insectoid machine sucking power from the battery array beneath it.

His partner, Chuck, tossed a pair of binoculars on his lap.

"Them things are a lot bigger up close."

"It ain't a mile in the sky," Chuck said. "Turn the camera on before we miss it."

Doug fumbled with the camcorder while Chuck studied the mechanized predator. Four missiles were clutched beneath each wing, with two larger bombs closer to the undercarriage. Six propellers spanned the top of the wings and sensors designed to sniff out humans hid somewhere within the nose, which faced away from them.

He spoke the details quietly for the recording.

Doug cracked open a skunked beer. "What now?"

"Recon only. Once we're clear, we get the footage back to the bunker."

Doug brushed the binoculars aside and picked up a rifle. "I bet I can knock off all six of them propellers in under a minute."

"Why not aim for the missiles?"

"Them things don't arm until they are launched," Doug said with unwarranted confidence. "I probably know more about military drones than anybody I know."

Chuck rolled his eyes and returned to scanning the drone for vulnerabilities. As militarized as the machine was, it was designed to hunt lightly armed humans at best. A glass cannon in the sky.

"Might be better to aim for the body," Chuck said. "It's some kind of plastic or carbon material, maybe even wood composite."

"Get ready to duck. I'm popping off a shot."

Doug pulled the trigger, and the shot rang out across the quiet countryside. They dove beneath the dugout's dirt ledge.

"You jackass! You're going to get us killed!"

Doug peeked over the ledge. The drone still sat

2

dormant on the pad.

"Sights ain't right. I'll pop off the rest and we'll step out and unload with the shotguns."

"The hell we are! You heard Trencher – recon only!"

Doug fired four more rounds in rapid succession. He set the rifle aside, grabbed a shotgun, and shimmied out of the blind on his beer gut.

Chuck cursed and grabbed his 12-gauge. They walked forty yards closer to the sleeping drone.

"Recon my ass," Doug said. "We cook this bird here and now."

They emptied their ammunition into the back end of the drone, hitting more often than not.

Chuck did not stick around to assess the damage. He turned to run before the last shell hit the ground.

Doug reloaded. When he bent to pick up the shells he had fumbled, the sickening *whirr* of propellers made him drop them again.

The drone disengaged from the vertiport and shot straight up as if it had leapt. It settled into a hover state fifty feet above before rotating 180-degrees to face them.

A spherical mechanism unfurled from the undercarriage. A barrel protruded from the sphere and gyrated as it took aim.

"Run!" Chuck yelled.

Doug froze.

The drone painted its first target with a green laser.

Chuck turned and continued his sprint to the dugout. He was fifteen yards away when his chest exploded. He fell face first in the mud, dead.

Doug managed to load a single shell. The drone watched him, as if curious. Then, the laser appeared just above his gut.

3

When he raised his shotgun, the drone fired, obliterating a softball-sized hole through his midsection. He remained standing and conscious for a spell before falling to his knees and folding to the earth.

The drone landed back on the pad and topped off its batteries.

Chapter One

Marcus Trencher sat at the bend of a U-shaped table in the newly designated War Room. It was once Ashley Cameron's suite before she was banished, and briefly served as the judge's chambers during the trial after Timothy Spencer discovered the separation between the two halves of the bunker.

Timothy sat to his right, Henry Plyman to his left. Robby Reed took up an end. The other seats were occupied by token representatives Marcus would have preferred not be there.

"We have a lot to cover, so let's keep it moving," Marcus said. "How are we on weapons?"

"The scouts brought in an arsenal," Robby said. "It's all stashed in houses up top, except for a couple gun cabinets for the guys watching the tunnel."

In the two weeks following his triumphant return to the bunker, Marcus deployed ten scout teams to the surface – two teams of three, the rest pairs. Too many traveling together would be too easy for drones to detect.

They only made moves under cloud cover, preferably during inclement weather. They were given a long list of supplies to gather in a sort of post-apocalyptic scavenger hunt. Their most important task, though, was to gather intel on the drones terrorizing the skies.

"Any word from the Bloomington?"

"Still nothing," Henry said. "Their engineers quit working on the tunnel rail gap. Kent said they disconnected the communications cable."

Their last interaction with the neighboring bunker beneath Bloomington – "the Quarry" – was a harrowing escape from it.

"I will head up an envoy."

"You're not going anywhere," Timothy said. "People there want you captured or killed."

"Y'all can stay put," Bill Douglass, one of the token members, said. "I'll go chat them folks up real good."

Marcus's face flashed red. Timothy cut in before Marcus could ridicule the man.

"Bill, your supervision in the mine is too valuable, but thank you."

"Type up talking points and I'll go," Henry said.

"I vote for Henry," Robby said. "He'll make a fine diplomat."

"Without a doubt," Marcus said. "But I've been there, I've established relationships. It's best I go myself. I do not foresee serious hostilities."

"Do you not remember the bullets whizzing by our heads in that rock quarry? You're too valuable." Robby turned to Henry. "Not that you aren't."

"Fine," Marcus conceded. "We will prep Henry for Bloomington. Moving on..."

"I'll cover surveillance," Timothy said. "We rigged a dozen looted doorbell cams around the elevator dome. Kent is setting up a live feed as we speak."

"And the train tunnel?"

"We snagged a hunting trail cam for that. It's a few miles past the train platform. We'll get notification if anything comes our way."

"Henry, how about the radio tower?"

"Not good. The tower was raised while the silo lid was jammed shut. The top was crushed before the motor burned out. Basically, it's broke on both ends."

Marcus rubbed his forehead. "Are the weather instruments salvageable? We need to know the weather if we want to travel. Praying for rain isn't cutting it."

"You know we have a meteorologist from WAYV 33 down here, right?" Robby said. "We should send a team to the station and steal the doppler radar or some shit."

Marcus mulled it over. The idea wasn't half bad.

"WVNI's weather reports were more accurate," Tammy Martin said, catapulting her to the top of Marcus's list of people he didn't want to hear speak. "...Their weather team had over 100 years combined experience. We should go to their station in Terre Haute."

Clay Boyle, another token appointee, guffawed.

"Their radar was junk. One time it snowed in downtown Terre Haute and didn't even show up."

"That was fake news perpetrated by WAYV!"

"People, please..." Marcus said.

Robby, Henry, and Timothy sat back and enjoyed the inane argument as much as Marcus despised it. The local weather wars somehow still sparked heated debate.

"...They could have 300 years' experience, but it don't mean a daggone thing if their radar can't tell snow from dingleberries!"

"You just like WAYV because of the bimbos they paraded up there!"

7

"I never cared for them liberal weather—"

"Stop *bickering*! We don't have time for this!" Marcus hunched over the table. "WAYV is closer. Clay, find the meteorologist and report to me within the hour. This meeting is adjourned."

The token representatives trickled out, sure to rush off and gossip. Marcus, Henry, and Timothy stuck around.

"They are insufferable. They bring nothing to the table."

"Best we keep them involved," Timothy said. "We are going to need them."

Marcus rolled his eyes. "Call me when they find the meteorologist."

He reached for the cord to pull the trapdoor ladder down to his suite.

"Not so fast. You're going the long way."

"We need you out and about," Henry said. "Public relations."

"Pat the kids on the head," Robby said, grinning.

Despite his popularity, not everyone in the bunker was happy with his return. He knew what he put them through – and he knew they knew.

Bunker denizens stopped to gawk the moment he left the War Room. They received quick nods and an averted gaze.

The entourage turned into the corridor linking the two halves of the bunker. Four men jogged in their direction. The first, Steve Mercer, was easily recognizable by his size. Two were scouts from the surface. The last, Kent Grieve, held a camcorder in his hand.

"You're going to want to see this."

Kent hooked the camcorder up to a laptop as they gathered around. The two scouts stood to the side, more enamored by the luxury of Marcus's suite than the footage they had retrieved.

The opening shot was that of a drone resting on a vertiport charging platform. It was grainy, but still offered intel. Marcus noted the propellers and munitions. He sketched out the shape of the craft and started labeling and estimating measurements.

The men behind the camera moved into view.

"They decided to shoot at it," Kent said. "Viewer discretion is advised."

They watched as a scout named Doug fired at the drone.

"I'm guessing he missed," Steve said. "Anyone know if drones react to sound?"

"Military drones do," Kent said. "The sensors are tiny and cheap. I can't imagine these don't have them."

"How do you know all this?" Robby said.

"I was a pretty serious hobbyist."

The scout fired four more shots in rapid succession and both men climbed out of the blind.

"What the hell are they doing?" Marcus said. "I told them recon only."

They popped off shotgun blasts from halfway across the field. One turned to sprint back while the other stayed and reloaded. The drone hovered from the platform and rotated to face them.

"Oh, shit," Robby said.

The fleeing man almost made it back to the dugout. If it were not so gruesome and real, the death scene could have been called cinematic.

"I don't need to see this," Steve said, stepping aside.

"Rewind it," Marcus said, unbothered. "Was that a laser?"

He added the gun mount to his diagram and noted the green laser. As the drone narrowed its sights on the other man, Henry and Robby bowed out.

"I don't want to watch these guys die," Robby said. "I knew them."

"What is it doing?" Marcus said, eyes still glued to the screen. "It's locked in but doesn't fire for several seconds. Why would it wait?"

"That's not very autonomous of it," Timothy said.

"A human decision is being made remotely," Kent said. "Definitely not autonomous."

"This has been very informative." Marcus closed the laptop. "Have the families been notified?"

One of the scouts cleared his throat. "Yes, sir. Happening now."

"What are your names? You guys deserve a reward."

"I'm Cal, he's Luke. It's fine we don't need nothing. We'd rather get back up there."

"We had cloud cover to work with, sir," Luke said.

Marcus was pleasantly surprised.

"In that case, I have just the mission for you."

* * *

Clay the committee member rang at the suite's ground level door. Marcus buzzed him up.

"Found your meteorologist, Mr. Trencher."

"Thanks, Clay. We'll take it from here."

Marcus welcomed her in and shut Clay out.

Cami Stinnett was a year into her first weather gig at

WAYV33 when the end times came. She lacked the decades of experience the Terre Haute news team had, but she would do.

The twenty-something year old blushed. She had never met such a formerly rich and famous person.

Marcus motioned for her to have a seat.

"As I'm sure you've heard, drones have been patrolling the area. Our scout teams move only when they have dense cloud cover. We'd like to gain a better understanding of the forecast for when we make bigger moves and longer trips. If we got you to the WAYV station, do you think you could operate the doppler radar?"

Her eyebrows raised in fright.

"Cal and Luke will be with you," Henry said. "They know how to move around safely."

"Didn't two guys just die up there? People are talking about it."

"They foolishly picked a fight with a drone," Marcus said. "Your guides will do no such thing."

Cal and Luke nodded.

"Even if my logins and the radar still work, how do we get the forecast out? There's a lot of tech stuff that I might not know how to work."

"We have a tower we are raising that will receive signals."

She thought about it with eight men eagerly awaiting her decision.

"Okay, I'll give it a shot."

There was a sigh of relief. Henry and Robby high-fived. Cal and Luke ushered her out of the suite. Marcus turned to his trusted team.

"She is right. They need someone tech-savvy."

Timothy and Kent looked at each other.

"Draw straws?" Kent said.

Timothy sighed. "No. I'll go." He looked at Steve, who he had been through so much with. "How about you, big guy? Want to gain some field experience?"

Steve smiled. "Count me in."

Chapter Two

It was early August, but the geoengineered tampering with Mother Nature made it difficult to predict the weather day-to-day. Temperatures had climbed as high as the 80's. Just weeks earlier, the ground was covered in snow and temperatures were in the negatives – in July.

Marcus opened the elevator dome man door to a blustery day of light rain and low-hanging clouds. Bad weather was good weather.

Cami was particularly enamored. It was her first time to the surface in over a year.

"Even better than this morning," Luke said. "Safe to drive in this."

The scout teams had accumulated a dozen pickup trucks at the site, bringing new vehicles back with every expedition. A camouflaged canopy was in the works, but for now, they tossed limbs and other debris on to hide them the best they could.

Cal and Luke cleared the brush from their truck while Timothy and Steve loaded provisions in the back. Cami climbed into the cab.

"See you guys in a day or two," Timothy said. "Check in on my daughters if you don't mind."

"Will do," Marcus said. "And Cami, these guys will have you back in no time."

"I'm just happy to see the sky again."

They waved as the truck departed and quickly turned their attention to the radio tower silo.

Henry and Robby backed up two trucks to opposite sides of the silo. The faulty lid was already pried open. Marcus returned to the dome to communicate with Kent via doorbell cam.

Henry and Robby fed long, heavy chains down the sides of the silo. When there were only a few feet of slack left, they whipped the chains to send waves down below until the hooks latched onto the tower cross beams.

They inched the trucks forward until fifteen feet of the tower peeked. Marcus jammed rebar through the tower to prop it up.

They unlatched the chains, dropped them down the silo, and relatched them four more times. When all said and done, the tower peeked sixty feet above ground.

"I feel like we just filmed a Chevy truck commercial," Robby said.

* * *

The scouts Cal and Luke, along with Timothy, Steve, and Cami, pulled into the WAYV News station after an uneventful journey across the county. Radio towers loomed above. One still had a functioning red light blinking at the top.

Cami punched in a security code at the employee

14

entrance and got a green light. Lights clicked on, illuminating the empty studio.

"This is so spooky," Cami said.

"You'll get used to it," Luke said. "Cal and I will have a look around. Y'all do what you've got to do."

Cami went to her old cubicle while Timothy and Steve checked out the on-air set. They took on their best news anchor postures and said stupid lines.

"I'm in," Cami said. "Can't believe my password still works."

After a few moments of troubleshooting, she pulled up a map of the local area. The first thin slice of a sweeping circle unveiled various shades of green. After a minute, green pixels covered most of the map.

"Looks like light rain."

"It works!" Timothy said. "Now see if you can broadcast it."

Cami ducked into the control room and powered the necessary systems. She made the rounds to the cameras and a monitor off-camera near the weather green screen. An On-Air light came on near the stage.

"Is this for real? Are we on?" Steve said.

Cami shrugged. "I think so."

"I'm breaking radio silence." Timothy grabbed his handheld radio. "Base, this is Scout Team One. Acknowledge."

A burst of static preceded competing voices.

"Bro, your radio speak is on point," Robby said. "We hear you loud and clear."

"Turn to channel 33. You should be able to see me, too."

Robby kept the button held down, letting everyone at the station hear the scramble to turn on the TV.

15

"We kind of see you," Robby said. "Don't you know not to wear green in front of those things?"

Timothy flipped them off with floating hands.

Marcus wrestled the radio from Robby. "Excellent work. Now get out of the way so Cami can tell us what we're looking at."

Half-invisible Timothy exited; Cami stepped into frame.

"As you can see, light rain across the viewing area." She waved a hand across the map. "It is breaking up to the west. Clear skies possible this evening, but it is hard to tell. We don't have data outside of doppler range."

"That'll have to do," Marcus said. "Go ahead and shut it down until Timothy sets up a more secure means of communication. Good work so far."

* * *

Marcus put out a call in the bunker to recruit someone who had experience operating a radio. As tech-savvy as Kent was, he was lost with the old "Boomer" technology.

Jack Pigg, a long-haul trucker that went by Big Pigg, and Eddie Cole, a 9-1-1 dispatcher, came directly from the mines. They tracked coal dust in with their boots.

"Gentlemen, our radio tower is up, and we need this station manned at all hours. You fellas up for it, or do you prefer the mine?"

"Mother always said I had a face for radio," Big Pigg said. "What are we listening for?"

"Anything and everything. We can always decide whether to reach out."

Jack and Eddie agreed to the no-brainer offer.

Marcus glanced at his watch. He motioned for Henry

and Robby to follow him down to the tunnel train platform, which to that point, had never welcomed a train. There, they met bored men armed with assault rifles.

"Any visitors from Bloomington?"

The sentries jumped to their feet.

"No, sir. No tunnel crew, either."

Marcus sighed. Whatever was going on down-tunnel was unlikely to be favorable.

"I don't like this. It's time we take precautions."

"Such as?" Henry said.

"Let's set up a barricade and rig it with explosives."

Chapter Three

Timothy rummaged through software code while Cami tinkered with the station's weather instrumentation and broadcast machinery. Steve tagged along with Cal and Luke to take advantage of the remaining cloud cover and scout the nearby town of Farmersburg.

"That third cup of coffee was a bad idea." Timothy pressed his palms to his eyes. "What are you up to over there?"

"Seeing what all we have to work with. You?"

"We had our own satellites – and by 'we' I mean *Trencher Industries* – and they're still up there. We should be able to route broadcasts through them and not have to worry about bad guys picking it up."

"Is it ready? I'm starting the doppler to let it get a few laps in."

"Let me give them a heads up." Timothy grabbed the radio. "Scout Team One reporting. Please acknowledge. Over."

Static blared, then an unfamiliar voice. "Scout Team One, this is Big Pigg. State your business. Over."

Timothy was baffled. "Is...Marcus around?"

"...Sorry, I'm here," Marcus said. "We brought in Eddie and Jack to man the radio. *Huh?* --Excuse me, Eddie and *Big Pigg*. Any progress?"

"We're linked to our satellites. Let me know when you're in the app."

Marcus logged into the old company portal and opened the stream. Cami was ready and waiting at the green screen.

"...rain has moved out of the area. Skies are partly cloudy and will continue to clear...and the wind has tapered down. I would say a drone advisory is in effect."

Unlike the old days when she reported improving weather, nobody was happy. Bad weather was good weather.

Oh, and I also wanted to show you guys something..."

She stepped off screen and the doppler graphic reset. A single pixel blipped southeast of Sherman, near the Knox County line.

"What are we looking at?"

"I found a setting that detects aircraft. That pixel is a drone, I'm assuming."

The radial line continued, revealing two more blips over Terre Haute.

Before Marcus could tell her how great it was, Kent caught on. He leaned across Marcus and pressed the push-to-talk button.

"Shut it down! If you can see them, they can see you!"

The doppler completed another lap while Cami went off camera.

All three blips appeared closer to the station before the feed cut out. It was all Kent needed to see to determine that the drones had the station pinged and triangulated.

"Get out of there! You have five minutes, tops!"

19

Timothy shoved his laptop in his bag and Cami powered down the control room.

"The guys took the truck," Timothy said. "C'mon, we'll have to run somewhere."

"No, we have the Storm Chaser!"

Cami pulled a set of keys from a drawer and tossed them. They ran outside and jumped into a satellite-topped news van.

Timothy floored it down the drive and turned north into the south-bound lanes on U.S. 41. Twilight was turning to dusk. A quarter mile from the station, they spotted a house. He slammed on the brakes and jumped out, leaving the van on the highway next to a fog-filled graveyard. The joyride lasted all of two minutes.

Cami hesitated.

"Get out! We don't want that thing parked next to the house!"

They sprinted across the highway to a common country home. He busted out a window on a side door to unlock it. Automated smart home lights clicked on. He opened the breaker box and cut power to everything, figuring it was the quickest way to turn them all out.

"There's a basement! Go!"

Cami got to the first step but lingered to see why he didn't follow. Instead, he went to the kitchen and emptied the refrigerator.

"What are you doing?"

"I want to watch. It's okay, get in the basement."

Cami hid below while he shimmied the refrigerator to the living room. He grabbed a roll of aluminum foil from atop the stove.

It was a tight squeeze, and it smelled awful, but he fit. He fashioned a foil hat and covered whatever else he could to further obfuscate his heat signature.

He mulled over whether to get out and pull the sheer curtains apart but decided against it. He had a filtered view of the Storm Chaser van beyond the front lawn, across the highway.

Five minutes passed with nothing but eerie silence.

Cami called from the basement steps with a whispery voice, "Are we okay?"

"I think so, false al—." A faint buzz interrupted. "...Never mind. We have company."

Outside, a menacing drone descended upon the news van. After close study, it rotated toward the house.

He held his breath, as if a murderer was in the room and he was hiding in the closet. He pulled the refrigerator door as closed as he could and draped another ribbon of foil across his body.

Light flooded through the windows. The house was under spotlight.

He squinted through the ajar door. The sheer curtains over the window were opaque in the light. Leaving them shut turned out to be a wise decision. The spotlight disappeared.

The whir of propellers faded. As much as he wanted to wait it out a bit longer, the cramping in his right leg became unbearable. He set a foot outside the refrigerator. As his toe hit the carpet, the eerie quiet was shattered.

A concussive blast blew in the windows and slammed the refrigerator door on his ankle. As the door swung open, he caught a glimpse of an unfurling fireball. The Storm Chaser was blown to oblivion.

He burst out of the refrigerator and scrambled to the basement door before leaping half the stairs in a single bound. He joined Cami beneath a work bench. He looked like the Tin Man in his foil armor. She would have laughed had she not been scared to death.

"That was a stupid, *stupid* idea," he said.

* * *

Marcus waited an hour in the media room for Timothy to radio in. An hour was reasonable considering the circumstances, but he worried. He then worried that his worrying looked bad.

"Call me when he radios in. I don't care if it's 2am."

Bigg Pigg nodded. "You got it, boss."

Marcus retired to his suite, anxious and foggy yet unable to sleep, and too groggy to be productive.

He tried drafting talking points for Henry's diplomatic mission to Bloomington. He scribbled a few bullet points but didn't make it far. It was difficult to find motivation when he thought he should be going instead.

He flipped the notepad back to his drone sketch. He completed it by adding in the charging platform and battery array beneath it.

There had to be a way to eliminate the drone threat, or at the very least alleviate it. Relying on the fickle weather wasn't good enough. For the most part, they were still stuck underground.

He had control over the power grid and could shut off charging platforms across the Midwest, but he wasn't ready to play that card yet. A more decisive blow could be dealt with that kind of power.

He set the notepad aside and grabbed a prescription bottle. He rattled it. One capsule left. His other medications ran out two days prior. He feared what withdrawal would bring. He was already struggling with focus.

Refills would have to come from Bloomington. Yet another reason he should be making the trip.

Just when he started to doze off, the intercom by his bedside buzzed.

"Hey boss, Big Pigg. Timothy Spencer made contact. They are safe."

Chapter Four

Timothy and Cami awoke to a creaking door and boots on linoleum tile and broken glass.

"Anybody home?"

They climbed the basement stairs to greet Steve, Cal, and Luke, who were in the living room doing mental math on why there was a refrigerator in the middle of it.

"We were a half-mile up the road when we heard the explosion," Cal said. "Looks like y'all might need a ride."

"Yes, but not yet," Timothy said. "Give me a few hours at the news station and I'll have it set up to run remotely."

* * *

While the men busied themselves with war and diplomacy, Brittney, Mariya, and Mercedes performed meal prep for the scout teams, alongside Brad and Becky Farris.

Mercedes had planned to leave the bunker but agreed to train a team to handle the water treatment plant before departing. Now it seemed she was stuck.

"Anyone else think it's sexist that the guys get to play

Drone Wars while we are stuck in the kitchen?" Mercedes said. "No offense, Brad."

"None taken," Brad said. "My manhood is secure. I got shot, remember?"

"If it's any consolation, we tend to live longer." Becky glared at her husband.

"They are Midwestern tech bros," Mariya said. "Smart, talented, powerful... but incapable of recognizing how much luck played a role in their success. At least they are nicer than the jackasses I dated in Silicon Valley."

"Marcus figured some stuff out when I was his assistant, like how to fry an egg, but he could barely function in about every other way," Brittney said.

"At least most of us only ran restaurants and backhoes and stuff," Brad said. "Not mega corporations buying off politicians."

"Don't act all high and mighty," Becky said. "You took a whole two minutes to accept Marcus's offer to buy our restaurant."

Brad shrugged. "Got me there."

"Why are we letting them lead us into a confrontation with a secret superpower that has supposedly already killed billions of people?" Mercedes said. "We should keep our heads down and survive."

"If we do nothing, people keep dying all over the world," Mariya said. "What if they are the only ones left that can do anything about it?"

* * *

Robby and Melonie walked hand-in-hand on the looping path through the bunker gardens. She was entering her third trimester and was as radiant as ever. He felt more prepared to wage guerilla warfare than to face fatherhood.

"I don't want you to go on any more missions," Melonie said.

"Babe, I can't just stay back while everyone else does their part. My life is no more valuable than theirs."

"It is to me! There are plenty of guys ready to fight. You can help in other ways."

He would have argued more vehemently, but he had the strange feeling of not wanting to. She cared about him, and he reckoned he liked that.

"...You're not saying anything! Promise me you'll stay with me."

"You're right, I can't run off and die and have some other man teach my son how to cuss and fight. My daughter, either, if it's a girl."

* * *

With a few final keystrokes, Timothy successfully programmed the news station to be operated remotely. The rest of the team was half-asleep. He was slightly dismayed by the subdued praise.

"Good deal," Steve said. "So back to the bunker?"

"What do you say, Cami?" Timothy said. "I haven't looked outside in hours."

"Rainy and windy, but clearing up soon," she said. "We better go now, because..."

"Bad weather is good weather," they said in unison.

* * *

Henry stood in a do-nothing managerial pose in the train tunnel as the crew began construction on a series of barricades. Marcus assigned him as the project manager for reasons that eluded him, and the men.

Marcus rolled up on his electronic motorcycle to check in.

"Hey man, these guys don't need me at all," Henry said before Marcus could even get off his bike. "Shouldn't we review talking points for Bloomington?"

"These defenses are important, so I wanted you supervise," Marcus said.

"I've not contributed a single thing." Henry laughed out of frustration. "If you want me to know what I'm doing tomorrow at the Quarry, we need to gameplan."

"Fine, I'll take you off the barricade project, but the talking points can wait until tomorrow morning. I'm battling a migraine."

"You've been having a lot of those lately."

Marcus got back on his motorcycle.

"Just a lack of sleep. Go ahead and release the men for the night. They can place the ordinance tomorrow. I'll see you bright and early."

* * *

Marcus watched the tunnel cameras from his suite until Henry and the crew departed. A teenaged kid in a ball cap was assigned sentry duty.

He shut his laptop and slid it in his backpack along with a couple snacks. He wouldn't be gone long.

When the hour was sufficiently late, he snuck through the passage behind his bathroom mirror. He glanced out at the bunker proper and gardens. Not a soul in sight. He unplugged his bike from the charger and rolled it into the train tunnel.

At the barricade, the bored teenaged sentry scrambled to his feet.

Marcus tossed him a snack size packet of Oreos.

"Mind if I borrow your hat?"

"Uh, no, here. Are...are you going to Bloomington?"

"You never saw me."

He rolled between the barricades and gunned it on the other side. He wanted to make good time to the Quarry.

Chapter Five

Marcus sped down the tunnel on his electric motorcycle, giddy like a teenager sneaking out in the middle of the night.

It was the middle of the night, not that one could tell underground.

He felt the thrill of rebellion. He felt free.

Undercutting Henry's diplomatic mission was not his intention, but it was just easier to do it all himself.

He arrived at the Quarry at half-past 4 a.m. He stashed his bike next to a padlocked maintenance room near the end of the tunnel.

The train station was open and empty. All quiet on the eastern front. He gazed up at the Indiana University championship banners above the east tunnel. They looked a bit dusty.

He climbed the right platform and entered the quarantine area in which he was sequestered during his first visit to the Quarry. Beneath the sterile mattress of his temporary room, he found the gun he had ditched all that time ago.

The coast remained clear on the platform, until he

was halfway over the crosswalk. Someone was approaching. He crouched and watched.

His fear subsided when he recognized that it was his bunker-architect friend, Jim Cox.

"Hello? Anybody there?"

"Jim, it's me, Marcus."

He came out of hiding and met Jim on the bunker side platform. The portly man was in still in his pajamas.

"What on earth are you doing here? You aren't safe!"

They climbed the subway-styled stairs that led to the rest of the bunker. At the top, the sound of a hand dryer in the nearby restroom let them know someone was about to step out.

"Let me talk to this guard," Jim whispered. "I'll meet you in the theatre."

As Marcus took off, Jim knocked on the bathroom door. He took on a jovial tone. "Got a notification of movement in the tunnel..."

Marcus sprinted across the atrium, onto the fitness track, and to the front of the theatre. A poster caught his eye. "Suspected undocumented visitors" were to be reported to the authorities. There was also a curfew.

A minute later, Jim joined him in the back row of the theatre.

"A family of raccoons got down in the tunnels and keep setting off our sensors. The guard won't suspect a thing."

"Wildlife has migrated back into the area after the thaw. Maybe they climbed down a shaft."

Jim was confused. He knew nothing of a thaw.

"Thaw? Never mind that. Why are you here?"

"There's been no communication between our bunkers. The crews that were laying the power line and the tracks to close the rail gap all left."

"Word got back to Carmel about your escape. The agents that fired at you were gunned down by the turret outside the vault doors. Quadruple the agents and soldiers showed up on the next train, and they keep coming. They've taken over."

"What are they planning?"

"To seize your bunker! They are going to take the train up to the rail gap, unload and start marching."

"That won't end well for anyone. It'll be Thermopylae meets Waco."

"Our higher-ups have begged for diplomacy, but they don't listen. They are calling you a terrorist. The people aren't buying the propaganda, but what can they do?"

"More than they think." He pulled his backpack over his shoulder. "We need to wake up my friend, Genie. It's time everyone knows the truth, including you."

* * *

They evaded the night shift patrols through the public spaces and "the Stacks" where the several thousand Quarry residents lived. Marcus knocked at Genie's door.

"It's bloody 5 a.m. Who is it?"

"Genie, it's Marcus and Jim."

She looked both ways in the empty hall and let them in. Her vibrant multicolored hair had faded since he last saw her.

"You're a popular guy these days," Genie said. "To what do I owe the pleasure?"

He tossed her a thumb drive. "I need you to load a video to the metaverse."

"Piece of cake. What's on it?"

31

"Something to make life difficult for our friends from Carmel. Release it this morning, after I leave."

He tucked his laptop back in his backpack.

"Where can I reconnect the communications cable between our bunkers?"

"There's a room off the tunnel, about thirty yards from the train station," Jim said. "Don't ask me what to do with the tangle of wires in there."

"Unlock it and I'll do the rest."

"What do you hope to spark with this video?"

"Revolution."

* * *

While Jim made his way to the tunnel, Marcus lurked two storefronts down from the Quarry Pharmacy. It was still early, but the bunker was stirring to life.

A tall, thin man strolled by, oblivious. He unlocked the grating in front of the pharmacy and sent it coiling above. He disappeared inside. When the neon sign lit up, Marcus stepped out of the shadows.

Bells jangled as he opened the door. The pharmacist was at the secure door leading behind the counter.

"Ah, an early bird..."

He turned and recognized Marcus. The ball cap wasn't much of a disguise.

Marcus pointed his gun. "Stop there. I need my prescriptions filled and that's it."

"This is totally unnecessary."

"Walk."

They went to the back. Marcus lined up his empty prescription bottles on the counter.

The pharmacist read the labels and went to the

computer. He found what was needed from the shelves and didn't try anything stupid.

"This should last you months."

Marcus shoveled the bottles in his bag and directed the pharmacist back to the front door. They stepped out to the concourse at a quarter past 6 a.m.

"Lock up and wait until I'm gone before you open back up. Everything you've heard about me is a lie."

"Whatever, man. I just want to live."

He backed away as the pharmacist pulled the metal grate down. He ducked into a stairwell and ran to ground level, emerging at the basketball courts. Early risers were stretching in the workout area but paid him no mind.

He encountered no guards in the atrium or at the train platform. His confidence swelled. Almost home free.

He hopped down to the tracks and turned right into the tunnel. His bike was still there, and thanks to Jim, the maintenance room was unlocked.

Inside, a blue cable as thick as a firehose lay unplugged from its obvious port. He plugged it in.

When he opened the door to leave, he was greeted by eight glowing yellow eyes.

"*Jesus...*"

A family of raccoons looked on with curiosity before ambling off toward the platform. He laughed.

He jumped on his motorcycle and lifted the kickstand, still amused by the minor scare.

"*Hey, you little bastards!*" a man yelled at the mouth of the tunnel. "Hey..."

Marcus looked back at the guard, who clearly saw him. The raccoons paused in the middle. He started the electronic engine and took off.

"*Hey! Stop!*"

Gunshots rang out and ricochets sparked off the tunnel walls.

Then, a bullet caught his right shoulder.

He yanked the handlebar, sending the bike into an uncontrollable wobble. The front tire caught when the angle became too severe, sending him flying.

He tumbled more than skid – he had not reached top speed – but still lost some skin. None of the abrasions, bumps, or bruises superseded the sting from the bullet.

The bike came to a rest ten yards back with only cosmetic damage. The guard was a tiny silhouette at the tunnel mouth. He crawled to the bike and got back on to continue his escape.

* * *

He rolled up to the barricades battered and bloody. The teenaged sentry stood, dumbfounded.

"Remember, you never saw me."

"Are you okay, Mr. Trencher?"

"I'm fine. Hit a raccoon. Here's your hat back."

He tossed the ball cap to the kid and finished the last leg of tunnel. He dragged himself up the steps to his trapdoor, unlocked it, and stumbled into his bathroom. He shut the door and looked in the mirror.

His right cheek and forehead were scraped. Blood ran down his forearm and his palms were raw. He turned to see the bullet wound. A red circle stained his shirt. His heart pounded and he was overcome with dizziness.

He grabbed a towel and went to his sofa. He balled the towel up, laid his wound on it, and passed out.

Chapter Six

Marcus opened his eyes and stared at the ceiling in a state of confusion, not immediately recognizing where he was or how he got there. There was a knock at his door.

"Marcus, wake up," Henry said.

Pain radiated from his shoulder. He stood, felt dizzy, and sat back down. The white towel was dyed deep red all the way through. He threw it in the bathroom and struggled mightily to put on an overshirt. He took a deep breath and let Henry in.

"About time. I went ahead and wrote some of my own talking points – *woah*, what happened to you?"

"Bike wreck in the tunnel last night. Hit a raccoon."

"Damn, that's random. Need to see a nurse?"

"I will, after you show me what you've come up with."

Henry sat on the sofa where the bloody towel was a moment before. Marcus groaned as he sat beside him.

As Henry spoke energetically about interbunker diplomacy, Marcus nodded off.

"...and then I was thinking...Marcus?"

Henry set his tablet aside and touched the wet couch. He lifted his hand and found it covered in blood. "What the? Marcus, wake up!"

"Huh? I'm fine. I'm f..." Marcus slumped forward.

* * *

Brad was keeping Becky company while she worked her nursing shift in the bunker hospital. A middle-aged man with high blood pressure occupied a bed, but it was an otherwise quiet morning.

That is, until Henry barreled in dragging Marcus with an arm over his shoulder.

"He wrecked his bike in the tunnel last night and tried to sleep it off. He's bleeding everywhere."

Brad helped prop Marcus on a bed and removed his overshirt. Becky began assessing his wounds and quickly decided to cut the undershirt off with scissors.

She rolled him to his side to see his back.

"The cuts and abrasions look worse than they are. We'll x-ray for broken bones – but the gunshot wound is a bigger issue."

"Gunshot? Are you sure it's not a raccoon bite?"

"Jesus, Henry. I can tell the difference!"

"He said he hit a raccoon! Maybe it ran up and bit him." He leaned over Marcus. "Were you shot?"

"Shot."

"Stings like a bitch, doesn't it?" Brad said with some satisfaction. It wasn't that long ago that Marcus had shot him in the shoulder during a bout of madness.

"Who shot you? How far down the tunnel..." Henry stood back as he connected the dots. "You went to Bloomington, didn't you?"

Marcus smiled weakly and shut his eyes.

"He's getting loopy," Brad said. "I think he's lost a lot

of blood."

"No shit, Brad," Becky said. "Go get Dr. Nora. She is going to have to work on him."

Henry leaned back over Marcus. "You couldn't let me handle the trip on my own, could you?"

"That's enough!" Becky said. "Out!"

* * *

Henry opted not to return to the hospital with Brad and Dr. Nora Weinstein. He took the elevator down to the ground floor on the other side. He needed someone to vent to.

A line of tables fixed with unlit grow lights cluttered the hall. A project was underway to expand the farm lab. He spotted Mariya transplanting a sprout.

"What are you doing down here? Done prepping for the trip already?"

"Marcus screwed me over. He couldn't let me handle any responsibility."

She tossed her gloves on a table. "What happened?"

He ranted for the better part of the return to the other side of the bunker. His grievances stretched all the way back to his days working for *Trencher Industries* when Marcus would constantly intervene on his projects.

When they stepped out into the bunker proper, they found Robby and Timothy chatting.

"Bro, Timothy rigged the weather station to work remotely," Robby said.

"It was nothing, really," Timothy said.

"That's great," Henry said, distracted.

"Are you about to head over to Bloomington?"

"Don't get him started," Mariya said.

37

"Marcus snuck out on his motorcycle last night and already paid them a visit. Oh, and he got shot and wrecked his bike."

"Why? Wait – he got *shot*?"

Robby and Timothy took off to the hospital. Neither Becky nor Dr. Nora appreciated the guests.

Marcus was already prepped for surgery, awake and semi-coherent, but still loopy.

"Everyone out," Dr. Nora said. "He is stable, but we need space."

They stood outside, collectively dumbfounded.

"Obviously since they are shooting at people, your trip is off," Timothy said. "Sorry, Henry."

Henry shook his head. "I don't know what he was doing there."

"Hopefully we get to ask him," Robby said. "Bummer about your trip, bro, and sorry but I need to go pick Melonie something up to eat."

"I better get some things done as well," Timothy said. "We're radioing weather reports to the scout teams. I'll check on Marcus in an hour or two."

Henry, clearly dismayed, was left with Mariya.

"Want to help out in the farm lab?"

Thoughts ran through his head. Mariya could almost see them racing by, but not the one that came out.

"I'm going...Do you want to come with me?"

"To that other bunker? It's too dangerous. You all agreed..."

"I did not agree," he snapped. "Sorry...we could do a lot of good reaching out. Plus, we can see my parents."

She looked around to see who would notice if they slipped away that very moment.

Henry met Mariya at the tunnel entrance on an ATV. He handed her a helmet.

"It's faster than the golf carts."

They covered the distance to the barricade where he expected the crew to ignore him like they usually did, but a foreman flagged him down.

"All set on the barricades," the foreman said. "Should we start planting the dynamite like Trencher laid out?"

"Sure, go ahead," Henry said. "And schedule two more sentries for the next couple shifts. Oh, and when you get back, tell Marcus that Mariya and I have departed for Bloomington. Diplomatic mission."

They walked between the barricades to a smart car on the other side.

"Not my first choice for a vacation destination," Mariya said, "but it'll be a nice change of scenery."

"I'll take you somewhere exotic on our next trip."

"Oh, on our honeymoon?"

"Might be skipping a step," he said with a blushing smile. "But I'll figure that part out."

He shifted into drive and took her hand.

They were off to the Quarry, unbeknownst to them that Marcus's brief overnight foray had already set off a storm.

Chapter Seven

Marcus called a meeting at his hospital bedside. A registry of blood types proved useful in getting a timely transfusion. The lucky donor was a teenager who had been working part time as a sentry in the tunnel.

"Heard you have your very own blood boy. That's so *billionaire* of you." Robby noticed that the teenager was still there, on the last bed to his left. "Oh, hey kid. Thanks for saving our dear leader."

"No problem. He hooked me up with some Oreos," the kid said lifting a cookie.

"We can handle things while you rest," Timothy said. "Give yourself a day out of surgery, at least."

Marcus waved dismissively with his good arm, which still made him wince.

"I'm fine," he said. "Don't want to delay our plans up top. Where is Henry?"

"Probably sulking after you sabotaged his diplomatic mission," Robby said. "What the hell were you doing in Bloomington, anyway?"

"I leaked the drone footage on the metaverse. Everyone in the Quarry and every other bunker in the network now knows the truth."

"The whole truth?"

"I laid out that there was no asteroid, exposed the depopulation program and how the weather was being geoengineered, the drones. All of it. I added text cut scenes and a voice over. Not the greatest production value, but it got the message across."

"A little chaotic," Timothy said. "Not worth risking your life – and you need to run this stuff by us – but overall...I like it."

"They sent troops in from Carmel after my previous escape. They are gearing up to seize our bunker. Hopefully an uprising keeps them occupied."

"We'll put our guys in the tunnel on high alert."

"What's our next move up top?" Robby said.

Marcus grabbed a sketchpad from his bedside table. "We're going to capture a drone."

"Hell yeah." Robby grabbed the drawing.

Before they could dive into the details, a foreman from the barricade knocked and peeked his head in.

"Mr. Trencher, the barricades are finished, and ordinance planted. Just up to y'all to wire the trigger."

"Excellent work," Marcus said. "One last thing – schedule two more armed sentries in case Bloomington sends trouble our way."

"Already done, sir. Henry Plyman told us to do so on his way out."

"His way out? Henry went to Bloomington?"

"Yes, sir. He and his girlfriend. Diplomatic mission, he said."

* * *

Henry and Mariya spotted a literal light at the end of the

tunnel. They rolled to a stop in the service lane and saw no one ahead. Henry backed the smart car into a recess designated for parking and turning around.

"Not the welcome I was expecting, but at least nobody is shooting at us."

Mariya found a squiggly tire track in the gravel and a broken mirror, presumably from Marcus's bike. They passed a maintenance room and the tunnel mouth into the train station.

They climbed the wider platform to their left. It was eerily empty, but they heard yelling – an entire crowd's worth. They jogged to a set of subway-styled stairs.

The swell of sound increased with every step. At the top, they found an angry mob filling a vast open space. Twelve stories of balconies teemed with more people. What they were upset about, they had not a clue.

Soldiers in riot gear held off a section of ground right of the stairs. The end soldier was too preoccupied to notice them. Officials behind the line were setting up a microphone and projector.

Mariya nudged Henry and nodded toward one of the officials behind the wall of soldiers. They both recognized one of the women.

Marcus exiled Ashley Cameron from their bunker shortly after his return. It didn't take her long to latch on to a new power. She stood with the enemy.

They melted into the fuming crowd of approximately 5,000 and pushed through to less density.

Mariya tapped on a man on the shoulder. "What is going on?"

"You haven't been on the metaverse today? Drones are hunting humans up on the surface, and the weather isn't what they told us. It said there wasn't ever an asteroid!"

Henry started to realize what Marcus had done.

"...You know Marcus Trencher, the billionaire? He leaked a video. He says everything's a lie, and I believe him! We want answers from these fuckers from Carmel!"

Henry pulled Mariya further back into the crowd until they found themselves on a patch of astroturf. It may have been a putting green.

A woman's voice came over a loudspeaker, provoking both boos and hushes. The crowd gravitated tighter towards the area blocked off by the riot guard.

"*Attention, attention. Please quiet down and we will address your concerns.*"

Hushes drowned out the boos and all eyes pointed to the limestone wall above the woman, where a projector beamed a freeze frame from the drone video. It was distorted and the lighting made it difficult to see.

"This morning, a video went viral across the interbunker metaverse. We have analyzed its source and would like to share our findings." She played a clip before pausing. "Our recognition AI matched the footage to a video from the conflict in Ukraine, Fall of 2025. The Russian drone landed on a helicopter pad, not a charging pad. The video has been heavily doctored..."

The video played on, showing the man shot in front of the camera, but now with a cartoonish blood splatter. The crowd, who had watched the video on repeat much of the day, were not fooled.

"*Bullshit!*" a man yelled.

"*That wasn't on the original! Y'all added that!*"

Projectiles rained down from the balconies and the crowd surged. Henry held onto Mariya as they were carried with the mass of bodies.

The woman and her team, including Ashley, fled

down to the train platform. The riot guard blocked the stairwell as the mob pressed forward. If they did not hold their ground, they were sure to be flung down the steps.

That is when the gunfire erupted.

Panic ensued in the form of a stampede. Henry was stunned by how loud the shots were, and the screaming.

Mariya pulled him by the wrist to run for *anywhere-but-there*. Hundreds fled alongside, leaving behind those who had been shot or trampled or both.

They rode the panicked surge deeper into the bunker, crossing a basketball court before entering a corridor lined with farm labs. They flew into a stairwell and climbed until they exited to a concourse on the sixth floor.

Emergency lights strobed and loudspeakers blared. All were ordered to shelter in their rooms. People were frightened, full of adrenaline, and out of breath.

The group they had fled alongside stopped to gather themselves. Henry approached.

"Could you help us find someone? We're not from here."

A man about his age looked them over and nodded.

"Follow us to the Stacks."

* * *

After a quarter-mile maze of hallways, they reached an apartment belonging to one or more of the trio they followed.

"I am Joel, this is Vance, and that is Alice."

Henry introduced Mariya and himself.

"What the actual *fuck*!" Vance said, ignoring them. "I thought mass shootings were a thing of the past."

"Something happened at the vault doors about a

month back and they showed up," Joel said. "More came after that video leaked this morning. They're all from Carmel."

Henry cleared his throat. There was a moment of awkward silence as the hosts were reminded of their presence.

"We're from the bunker to the west. We arrived right before the riot."

"Yeah, and what do you do?" Vance said.

Henry was confused by the question.

"Everyone here has a skillset, or they wouldn't have been chosen to survive. We are research pharmacists and Alice is a phlebotomist. What do you do?"

"He's a *diplomat*," Mariya said, offended on his behalf. "We're human beings and deserve to live regardless of merit."

Vance rolled his eyes.

"Do you guys know Marcus Trencher?" Alice said. "They keep saying he is a threat to the bunker network. Then this crazy video came out."

"The drone video is real," Henry said. "And I've been to the surface. It was freezing, but we believe the cold was geoengineered. It's warmed in the last couple weeks. Was that in the video?"

"Yes, and a whole batshit crazy depopulation conspiracy theory," Vance said. "The no-asteroid-thing is ridiculous – we felt the place shake."

"Your bunker's anti-seismic machinery was programmed to create rumbling rather than counteract it. It is all a conspiracy, and it is all true."

"Yeah? And how do you know this?"

"Marcus is my best friend. He was brought in on the conspiracy, to a degree. By the time he learned what was really happening, it was too late to do much about it. The same people that shot up that crowd down there planned to seize his bunker before he was tipped off and outsmarted them.

"Our bunker is not all they wanted. The *Trencher Industries* power grid is still mostly intact up the surface, and we have control over it. The people orchestrating this mass kill-off of the population want to take it from us."

"Then they should march right past the Quarry to your bunker. What do we have to do with all this?"

"Ask your own question. What do you do?"

"I told you, we are research pharmacists."

"Specifically, what are you creating?"

Vance and Joel look at each other, entering a nonverbal negotiation on disclosure.

"They are making an anti-aging serum," Alice said.

Vance was flabbergasted. "Seriously, Alice?"

"What? Were you really going to keep that a secret after what just happened?"

"She's right," Joel said. "We've essentially cracked the code of biological aging. We can freeze it, we think, for decades, if not longer. We can even reverse nearly every effect of aging. A small number of very fortunate residents in the bunkers have access to it, and most of them are in Carmel."

"Is it clear now?" Mariya said. "These people are depopulating the earth, extending their own lives with your serum, and preparing to rebuild the world according to their vision."

"The serum is your leverage, your bargaining chip, just like we have the power grid," Henry said. "We can't let these people win. We have to fight back."

* * *

They left the pharmacists with plenty to think about. They had something of extreme value to those in power. Henry hated how much he wanted to talk it over with Marcus.

People in the halls were discussing the day's events. A blood-splattered woman was being consoled by friends, one of the many traumatized victims of the massacre earlier that afternoon.

As important as it all was, though, he easily put it all aside when he found the room number he was looking for.

He took Mariya's hand and knocked on the door.

Cheryl Plyman burst into tears of joy as she hugged her son. Harold Plyman welcomed Mariya inside before hugging his son as well. It was the first they had seen each other since they were forced underground.

"Come in," Mr. Plyman said. "We have so much to catch up on."

Chapter Eight

Robby offered token help while Cal and Luke loaded supplies into two heavy-duty trucks. He wore a rain poncho and manned the radio so Marcus could micromanage from down below.

"Ask if they found enough gravel," Marcus said. "Did they check if the fuel is still good in the backhoe?"

"They have a truckload of gravel waiting at the vertiport," Robby said. "Relax, it's under control."

Robby clipped the radio to his belt and helped Luke load a length of heavy chain.

"Are you going to be able to pull this off before the weather clears?"

Luke shrugged. "We're going to try."

"Mind if I tag along?"

"Depends," Cal said. "Can you follow rules? We don't like excitement up here."

"Rule-follower is my middle name."

Cal laughed. "I saw your name in the arrest column in the *Daily Times* so many damn times. But if the boss gives the okay, it's fine by us."

Robby retrieved the radio. "Marcus, I'm going with

them. Make something up to tell Melonie. Over."

* * *

Kent confirmed that Marcus had successfully reconnected the communications cable at the Quarry. Marcus had VR headsets fetched from the storage tunnels.

When Kent tried to give him a tutorial, he cut him off. "Metaverse, call Harold Plyman."

Marcus was warped to a mountainside chateau where Harold Plyman's avatar greeted him in a great hall. After Timothy rushed through the setup menus, he appeared as a generic male avatar.

"I'm here with Cheryl, Henry and Mariya, and Genie is joining as well," Mr. Plyman said. "I'll hand the headset over to Henry now."

Genie materialized as her patented centaur avatar with multi-colored hair.

"Gene Granlund, is that you?" Timothy said as his avatar floated toward her.

"I go by Genie these days. Nice to see you, Timothy."

"Genie and I leaked the drone video on the metaverse yesterday," Marcus said. "I was hoping to hear if anything has come of it."

"There was a riot," Henry said. "Soldiers from Carmel fired into a crowd."

"That's terrible," Marcus said in monotone. "...But we could use this. We'll call it the Bloomington Massacre."

Henry thought about revealing how narrowly he and Mariya escaped the shooting, but didn't bother.

"What is your grand plan?"

"We need to overthrow our oppressors underground before we can do so on the surface, and by 'we' I mean the you guys and the rest of the people in the Quarry."

* * *

Robby, Cal, and Luke met four other scouts at the vertiport where two of their colleagues had died. Cal and Luke were the ones to retrieve their bodies, and the footage. This time, they were there to set a trap.

They dug a pit north of the platform and poured gravel in the bottom. They covered it with plywood, and then covered the plywood with dirt.

The hole was just big enough to house a full-sized pickup truck.

Another truck was backed in on the gravel utility road on the opposite side. They did their best to camouflage it with extra gravel and tree limbs.

The weather became less dreary as they worked. The wind died down and clouds were thinning. The other scouts took off.

"Where are they going?" Robby said.

"We're calling it," Cal said. "Drones can fly in these skies. There's always one that comes to charge up first thing. Best we get to cover."

"What else is left to do?"

Cal showed him the diagram. "According to Mr. Trencher's plans, we have to lay the chains out on the charging pad like so."

"Hell, that's five minutes of work. I'll do it."

Cal looked skyward. He didn't like what he saw, but when Luke agreed with Robby, he caved.

If all went according to plan, a drone would land on the vertiport and shut down for charging. Drivers would run out to each truck, pull the chains from each direction, and lasso the drone's skids.

Robby lugged the first chain from the buried truck up grated metal stairs and carefully laid it along the edges of the pad. He repeated the task, overlaying the second chain from the second truck so that they crisscrossed.

"Nothing to it."

"Everyone under the pad!" Luke said. "We got company!"

"What did I tell you guys?" Cal said, furious.

A dot in the sky was approaching fast. They hid beneath the vertiport, between the Stonehenge-like battery units that held it up.

The whir of propellers grew until the skids scraped onto the platform above their heads. They heard the cleats click into the charging mechanism. The machine powered down and began to charge.

"What now?" Robby whispered.

"We wait the damn thing out."

"The trap is set. What is there to wait on?"

"That wasn't the plan. We were only here for set up."

"We've watched a dozen of these things charge," Luke said. "I think we can pull it off."

"I ain't getting blasted like Chuck and Dougie."

"Luke and I will drive the trucks," Robby said.

Cal was outnumbered. If they were going to do it, they needed to do it right.

"Fine, but let's be smart about this. Don't accelerate like a bat out of hell. Ease forward until the chains are taut then throw it in park."

"Got it. Then what?"

"Luke and I will sprint out to the getaway car. You run the other way and get into that tree line across the road. We'll swing around and pick you up."

51

They got to their mark on each side. Cal counted down, and they sprinted out to the trucks.

Robby slid in the muddy field as he turned to descend the ramp. He shimmied by the door and climbed into the bed, then through the back window. He turned the engine on and signaled over the radio.

He gave it some gas and cleared the gravel ramp. Near the top, the chain flipped the plywood cover off from over the pit. He rolled forward until the chain drew a straight line up to the drone. His lasso was latched. He prayed Luke's was as well.

"See you at the tree line!" he said into the radio.

The ominous buzz of propellers started again before his foot hit the ground.

The drone bucked like a bronco – scraping and bouncing off the pad – but the chains held.

The tree line looked a lot closer before he had started for it. At the edge of the field, he heard the roar of missiles fired in rapid succession. He turned to see the drone still angrily thrashing atop the pad, and trails of smoke leading off to nowhere in particular. The drone was trying to shed weight, or jolt itself free, but it was unsuccessful.

He crossed the road, splashed through a flooded ditch, and plopped down behind a tree. Had had barely caught his breath by the time Luke and Cal circled around to pick him up.

"That thing is liable to call for backup," Cal said. "We better haul ass back to the bunker."

Chapter Nine

Henry and Mariya sat on the edge of the bed after a restless night. The cramped apartment in "the Stacks" was not designed for four, and he refused to make his parents sleep on the floor.

Mrs. Plyman readied a pot of tea while Mr. Plyman was already plugged into the metaverse. Henry was in awe of his father's adaptation of modern technology.

"After all the times he kicked me off my PlayStation growing up..."

Mr. Plyman removed his headset. "My pals in the 101st Airborne tell me there were five dead and twenty injured in the shooting. They're patrolling the public spaces and have the train station locked down."

"101st Airborne? You have contacts in the military?"

"It's a group I run with on the World War II metaverse game."

"He is on there all daggone day ranting like a lunatic about Nazi bunkers on the beaches of Normandy!" Mrs. Plyman said.

Henry and Mariya laughed.

His father blushed. "Marcus left a message this

morning. He wants you to meet a contact, Jim Cox. He plans on releasing his next message tonight at 8pm. Needless to say, it'd be best you were not out and about."

A buzz at the door made Henry jump, but it was only a meal delivery bot. Henry's father retrieved a tote bag off its back and brought it inside. He pulled two booklets from the tote and handed them to Henry and Mariya.

"Breakfast is served, and a few things that might come in handy."

"You scored us fake IDs? How did you pull that off?"

"We had a digital photo of you lovebirds that I passed along to one of my metaverse war buddies. He made those first thing this morning."

"Thanks, dad. Think your pals would be willing to fight a real war?"

"Sure, but you should pursue peaceful means. This isn't a video game, or World War II."

"It's arguably World War III, and it's already gotten un-peaceful."

"Fair, but don't get into a gunfight without any guns, literally and figuratively."

* * *

Mariya and Henry ventured out of the Stacks after breakfast. Gatherings broke up as they approached. People walked with their heads down. Paranoia in the wake of the massacre was palpable.

After a maze of administrative hallways, they found a tiny office belonging to Jim Cox. He was an architect, which explained why Marcus took a liking to him.

Henry and Jim became mired in small talk about Marcus before Mariya cut to the chase.

"We want to spark an uprising," she said. "There weren't many soldiers at the protest, but they had guns. Are there any weapons we can get ahold of?"

Jim blinked in surprise. "They've seized our guns. There were less-than-lethal arms in the bunker police department, but I imagine they've taken those as well."

"What if we all just left?" Henry said. "Could you open the surface doors again?"

"Not after what Adam Terry pulled when he broke Marcus out a month or so back. A team from Carmel occupies that control room."

Henry didn't feel he was cutout to be a revolutionary leader. He was given an impossible mission.

"Well, we'll keep in touch and see what Marcus has in store," he said, standing. "Before we go, do you think you could hook us up with a room? I love my parents, but it's awfully cramped."

* * *

They wandered out to a balcony overlooking the atrium where the massacre took place. A procession of forklifts carried pallets of food across the space, disappearing through a cargo door to the loading docks. There were no bunker denizens in the area, only soldiers hitting golf balls, and one posted at the stairway.

"The train must've arrived today," Mariya said.

They took a zigzag of escalators down to ground level. The golfing soldiers watched with amusement as they approached.

"The platform is off limits," the soldier before the stairway said.

"We want to see the train," Mariya said cheerfully. "We've lived here all this time and we've never been down

55

to see it!"

"It's just a train."

"C'mon, Kyle," a soldier said from the tee box. "Let the nice couple have a look."

The sentry shrugged. "I'll take you to the bottom of the steps, but that's it."

He escorted them down to a hub of activity. Three passenger cars peeked out from the east tunnel. Dozens of newly arrived troops filed onto the platform where they wrangled tactical gear and checked their rifles. The occupying force had grown substantially.

An elevator dinged to their left. Joel and Vance, the research pharmacists they met in the aftermath of the massacre, stepped out wearing white lab coats. They carried Styrofoam coolers stickered with warning labels. A soldier hounded them for IDs and shipping paperwork.

Henry made fleeting eye contact with Joel. The soldier moved aside, and they delivered their precious cargo to the train's caboose.

"We've seen enough," Henry said. "Thanks, Kyle. You guys aren't so bad."

Chapter Ten

Marcus pre-recorded his video message to ensure it met his standard of perfection. He left the infirmary against Dr. Nora's advice to make his speech from his suite. Despite the recent gunshot wound, his energy was boundless. His prescription refills helped.

"Should I be wearing makeup?" Marcus said after yet another take. "They always put stuff on me when I did TV interviews. We should get one of the girls up here."

"Nobody cares," Robby said. "But you did forget to tell everyone to smash that like button and subscribe. Maybe you should do another take."

"No, you nailed the last one," Timothy said, glaring at Robby. "Also, Kent needs time to load it up with graphics and have it ready for release tonight."

Marcus gave the okay. Kent took his laptop.

"Let's get to the important topic," Robby said. "What are we doing with the drone I heroically captured?"

"We cut power to the vertiport," Marcus said. "We don't need to wait until the batteries drain, but we do need weather coverage. The skies are too clear right now."

"Why haven't you cut power to all the charging

platforms? I'm sick of living in this bunker."

"Don't worry, we will play that hand. All in due time."

* * *

Henry and Mariya loitered a semi-safe distance from the Quarry pharmaceutical labs, pretending to show interest in a screen outside a neon-lit lounge. When Joel and Vance returned from the train platform, they made their approach.

"Hey, do you guys have a minute?" Henry said.

"Are you crazy?" Vance said with darting eyes.

"Not here, never here," Joel said. "Meet us at my apartment in an hour."

The two men hurried into the labs as a group of soldiers exited.

Henry and Mariya ducked inside the gaming lounge. People of all ages wore headsets and slouched in chairs. A younger crowd gathered around omnidirectional treadmills for more active gaming. It was a strange social space, as so few spoke face-to-face. They found and claimed two open stations.

"Maybe we can touch base back home," Henry said, wiping down a headset. "You ever use these things?"

"Avoided them like the plague," Mariya said.

They created avatars with pseudonyms. Henry spawned on the streets of a dystopian megacity before accepting Mariya's invitation to the Golden Gate Bridge.

"Never thought I'd see San Francisco again."

"Let me see if I can get ahold of you-know-who." He pulled his headset up to see if anyone was near enough to hear. All were engrossed in their own worlds. "Metaverse, call Marcus Trencher."

The search was unsuccessful.

"He probably has a fake name," Mariya said. "Your dad knows it, call him."

He prompted the virtual universe to contact Harold Plyman. A youthful digital clone of his dad appeared on the bridge, in uniform.

"Dad, we're in a gaming lounge. Are you busy?"

"The boys and I were running the Battle of the Bulge, but they have me covered. What can I help you with?"

"I can't seem to get ahold of Marcus."

"Let me reach out." After several *hmms*, his avatar shook its head. "That's strange. His profile doesn't even show as offline."

"I bet they disconnected the communications cable again," Mariya said.

* * *

Henry let his dad get back to virtual warfare after confirming dinner plans. He and Mariya killed time playing a cart racing game for an hour before departing for the Stacks. They had a lead to follow with the pharmacists.

Joel answered the door and welcomed them in.

"Sorry I was curt with you earlier. The labs were swarming with soldiers."

"I'm not," Vance said, arms crossed. "If they find out we're talking with Marcus Trencher's pals, they'll kill us."

Henry ignored Vance. "Those Styrofoam coolers you had at the train station, was that the anti-aging serum?"

"A small batch," Joel said. "The train was a week-and-a-half earlier than our normal schedule. That was all we had ready."

"The half-life in super short," Vance said. "Efficacy starts ticking down the moment we make it."

"Can you explain like I am five?"

"The serum essentially expires in a week," Joel said. "It works best when taken immediately. We store it in ultra-low temperature freezers and ship it on dry ice, but it still rapidly deteriorates."

"Before the world ended, we shipped overseas weekly to a Saudi prince. We sent that shit on supersonic fighter jets. $40 mil a pop. A six-day old batch will make you feel good, but when it's fresh, it will straight up reverse your biological clock."

"What happens if you miss a shipment?"

"Patients in the network get one shot per month," Joel said. "Missing one won't do much, but any more than that and they might see and feel regression."

"I know what you are thinking, and it won't work," Vance said. "We are literally working under gunpoint. Nothing is going to interrupt production."

"Is there anything we can do to gain leverage? The time to act is now before they totally lock the place down."

Vance immediately declared nothing could be done, but Joel had an idea.

"The serum is a gene therapy, DNA drug. Each dose is catered specifically to the individual. The patient information is encrypted, but it is something we might be able to extract."

"I know someone who can probably crack it," Henry said. "How difficult would it be to get it off your system?"

Vance laughed. "We've been using an Excel spreadsheet and uploading it to the terminal at the end of the week. Helps us avoid using the clunky software they gave us as much as possible."

"An Excel spreadsheet?" Henry said. "So, like, a USB drive and a minute of privacy is all you need?"

Vance shrugged. "Yeah, that's about it."

* * *

Marcus eagerly awaited the release of his fiery message across the bunker metaverse. He wore a sling on his left arm and paced about his suite. The countdown was nearing 8 p.m.

Kent sheepishly entered with his laptop. Timothy followed. Robby sat up from the sofa.

"Let's put it up on the big screen," Marcus said. "You can broadcast my avatar's feed."

Kent cleared his throat. "There's been an issue. We're no longer connected to the network. They unplugged the communications cable again."

Marcus tossed his headset then grimaced in pain. "This is a disaster. We're losing momentum from the first video. We have to send someone..."

"We already have someone there," Timothy said.

"Yeah, Henry will pull something off," Robby said. "Have faith."

Chapter Eleven

A streak of clear skies bound them to the bunker while scout teams on the surface were stuck in the basements of their safehouses.

There was an uptick in drone sightings. They had attracted increased attention. Robby's trophy drone was still chained to the vertiport, but too dangerous to retrieve.

When Cami finally forecasted dark clouds on the horizon, plans were put into motion.

Robby met Marcus, Timothy, Steve, and Kent at the surface elevator. He was surprised to see Marcus dressed as if he was coming along.

"You're going up? And Kent?"

"The drone won't fit in the bunker, and I want to see it," Marcus said. "And Kent knows more about these machines than any of us."

They stepped outside and looked west. A rolling wall of dark clouds dominated the skyline. Marcus tossed a set of keys to Timothy, but Robby intercepted.

"I'll drive safe, I promise."

They kept ahead of the storm – thanks to Robby's

unsafe driving. By the time they arrived, scout teams were already gathered at the end of the access lane to the vertiport. The drone was still perched there, tethered by chain to two pickup trucks. Rain started to fall, and rumbles of thunder shook the landscape.

Cal ran up to the truck, holding onto his jacket hood. "Hey, boss. You ready to do this?"

Marcus gave the thumbs up.

They watched from the comfort of their pickup as a yellow boom truck turned into the lane. A semi tractor with a flatbed trailer expertly backed in behind it. Another scout moved the pickup truck anchored to the drone, before quickly situating it so that the chain was taut again.

A bolt of lightning crashed terribly close. The scout in the crane called over the radio.

"Should I get out of this thing? I don't want to get struck."

"Negative," Marcus answered. "I suggest you work quickly."

The chains around the skids were relinquished and another apparatus was tied around machine. The crane picked it off the pad and swung it to the flatbed truck. A crew clamped the ratchet straps and chains were reapplied for good measure.

"Looks like we're up," Marcus said to Kent.

They jumped out and jogged to the flatbed.

Kent climbed up and examined the drone. He found what he was looking for and requested a tool. He cranked away at a panel until it was freed.

He climbed halfway inside the drone, legs flailing. When he re-emerged, he held up an electronic device. Marcus gave a thumbs up and they returned to the truck.

"GPS beacon," Kent said tossing the black box to

Timothy. "It's disabled."

"You were a drone hobbyist, you said?"

"I flew surveillance drones for the Army. *Not* the ones that killed people. I don't talk about it much."

The flatbed departed with the drone in tow, and a convoy of pickup trucks.

"Follow them," Marcus said. "We're taking it to the warehouse north of town."

* * *

Parts were methodically removed, labeled, and laid out on a tarp until the drone was a mere shell. Kent was the expert, but Marcus was a genius who could learn on the fly. Steve had an engineering degree, so he added value. The rest of the men provided muscle and tools, but mostly stood around.

"This is interesting." Kent held up a section of the drone's carbon composite body. Characters were written in blue marker on the interior. "Is this Chinese?"

"A translation app should pick it up." Timothy aimed his tablet at the text until the program recognized it. "Korean. It says, '*Seok Lee, Chongjin.*' Ever heard of him?"

"Chongjin is a city in North Korea," Robby said to immediate skepticism. "What? I got on a North Korea documentary kick a couple years ago."

"A factory worker probably felt like putting his name on one." Timothy pulled up a map and confirmed that Robby was correct. "Where else would be better to quietly mass produce killing machines than North Korea?"

"It would also explain why this thing is such a piece of crap," Kent said. "Everything is cheap. All the chips are

Chinese; none of the good Taiwanese stuff, nothing American. Software looks like shoddy Russian code. The drones I flew 15 years ago put this to shame."

"So definitely not autonomous?" Marcus said.

Kent shook his head. "Somebody is flying these things, pretty much manually. I'd say from anywhere, but judging by the equipment, probably not far."

"Can I get a look at that shoddy Russian code?" Timothy said.

They gathered around a workbench where Kent's laptop was linked to the drone's motherboard.

"Wow, this is trash," Timothy said ten seconds into his code review. "We can pull flight data and tell you where it's been."

Robby was crowded to the back but had a question. "Can you hijack its controls and fly it?"

Kent pointed at the screen. "...You can pull all its footage. There's a log of every time its landed to charge and what charging pad. That's how we used to bill customers back in the day, there was a data exchange..."

"But can you fly it?" Robby said.

"Even the infrared sensors are twenty years old..."

Marcus put a hand on Kent's shoulder.

"Can you fly the thing?"

The idea somehow hadn't crossed his mind.

"Loan me Timothy and Steve and give us a week. Then...maybe."

Chapter Twelve

Henry and Mariya kept to their apartment for the better part of two days as the Quarry entered a "soft" lockdown. New reinforcements gave the occupying force the manpower to extend patrols and perform door-to-door searches in the Stacks.

Their apartment was in an otherwise vacant hall full of other empty apartments allocated for future population growth. It was off the books, thanks to Jim Cox.

The room's virtual-reality headset lit up neon blue and played a jingle. Henry scrambled to put it on.

"It's one of the pharmacists."

He nearly poking Mariya in the eye as he motioned to accept the incoming call.

"We need to meet," Joel's avatar said. "Come by ASAP. Curfew's not for another few hours."

* * *

Joel was calm and serious as usual. Vance sat at the kitchenette, hands folded, left leg bobbing. Alice the phlebotomist joined them, eager to help if she could.

"You got the patient data?" Henry said.

"Yes, but the USB is still in the lab – for a few reasons," Joel said. "The first being increased security. The second...Vance is having second thoughts."

Henry and Mariya couldn't hide their dismay.

"What? I'm the one risking my life here, "Vance said. "I also happen to like the fact that I get to take the serum. I feel ten years younger. My hair grew back!"

"We can't fault you for that," Henry said. "But—"

"Evil fascists are imprisoning us while they systematically wipe people off the face of the earth," Mariya said. "You're worried about your hair?"

"Give me a break." Vance looked at Henry. "You need to get her under control."

Mariya bolted forward and shoved him off his stool. "Your immortality drug is bullshit!"

Vance put his hands up. "I must be an idiot for thinking the greatest advance in medicine in the history of mankind was a good thing."

"Good for the super-rich and powerful. You don't think your drug is playing a part in all this? They are resetting civilization to calibrate for their extended lives."

"That is for the politicians to figure out."

Mariya was unleashed. Even Henry was intimidated.

"Politicians? You think twelve-term senators would have legislated for the common people while your big pharma company pumped them full of serum and lobbying money? Imagine if we had it in the recent past...Putin in power for forty years, 120-year-old Henry Kissinger, Billionaires becoming trillionaires after decades of doing jack shit..."

"Fine, you got me. Bad things were inevitably going to come of it. The rich get richer, and all that."

Henry put a gentle hand on Mariya's shoulder. She was burning hot to the touch. "All we're asking is you get us that patient data and we'll take it from there."

Vance wasn't sold. "And in two days they trace it back to me. Then what?"

Alice cleared her throat. "I'll take the fall for it."

"Alice, I can't ask you to do that."

"What they are doing is wrong. If we get this list out, the people will rise up."

"First things first," Joel said. "We can't take the USB drive into the Stacks. They've searched our apartments twice already and we get frisked every time we leave the lab."

"Not necessarily," Vance said, hesitantly. "When I stepped out for coffee today, they didn't check me. If I'm getting that thing out of the labs, it needs to be midday."

"We can hand it off discreetly and save a copy on the metaverse from the gaming lounge," Henry said.

"That could work, if you are allowed out of the Stacks. Essential workers only during the lockdown."

"I'll take care of that." Joel checked the clock on the wall. "Curfew is about up. I'll order Chinese food to your room, and hopefully a few other items.

"Tomorrow at noon – one of you needs to be in the Green District Café, a few storefronts down from the labs. Vance will be there."

Joel made the last part more of a question.

Vance sighed. "Yeah, yeah. I'll be there."

* * *

Later that night, as promised, a delivery bot arrived at their door with bunker Chinese cuisine – and other items.

Joel scored Henry a janitor's uniform, and Mariya a

white lab coat.

They donned their disguises and left the room at 11 a.m. the next morning. When they turned the corner into the main hall, they met a long line of workers snaking back from the checkpoint between the Stacks and the public spaces.

"Move it! I have a nuclear reactor to get to!" A man yelled before cowering behind them.

"The line is too slow," Henry said. "I don't think we're going to make noon."

Just as he spoke, a soldier at the checkpoint called up the line, *"White coat, you!"* He was looking at Mariya and motioning for her to skip the line.

The nuclear scientist behind them groaned.

"Get to the café," Henry said. "I'll meet you at the gaming lounge."

Mariya received a few boos, mostly in jest. She was let through after a cursory search while others received the full TSA treatment.

Twenty minutes later, Henry underwent an invasive search, even though his tight-fitting janitor uniform left little to the imagination.

"You should check the men's room by the train platform," the soldier said as he frisked him. "The boys have been blowing it up down there."

* * *

Mariya rushed to the café, crossing before the pharmaceutical labs right as Vance was exiting. He was stopped for a mandatory search.

"I don't have time for this," Vance said.

"It is protocol..." the guard said.

69

"I'm getting lunch two doors down. You can watch me eat if you want."

The guard looked around for his superior before letting Vance through.

Vance spotted Mariya and looked surprised that she was the one sent to meet him, considering how poorly they had hit it off.

They took a table away from the other patrons. A robot waiter approached, and they put in their orders.

"The grilled chicken salad ain't bad," Vance said. "If you don't mind the lab-grown stuff."

The robot brought two waters and zoomed off to wait for the robot chef to prepare their salads.

Vance's hand shook as he took a sip of water. Mariya looked out of the café, hoping Henry could come in and take her place. She could handle the USB hand-off, but a conversation with Vance was another thing.

"You were right about everything last night," he said. "Immortality isn't meant for humanity. But I hope you can understand it's difficult to pass up when you are in on it."

"I can't fault anyone for the pursuit. But it is all too predictable who will get access to it."

"Who *has* gotten access to it. It's been around longer than you'd think. There were more than a few in the public eye that were starting to push the boundaries of suspicion. It wasn't botox, fillers, and surgeries doing all that."

The robot waiter brought their grilled chicken salads. Vance asked for a to-go container.

"I won't keep you. Only wanted you to know I'm not evil, just human. I'm at peace with burning the whole thing down."

Vance reached into his pocket and slid his hand into a cloth napkin. Then, the napkin across the table. Mariya tucked it away.

* * *

Henry approached the café as Vance was scraping a salad into a to-go container. He contemplated on whether he should join them and potentially draw attention. Surprisingly, the conversation inside appeared civil.

"*Hey, you.*"

Henry turned to face an occupying soldier.

"Think you could do something about the restrooms over here? It's like a bomb went off in there. Same down at the train station."

"I'm on it, sir. I'll be right in there."

Was he really about to clean a public restroom? The soldier stayed nearby, so he didn't feel he had a choice.

The restroom was unpleasant, as expected. Two soldiers stood at the urinals. He found a cleaning supply closet and opened it to look busy.

A soldier looked back over his shoulder. "About time one of you got in here...*Anyway, sounds like we might get called back to Indy. The Speedway bunker is in a full-on revolt. That video got everyone riled up.*"

"*I hear Louisville is a mess, too. This place ain't nothing. Don't know why they sent so many of us here.*"

"*Gotta be something in those labs.*"

The two soldiers left without washing their hands, Henry mentally noted. He also took note of their discussion.

He dipped a mop in a bucket of soapy water and ran it over the tiles to make it look like he did something before leaving. He didn't want to blow his cover, but he also didn't want to go anywhere near the toilet stalls.

He met Mariya in the gaming lounge. Without saying

a word, she discreetly unfolded a cloth napkin, revealing a USB drive.

"It's time to bring Genie in," Henry said, grabbing a headset. "In the meantime, I found a place we can stash the drive."

Chapter Thirteen

Marcus returned to the bunker in case word got back on Henry's status in the Quarry. They were still left in the dark. Kent, Timothy, and Steve stayed up top with the captured drone.

It became consensus among the tech-savvy trio that the drone's data was at the very least just as important as the capacity to fly it.

Timothy threw together a program to process raw coordinates data and overlay it on a map. He pinpointed every place and time the drone had fired a missile.

"Looks like it fired one west of Bloomfield," Timothy said. "Robby will be thrilled to know he captured the very drone that nearly killed him."

Timothy dropped another digital pin on the map. Bombs were also released over Paoli, Jasper, Princeton, and a dozen other towns across southern Indiana. Never did it travel north of Indianapolis.

It stayed out for days at a time, charging at vertiports across the region and occasionally sitting out poor weather. Eventually, it always returned to one location.

"Crane Naval Facility," Timothy said. "That is where

it is getting refitted with bombs."

"What the hell is a naval base doing in the middle of Indiana?" Steve said.

"Military industrial complex," Kent said. "Can't have a non-coastal congressman voting to cut the Navy budget."

"Marcus mentioned this place," Timothy said. "I hope he doesn't gloat too much when I tell him he was right."

* * *

Just as Marcus suspected, the drones were being deployed from Crane, deep in the heart of southern Indiana. He was pleased to tell Timothy he had told him so.

Trencher Industries installed the smart grid around the naval base, but it was not part of the greater grid that they controlled – a stipulation of the military contract for national security purposes.

He could not simply cut its power, but he did have a plan to take it out, the old-fashioned way.

He pressed the intercom button at his suite desk to address the entire bunker.

"Good afternoon, Marcus speaking. Every able-bodied man or woman capable of operating a firearm, please report to the chamber on seven in ten minutes."

He took the stairs from his suite, his left arm still wrapped in a sling. Robby was first to greet him, having run across the bunker the second he heard the message.

"Is it time for the grand finale?"

"We're just getting started."

The chamber was filled by the time he arrived. Not everyone was able-bodied, or of appropriate age, but they all wanted to hear the latest.

He walked up the ramp before the War Room.

"As I am sure you have heard, we captured a drone earlier this week. We extracted data telling us where it has traveled. Evidence shows it was deployed from the Crane Naval Base, approximately 45 miles from here.

"This is what we've been gearing up for. When the next major storm system rolls through, we will use it as cover to attack the base. It will be dangerous, but it is the only way we can break free and begin to retake the surface."

The people volunteered in great numbers.

* * *

Henry and Mariya made it out of the Stacks for a second time, again thanks to their disguises.

Henry made a stop at the restroom near the labs to retrieve the USB device. He had stashed it on a tile in the ceiling above a particularly gruesome toilet.

"Ugh, that was your hiding spot?" Mariya said.

"Nobody found it, right?"

They coordinated a meeting with Genie at Jim's tiny office in the engineering department.

"I can't be gone long," Genie said. "These jerks from Carmel are undoing all the metaverse privacy measures I built out."

Henry handed her the USB. She opened her laptop and plugged it in without hesitation. Before he could explain what was on it, or what to do with it, she was already hacking away.

"We need you to decrypt the Excel file. It is from the pharmaceutical labs. There should be a—"

"Done," she said with a triumphant keystroke. She

75

squinted at the screen. "I recognize that name...and that one. CEO, CEO, Congressman, Celebrity...NFL QB...What is this?"

"Everyone on that list is receiving a gene therapy produced in the pharmaceutical labs. The serum can supposedly add decades to their lives, even reverse aging."

"Oh, and I can't even get the right hormone medicine for my transition...but I digress."

"I never knew such a thing existed," Jim said. "Reverse aging?"

"Everyone needs to know," Mariya said. "It'll push our message over the top."

"Marcus was going to release another video, but the cable got disconnected," Henry said. "We will release our own, with this list being the centerpiece."

Genie contemplated the technical aspects of the plan.

"We can still get a video out anonymously, but the sooner the better."

Jim shimmied by and checked the lock on the door.

"Now is as good a time as any, right?"

* * *

Henry and Mariya hustled back to the Stacks, delayed only by a brief harassment at the checkpoint. They went straight to his parents' room.

His mother's first concern was that he had plastered his face all over a video that would get him killed.

"Mom, it's all AI-generated. It won't be my voice or face or anything."

"I can't bear to watch. Mariya, you can use my headset."

Mariya donned a headset, and Henry invited her to

the dystopian virtual megacity in which he spawned. Neither were sure what to look for. A flying car sped overhead, pursued by six flying police cars. A jetpacked avatar leapt from the car before it exploded into the side of a building. He fired a rocket launcher before being gunned down by a hail of lasers.

"*Grand Theft Auto 2169*," Henry said. "Will the message get out here?"

The virtual world suddenly reset. The carnage and police cars vanished. In the virtual distance, a projection appeared on a massive, monolithic building. A figure sat before a glowing red background. Other avatars on the street stopped their chaotic crime sprees and turned their attention to the screen.

"Good evening. A list of names has been sent to your inboxes. The people on this list are more privileged than you and I. Pharmaceutical labs located in the bunker beneath Bloomington, Indiana, are producing a miraculous serum capable of adding decades to one's life. The people on the list have access to it. You do not.

"A force has taken over the Quarry to protect their precious drug. They massacred a crowd of protestors after the release of Marcus Trencher's message. We must not let these tyrants hold power over us any longer. We must stand up to our oppressors. We must retake—"

The world glitched and cut the video short. Whole skyscrapers disappeared and reappeared, and polygons blinked through different textures. A second later, they were booted out of the world.

"Check your inbox, see if the list is there," Henry said, frantically trying to figure out the overlay of menus.

"I have it open," Mariya said. "It's there. All the names are there."

He found it soon after. After 30 seconds of scrolling, the screen went black.

"It's gone. Is it gone for you?"

"They shut the whole thing down."

They peeled off their headsets. Henry's parents had faces of grave concern, despite not seeing or hearing the message directly.

"We did it...I think I'm going to throw up."

Across the bunker network, the metaverse went dark. The virtual bread and circuses that sedated so many – gone in a flash – but not before the message was received, and the list of names seen. Not before the flame was lit.

Chapter Fourteen

Bunker denizens congregated in the halls, headsets still in hand. Henry and Mariya cautiously stepped out of his parents' apartment.

"Did you see that?"

"We need answers. Did you see the list?"

Lights strobed, and lockdown announcements commenced. The passing conversations heated up as they got closer to their apartment.

"That insider trader Ohio senator was on the list!"

"I pulled it to my personal drive before they shut it down. I'll show you..."

More and more crowded into the halls, ignoring the commands to stay in. Henry felt like he was in Third Class aboard the Titanic. He was Jack and Mariya was Rose. And the ship – it was going down.

They worked through the crowd until they were suddenly confronted with a wall of riot gear. The occupying forces were making a sweep.

"Back to your rooms! We are under lockdown!"

"Fuck you! We're not going anywhere!" a man said.

The soldier struck him with a baton. Others surged

forward to even up the fight. Henry and Mariya retreated from the line of scrimmage, doubling back to find another way around. Joel and Vance waved them down.

"It's anarchy out here," Joel said. "You need to get to your room and lay low."

"We're trying," Mariya said. "Your room is closer. Can we hide there?"

"Where do you think those assholes are headed?" Vance said.

"Take the next left up that way, then another," Joel said. "That'll get you close to your room. We're going to the labs to try and head off suspicion."

* * *

Marcus stayed in his suite while his volunteer army practiced shooting on a makeshift gun range up top. A light rain provided enough cover for the exercise, but not the stormfront necessary for the Crane mission.

He felt idle. Henry was in Bloomington and the others were at the warehouse working on the captured drone. Robby was around but was spending time with Melonie.

He was usually fine with seclusion in his suite, but he was out of coffee.

He made it halfway to the café before his former assistant, Brittney, jogged up to greet him. She had just finished a fitness class, judging by the flock of women carrying yoga mats behind her.

"Walk with me," Marcus said. "I need my coffee."

"The ladies wanted me to ask if people could start moving into the empty apartments, like the couple that just had the first bunker baby. It doesn't look like we'll be down here for decades like we thought, so..."

"I don't have time for domestic issues," he said before coming to a stop. "A baby was born? When was this?"

"When you, um, reserved the hospital. A girl gave birth in one of the rooms. Young couple, I think teenagers, but anyway they want to move in together."

"We should have one of those parties."

"Baby shower – already happened. It's a boy. Want to know his name?"

He shrugged.

"They named him Marcus."

He rolled his eyes and continued to the café. "Let people move wherever. Room keys are in the War Room."

She pecked a kiss on his cheek and ran off. Across the way, men began filing back in from target practice.

He started a fresh pot of coffee, watched the drip, and enjoyed the aroma for an entire minute before the next interruption.

"Yo, Marcus," a deep voice said.

He turned to find Steve, Timothy, and Kent.

"What are you guys doing back?"

"The weather girl didn't tell you?" Timothy said.

Cami hurried up to them, excited and out of breath. "A front is rolling in! It's a solid line of heavy storms over western Illinois. We have maybe two hours."

He rushed out of the café, ignoring the splashes of burning coffee on his hand. He didn't want the men returning from target practice to disperse.

It was time to gather the troops.

Chapter Fifteen

Marcus triple-checked the radar until he was convinced that the storm was the real deal. His troops were up top and ready to go.

Timothy agreed to stay behind. If something were to happen to Marcus, he would be the only one capable of operating the power grid – their ultimate asset. Despite his importance, he still didn't want to sit underground during their mission.

"While you guys are gone, would it be alright if I take the girls up top for a little overnight trip? I want to fly our captured drone out to the bunker. The girls have hardly seen the surface in years."

Marcus mulled it over. "The storm will give you cover, and if all goes well, you'll have nothing to worry about tomorrow. Be safe and return by sunup."

Timothy thanked him and stopped him before he could get on the elevator.

"You're going to hate me, but I'm going to need some blood before you go."

"Now?" Marcus said. "I've got to get up there."

"We programmed expiration resets to the blood key,

and it's time to re-up. This will be the last time – I've already patched the code – but we do need a fresh deposit. Becky is on her way."

He was annoyed, but knew Timothy was right. If something were to happen to either of them, they needed to be able to pass on their control over the grid.

Becky entered the room with a tube and needle in hand. Marcus offered his arm. She rubbed alcohol on it and drew his precious blood.

"All good." She handed the tube to Marcus.

Timothy lugged the blood key up to the table. He ejected the one tube of blood still in the machine. The other was removed several weeks prior when Marcus tossed it at Ashley Cameron before exiling her from the bunker.

Timothy realized the remaining tube was Marcus's blood, and not his.

"Uh, Marcus. Remember when you tossed your blood tube at Ashley and told her to get a DNA test? Did you mean to give her my blood?"

"I must have grabbed the wrong one. Doesn't matter. The kid isn't mine."

"Were you bluffing? Because, man, if you might be responsible for bringing a life into this world, even if it's with a person like Ashley, you should take responsibility."

"I told you I had a vasectomy. That kid isn't mine and this is the last time you ever bring it up."

Marcus broke his gaze and moved to the elevator.

"Hey," Timothy said. "Take down every last one of those drones, will you?"

* * *

Fifty rifle-wielding men and women lined up a convoy of trucks on the bunker site access road. It was calm before the storm, and for a moment, the pale sun peeked through the filmy clouds.

"I'm sure the drones are grounded," Kent said.

"They better be," Robby said. "The storm is here."

A wall of deep blue and grey swept the distant horizon like a tidal wave. The first rumble of thunder rolled across the landscape. Marcus arrived late and gave the signal to depart.

Robby led and set a blazing pace, only slowing to swerve around fallen limbs and the most egregious of potholes. Kent served as his brave passenger. Marcus rode in the second truck with Steve as his driver. Twenty more trucks followed.

The storm started nipping at their heels between Linton and Switz City.

Before the White River – where a month prior Robby nearly drowned after narrowly evading a drone strike – he spotted a familiar man out by the road. He slammed on his brakes, risking twenty fender benders behind him. He rolled down his window.

"Farmer Brant! How are you?"

"Good! Looks like you've got yourself a convoy."

"We're headed to Crane to get revenge on the drones."

"That's where they've been flying out of? Be safe now. Helluva storm on the horizon."

Brant gave a salute and waved to the parade of pickups. Robby flipped the White River off as they crossed. Near the edge of Bloomfield, he picked up his radio.

"Look alive. There were a bunch of jackasses in this

84

town last time we were here. Over."

There were no immediate signs of life, or jackasses, as they entered the town. He slowed to observe the missile-damaged tower where most of the townsfolk lived during the protracted winter. The strike was the first escape from death he and Henry lucked into that day.

A man on a dirt bike shot out in front of them, stopped to get a look, then sped off.

"We have company."

The convoy turned at the courthouse square and came to a planned stop. The rider made another appearance, and shortly after, a truck apart from the convoy pulled up to observe. Robby jumped out and walked straight toward them.

"I was passing through and wanted to know if I could bum a cigarette off that asshole CJ."

A familiar man named Ricky popped out of the passenger window. "Welcome back, you crazy sumbitch! Can't believe you made it out alive. Them drones bombed the shit out of us."

"They about got me. Farmer Brant dragged me out of the river. Is that Joe driving?"

"Sure is. You might recognize the boy on the bike, too."

The rider removed his helmet. It was Cameron, the loner teenager they met in Linton. Robby bearhugged him. Joe got out of the truck and gave Robby a manly handshake.

Marcus joined the reunion. Steve was a stranger to the men, but he joined as well. Ricky, Joe, and Cameron stared at him in awe.

"CJ didn't make it," Ricky said. "He got blowed up same day y'all skipped town. I hate to speak ill of the dead, but we should've never let him run things. He had crazy ideas. Plus, he was a, you know…"

"A neo-Nazi white supremist?" Robby said.

"Uh, yeah, that."

Marcus cleared his throat. "We're on our way to resolve our mutual drone issue. They've been flying out of the Crane Naval Base."

"Damn, I never thought of that."

"What's a naval base doing in Indiana?" Joe asked. "Ain't no submarines around here."

"They used to test sonar equipment and store bombs and shit," Ricky said. "My brother-in-law's cousin worked there."

"It is a drone base now, and we are about to take it over," Marcus said. "You are welcome to join."

"Right on, brother. Let's go fuck up some drones."

* * *

Gusting wind and spitting rain soon turned into a downpour and dime-sized hail. The storm was certainly going to mask their approach. They soon became concerned it would prevent it all together.

Road conditions were poor irrespective of the weather. There was no highway department in the post-apocalypse. But after slow going and a brief stop to clear a tree from the road, they hit the outskirts of Crane.

"Time to go dark," Robby called over the radio. "Headlights off."

The blacked-out convoy crept up to the entrance gatehouse. The third and fourth truck pulled ahead to clear it. There was nobody there.

"Stay on this road," Kent said with eyes on his laptop

map. "We should start seeing buildings."

They passed several identical warehouse structures.

"What are in all these?"

"Munitions, I think. There are about 200 missile bunkers just south of us."

They approached a complex near the center of the base. Robby turned right and drove parallel to a parking lot large enough to fit 200 cars. Instead of cars, two dozen drones were spread equidistant across the pavement. The next lot was twice the size, with twice as many. He pulled forward until the entire convoy fit on the road.

Beyond the lot were several buildings, but only two with lights on, and only one with a door propped open.

The volunteers got out and waited for orders. A group of ex-military and former police congregated outside Marcus's truck, the scouts Cal and Luke among them.

"We're going to hit the building on the right first," Cal said. "Everyone else keeps an eye on the other. Standby on radio."

"Kent and I are coming with," Marcus said.

"What?" Kent said.

"You're the drone expert. We might have a limited opportunity to do damage, so we need you there."

"We'll watch the second building," Robby said.

"Stay right behind me." Cal plugged in an earpiece. "The hotshots up front will do the heavy lifting."

* * *

Marcus and Kent trailed the team as they crossed the lot, weaving between the sleeping drones and stepping over the thick cables laid out to charge them. Deafening rain pelted their poncho hoods. Adrenaline spiked in their systems.

87

They lined up against the wall outside the open door. The lead soldier held out his fist. When he dropped it, they made tactical entry.

Fluorescent lights lit an unmanned lobby with a slick linoleum floor. Security was lax. The next door was propped open as well.

They crept down the hall, guns pointed, clearing each room as they passed. They found no one. Marcus peered inside to see stations with panels, six screens, and joystick consoles. They were in the right place.

As they neared a T-Intersection in the hall, faint music gave them something to follow. They took a right and passed more vacant control stations. The volume of an electronic beat grew. Someone was in the office at the end of the hall.

The lead, an ex-marine they called Cooper, put up his fist and, through nonverbal communication, laid out a plan of attack. *Three, two, one...*

They rushed in. There was no yelling, no struggle. Marcus assumed it was empty and began mentally drawing up a new plan. Then he stepped inside.

A man sat in a computer chair, back turned, obliviously engrossed in a video game. A bottle of vodka and a mess of snacks cluttered the table beside him.

Cooper nodded toward Cal and Luke, who understood to step out and watch the hall. He then nodded at Marcus and the rest of the men.

"Hands up! Don't move!" Cooper yelled.

He grabbed the chair and spun the man around. Another squad member turned the music off.

The pale soldier, in a wifebeater and camouflage pants, looked blankly at the guns pointed at him. He put his hands up, still holding his video game controller.

In a heavy Russian accent, he said, "Who the fuck are you?"

Chapter Sixteen

Marcus placed a hand on Cooper's shoulder before he could punch the Russian. His brief interrogation gathered that he was the only one on duty during the storm. Men split off to search the building and verify.

Marcus stepped in front of the soldier.

"What is your name, soldier? Where are you from?"

"Sergei Vasiliev. Vladivostok."

"Do you know who I am?"

Sergei scrutinized his face. "You are American oligarch who invent intelligent power grid everybody get except Russia."

"Close enough. Can you tell me what it is you do here?"

"We fly drones and find survivors..." He looked around and knew the abridged version wouldn't fly. "...and we eliminate them."

"Who gives you these orders?"

"To us, it is *Command*. We don't ask question."

"You must know something. I find it hard to believe you blindly follow orders to hunt humans. Are the Russians orchestrating all this?"

Sergei laughed. "Russians are not in charge of shit. *Command* speak English only. All we know is they kill our family if we don't follow order."

"Why are Russians on American soil hunting Americans with drones?"

"They tell us it is easier for Russians to kill Americans. They tell us in Russia, Americans are doing same thing."

"Do you find it easier to kill Americans?"

Sergei laughed grimly. "Being Russian does not make easier to kill. Only vodka does." He grabbed the bottle from the table and took a swig. "I am typical Russki."

"How many others are on the base?"

"Twelve, all Russian. Big storm give us night off. My comrades are drunk in the commissary. I pick short straw and have to listen for radio."

Marcus turned away and took out his own radio.

"Robby, there are twelve men in the other building, possibly all drunk. I'm sending Luke and Cal to meet you there. Do you copy?"

"Copy. We'll bring in the brigade."

* * *

Robby and Steve rounded up the troops, who had all gotten back in their trucks to stay out of the rain. They fanned out and crossed the drone parking lot before meeting Cal and Luke outside the lit-up building. They heard music and laughter inside.

"Move as far into the room as quickly as possible so the next guy can get in," Cal said. "Marcus said there are only twelve of them, but we don't know that."

Luke crept to the door and peaked through a window.

He gave a thumbs up. Cal grabbed the door handle and motioned a countdown before bursting into the building.

They followed Cal and did as he ordered, rushing deep into the cafeteria. At the tables in the middle, twelve befuddled and thoroughly inebriated soldiers barely reacted. When the commotion settled, thirty guns were trained on them. They spoke what were presumably curse words, but in a foreign language.

Robby scanned the room frantically, attempting to account for each enemy soldier. At first, all seemed calm. They were frozen by the ambush – all except one man who sat at a table apart from the rest.

Robby did not see it, but he heard the gunshot. He turned in time to see the man fall, and the handgun fall from his hand.

Joe was the one who pulled the trigger. He looked pale white.

"Sumbitch pulled a gun on me!"

Heightened attention turned back to the others. None moved, and none seemed particularly moved by the death of their comrade.

One of the men stumbled forward, testing how twitchy their trigger fingers were. He offered a bottle.

"*Vodka*?"

Cal motioned for everyone to lower their guns. They searched the soldiers and found none of the rest were armed. Robby got on the radio.

"All secure, we count twelve. Well, eleven now, one resisted. Dude, I think they're all Russian."

* * *

Sergei Vasiliev hardly knew where or what Indiana was.

91

He only knew his assigned geographic sector. Previously, he was in New Mexico, and then Oklahoma, doing the same work. His team moved with the warm weather. Shortly before the freezing temperatures were lifted over Indiana, his team was relocated to Crane.

Marcus had Sergei pull up the map he was charged with sweeping. They flew as far west as Illinois Route 1, and east to the Ohio border. They never crossed the Ohio River to the south, or north of lower Indianapolis. It matched with the data Timothy and Kent pulled from the captured drone.

"Electric drones have piss range," Sergei said. "We fly low because they fill atmosphere with chemicals to block the sun and it stays long time."

Marcus pointed to Indianapolis in the center of the state. "Why don't you fly there?"

"There is another base north of *Ko-ko-mo*. Indiana*polis* is their territory. We do not destroy big *infrastruktura*. Small town, no problem, but not skyscraper."

"Do you coordinate with Kokomo?"

"All communication goes through *Command*."

"And to the south?"

"We do not fly over the *oblast* of – how you say? – *Kyen-tuck-ee*. Big base, Fort Knox. That is where *Command* is."

Marcus stroked his chin.

"First break in the weather, we attack Fort Knox and the other Indiana base with everything we have."

Sergei shook his head. "You mess with wrong people."

Chapter Seventeen

Henry and Mariya spent the night holed up in their off-the-record room in the Stacks. Outbursts of shouting echoed down the halls at all hours.

Henry helped sow the seeds of discord, but he wanted no part in a violent struggle. He peered through the apartment door peephole.

"We need to start thinking of an exit strategy."

"We can't get out of the Stacks, let alone past the train station," Mariya said. "The revolt has to work if we want to escape."

"Maybe, but we're staying out of it from now on."

They left the sanctuary of their room to gauge the situation and check on his parents.

At the first hallway intersection, a young man, bleeding from his forehead, jogged by with a frying pan.

"Hey! Excuse me," Henry said. "What's the latest?"

"We beat them out of the Stacks overnight, but they've blocked the entrances on every floor. We have spies looking for weak points. We're collecting frying pans to use as weapons. You two want to join?"

"We need to check on an elderly couple. Maybe after

that."

"You do you, but don't be a slave. This is going down."

The man shrugged and jogged off.

Mariya stifled her laughter until the man was out of sight. "If he only knew he was talking to the very man that sparked the Frying Pan Revolution."

"Yeah...we're not taking part in that."

The light-hearted moment was instantly ruined. They turned the corner and found a woman weeping over a dead man. Blood was smeared wall to wall, as if multiple people had slipped and fallen in a skirmish.

They skirted by the puddle of blood. Inside the stairwell, they passed two more men wielding frying pans.

Henry knocked at his parents' door and waited for his mother's frantic greeting. He knocked again.

"Are you the Plyman's son?" a woman said from across the hall.

"Yes, do you know where they are?"

"They took them away last night. I'm so sorry."

"They? Who do you mean, 'they'?"

"The men with guns. They said your parents were affiliated with Marcus Trencher. That's all I heard. I don't know what else I could've done..."

He turned abruptly and walked the way he came. Mariya thanked the woman and caught up with him.

"Henry, where are you going?"

"Back to the room. I need a frying pan."

* * *

Mariya pleaded. He had his flimsy frying pan, not even cast-iron, and was on a mission to find the stairwell where the revolutionaries were gathering. She finally stopped tugging on his arm and simply held on.

They turned into the last length of hall before the guarded gateway between the Stacks and the rest of the bunker. They caught a glimpse of the enemy's mounting defenses. He tucked the pan behind his back.

A group of women were at the checkpoint chastising the soldiers, or purposely distracting them.

They slipped into the stairwell where a mob of men waited quietly, sitting on the steps, leaning against the walls, on all twelve floors. They received silent nods. All wielded frying pans or equally absurd weaponry.

He hoped they would go soon. He was angry enough to go through with the attack, and it was stifling in the stairwell.

An exhausted man dripping in sweat jogged up from a lower floor. Men cleared out of the way. When he hit the landing, he stopped.

"Floors three, five, and ten," he said, panting. "Go on three loud bangs on the railing. ETA, four minutes." He took a deep breath and sprinted up to the next floor.

Men lined up on the descending flight of stairs. Henry and Mariya were carried down to the fifth-floor landing. A muscular man all of six-foot-five took charge.

"No yelling until we see the whites of their eyes, or they point their guns – whichever comes first. Once we break through, spread out in teams. Take out any soldier you see, take their weapons, and take it all the way to the train platform. This bunker is ours."

Mariya cowered in the corner, clinging to Henry's arm. He had to jostle to keep her space.

"Will you stay with me?" she said.

Three discordant pan strikes rang down the railing like a ceremonial gong. Men pressed against him, forcing him forward, and forcing her to let go.

"...Stay...I'll find you..." Henry said.

Fifteen men flooded into the hall before him and countless more after, like a nightmarish Black Friday sale. The strange silence and overwhelming fear put him out of body, but his body kept moving.

The first primal screams erupted from the front, which could only mean they saw the whites in the enemies' eyes, or guns were now pointed in their direction. Two shots were fired, but they were too late to slow the stampede.

A violent clash played out before him, and then around him. The first thuds were body-to-body, frying-pan-to-protective-plastic. They quickly became more visceral and involving flesh.

The initial wave leveled the soldiers, but all went down in a dogpile. Henry was in the second wave. He watched a man claw the helmet off a soldier in a desperate struggle.

What was he to do? Bash the soldier's head in with a frying pan?

Someone else did it for him. The follow-up strike split the soldier's scalp open. He had to look away. The mob pressed him forward, until he was beyond the skirmish, and out of the Stacks. They broke through.

He hobbled to the side of the checkpoint, confused on how he hurt his ankle. Men flooded into the concourse like a barbarian horde.

He waited for an opportunity to go back for Mariya, but a man grabbed him and yelled in his face, "*Keep moving!*"

Ahead, five enemy soldiers swung around the corner and formed a firing line – too far away to melee. The man beside him threw his frying pan end over end like an axe. The soldiers returned a hail of bullets.

Henry's pan was shot out of his hand. He hit the deck. Men around him did the same, but mostly because they were struck.

He scampered into a shallow smoothie shop full of pastel colors, dragging in a smear of someone else's blood as he flopped across the tile. He crawled around the counter and hid.

A resistance fighter wielding a looted gun fired wildly from somewhere near the checkpoint. He hit everything but the soldiers, forcing them to seek cover in the same smoothie shop.

They did not notice him. He opened cabinets to see if he could fit, but they were all shelved. He cowered helplessly as they exchanged fire.

The volleys ceased. The revolutionaries moved on to paths of less resistance, scattering into other hallways and stairwells to continue the fight.

A soldier turned around and did a double take. He tapped on his superior's shoulder. "What should we do with this one?"

"Put a bullet in him," the superior said. "We've got assets to secure. We don't have time."

Henry lost his breath, gasping for air when he wanted to beg for his life.

Another soldier looked him over.

"Hold up, I recognize him. This guy was super rich, maybe even a billionaire."

"That's half the people down here, including these hedge fund fucks coming at us with frying pans. Waste him and let's move up!"

"No, I mean he was part of *Trencher Industries*. He

was in Marcus Trencher's inner circle."

The soldier removed his helmet – and Henry recognized him.

"Remember me, buddy?"

It was Grant Maniego, the self-proclaimed former Navy Seal who Marcus had exiled from their bunker, nearly naked, months prior. He could hardly make sense of how he ended up where he was, but he was always a sleazy opportunist.

"Drag him to the train platform," the superior said.

Maniego offered Henry a hand. When Henry reached out, he withdrew, and in one fluid motion, slammed his rifle butt into Henry's forehead.

All went black.

Chapter Eighteen

The storm passed Crane in the early morning hours. Robby awoke from a brief nap after his shift watching the Russians. The mercenaries never stirred after a night of such heavy drinking.

He meandered over to the other building, the drone control center. He found Marcus grilling a tired Russian soldier for every detail on how the operation worked. Kent and Steve were in the room as well, but half asleep.

Marcus was hunched over a console studying a panel of screens as the Russian pointed things out. A quick nod is all he got.

"The skies are clearing, and we need our drones in the air before the other bases," Marcus said. "Can you wake the Russians and march them over here?"

Robby sighed, turned around, and walked back to the other building.

In the commissary he yelled, "Rise and shine, comrades. It's time to blow shit up."

The Russians ambled to the control center under armed escort. None resisted. They were even polite. Marcus met them in the hall.

"Allow us to formally introduce ourselves," Marcus said. "We have been your targets – those pesky heat signatures you've been tasked with snuffing out. We realize you were coerced. No hard feelings. Now you are being coerced into attacking two new targets: Grissom Joint Base in northern Indiana, and Fort Knox in Kentucky – or what you guys may know as *Command*."

Sergei translated for those that needed it. The groggy Russians grumbled amongst themselves.

"We will split the fleet and attack both bases simultaneously. You will target grounded drones, battery arrays, and charging infrastructure."

He assigned four Russians to the Indiana base and the rest to Fort Knox.

"After the mission, I will radio Command and notify them that you are all deceased, and you will be free to go. If you do not comply, you will be shot."

The Russians reacted with indifference. They had assumed as much.

* * *

Each drone pilot was accompanied by two armed men. Marcus stayed with Sergei, while Kent volunteered to commandeer a few drones at a station across the hall. The Russians controlled up to six drones each.

Marcus watched the radar blips disperse in opposite directions, with the northbound cluster taking a fifteen-minute head start.

When each fleet was three-quarters the way to their targets, the radio crackled, and a voice came across.

"*Crane, be advised you are not yet authorized for flight, pending weather clearance. Ground your fleet.*

Over."

"Ignore it," Marcus said.

"Approaching *Kyen-tuck-ee* airspace over Fort Knox," Sergei said.

"Got a visual on Grissom Air Force Base," Kent announced from across the hall. "Their whole fleet is still grounded. Ready to engage."

"Fire away," Marcus said.

Robby darted across the hall to witness the carnage. A bright white air strip with dozens of black dots – drones – cut diagonally across the monochrome screen. A friendly drone hovered into view in the lower righthand corner and fired the first two missiles. The flash of impact was spectacular.

Kent flew in closer. "Ah, there they are. Ever seen a battery array get blown up?"

"I've seen a few electric vehicles catch fire."

Kent flipped a switch and pressed a button. A square appeared, framing his target. He pulled the trigger on his joystick and lit up the base.

He unloaded the rest of his payload along with his comrades, and in a matter of minutes, the primary objective of their half of the mission was complete. The base and drone fleet of northern Indiana was obliterated.

Their cheers were interrupted by loud Russian cursing. Two of their drones were shot down over Fort Knox before they had even gotten a shot off.

"We're getting anti-aircraft fire," Sergei said. "And they have drones in air."

"Focus on what's still on the ground," Marcus said. "Kamikaze if you have to. Just get it done!"

Glowing strands of anti-aircraft fire swayed across Sergei's screen. One of his monitors went black. Five seconds later, another. They were dropping fast.

"Fire at will!" Sergei said.

Sergei abandoned evasive maneuvers and zoned in on the fort's crisscrossing of airstrips. He dove his four remaining drones in unison and fired four salvos in rapid succession. Once the blinding flash died down, he hunted his next target.

Marcus jabbed one of the screens with his finger. "Battery array!"

Explosions lit up the air strip. The men were getting their shots off. Another of Sergei's screens went dark. A cluster of squares framed the array and several vertiport platforms. He unleashed all he had left. The three remaining screens burned bright white from the explosions.

They broke out in cheers. A Russian down the hall yelled out that he took out a row of fighter jets.

Two more of Sergei's screens went black. He was down to one drone with zero missiles and only his gun turret.

"Kamikaze, you say?"

He strafed a row of helicopters, emptying out his turret ammunition. He crashed into the last helicopter, turning the last screen dark.

A single drone was set to hover high above, out of the action. They ran down the hall to see what he saw.

The Fort Knox aircraft squadrons were decimated. The battery array and vertiports were destroyed.

They set the few surviving drones left on an auto-piloted course to various vertiports across southern Indiana. They didn't want to bring them all back to Crane, at least immediately.

Retaliation was expected – and expected soon.

Marcus stepped out into the hall. "Alright, everybody! We are relocating to a bunker on site! Move it!"

They hustled out of the building and out to the convoy of trucks. Sergei led them down the road to a row of munitions bunkers. They divided up and sheltered inside two of them. There were enough missiles stockpiled in each to take out a couple Indiana counties.

Outside, not two minutes later, a deafening blast shook the earth. The bunker door was still open, giving them a glimpse of the gigantic fireball plume over the complex. Sergei surmised that it was a ballistic missile.

"Holy shit! What did we just do?" Robby said.

"Declared war, I'd say." Marcus shut the bunker door.

"Thank you for good time," a black-bearded Russian named Rodion said. "Fuck Command!"

The others cheered, "*Fuck Command*!"

"Thank you all, and I am sorry about your comrade last night," Marcus said. "I wish it didn't go down like that."

"Anton?" Rodion said. "You did us favor! He was a Wagner asshole!"

The others agreed.

"Mr. Trencher, I have surprise for you," Sergei said.

He lugged an armored briefcase onto an old aluminum desk.

"Don't worry about building. All you need is here. It is computer."

Kent gravitated forward at the mere mention of a computer. Sergei opened the case.

"What is on it?"

"Access to remaining drones. You can fly them from anywhere. I have all passwords on paper. And it has communication link to Command, so you can tell those bastards all the Russkis are dead."

The Russians laughed.

"Sergei, your surprise is shit," Rodion said. "I have better surprise..."

Rodion pulled two bottles of vodka from his coat and raised them up to more cheers. They passed the bottles around in a celebratory toast.

Chapter Nineteen

Henry awoke handcuffed to a chair in a white room. When he blinked away the tears and let his eyes adjust, it looked like a doctor's office.

He tried to jog his memory – his parents were taken, the frying pan revolt, the... *oh, right, the rifle butt to the face.*

He next wondered if Mariya was safe.

The door opened to a flurry of activity. A man in a suit exchanged words with two soldiers before shutting the door behind him. Henry gathered he was somewhere near the train platform. The agent took out his fake ID card and tore it in half.

"Henry Plyman, you've been busy during your stay at the Quarry," the agent said.

"Where are my parents?"

"Down the hall. We also have Gene Granlund, or Genie. Oh, and your co-conspirators Joel Witt and Vance Rizzo from the labs, Alice something-or-other, and Jim Cox. I'd say that puts your whole network in our custody, except the young lady you've been running around with, but we'll find her, too."

"I'm sure you'll land a big promotion for this."

The agent smirked. "Let's cut to the chase – You get out of this alive under one condition – you hand us the controls over Marcus Trencher's electrical grid. We know he can manipulate its power distribution. Your mother, of all people, let that slip."

Henry was knocked out of the rebellion – early, and literally – but he sensed that it was still underway. The running and shouting beyond the door, the nervous agent trying too hard to be cool. Something was off.

"You're nothing but a pawn."

The agent exhaled a deep sigh through his nostrils.

"...In exchange for control over the Trencher grid, you get to live, and we leave your bunker alone. We'll even throw in the anti-aging serum for ten individuals. Your parents are getting up there. Trencher pulled quite a few strings getting them bunker bids in the first place..."

The agent glanced at the door. A bead of sweat dripped down his temple.

Henry's instincts screamed to waste time.

"Who is orchestrating this holocaust you're so gung-ho to play a part in?"

"A greater human race will emerge from these bunkers, and one that will build a greater civilization fit for the next thousand years. Cooperate, and you will be compensated beyond your wildest dreams, and this will all be over much sooner."

"You don't even know who you are working for, do you? Just a grunt hoping the elites give you a crumb."

"Fine. We do this the hard way."

The agent went to the door and leaned out into the hall. Soldiers ran by, shouting and yelling. Henry grew even more confident that the rebellion was still in motion.

"Bring them all in here. What? I don't care, this takes precedence..."

Henry's parents, Genie, Joel and Vance, Alice, and Jim were hauled into the room, all handcuffed. Joel and Vance looked as though they had been beaten.

"Enough with the games." The agent took out his gun and cocked it. "Tell me how we can transfer the controls of the Trencher power grid, or they start dying."

"Okay, okay..." Henry said, no longer willing to push his luck. "Marcus holds the key to the grid. If you take us down the tunnel, I will talk him into handing it over. Our lives are worth more to him. He'll do it."

"You and the computer whiz can't do it from here?" the agent said, waving the gun at Genie.

"It doesn't work like that," Genie said. "You need the physical key. No way around it."

The commotion ratcheted up outside the room.

"We can pick this up later if you need to handle your business out there," Henry said.

The agent pointed his gun at Henry. "Your little rebellion will be squashed by dinner time." Still, he stepped halfway out of the room, and after a moment, leaned back in with a grin. "Shh, listen, listen! I want you all to hear this..."

The distinct gasp of air brakes, then, a train whistle, reached the room.

"Reinforcements! Safe to say your rebellion is—"

A burst of gunfire interrupted his gloating. Within seconds, a full-on gun battle erupted on the train platform.

The agent stepped all the way into the hall, and as he turned to the train platform, was blasted by machine gun fire. He slammed against the open door and fell back into the room, sliding down the wall. A sash of bullet wounds grew red across his white shirt and black tie. He died instantly.

"Solves that problem..." Vance said.

They crowded into the back corner of the room. Armed men – not the oppressors – ran by in the hallway. One of them entered the room, stepping over the agent's legs. He wielded a machine gun.

He looked them over and flashed a friendly smile.

"Y'all in handcuffs, so y'all probably on my side."

He dug into the agent's pocket and pulled out a set of keys. He uncuffed Harold Plyman, handed him the keys, and politely said, "There you are, sir."

"Did you fight your way down from the Stacks?" Mr. Plyman asked after thanking the man.

"Nah, we're from the Speedway Bunker, and a few guys from Louisville. We just hopped off the train we jacked. Name's Taveon Hunter."

They thanked Taveon profusely as they shed their handcuffs.

"Happy to help, but we ain't done yet. We're headed down to my man Marcus Trencher's bunker. We starting a revolution. Y'all welcome to join."

Chapter Twenty

The expeditionary force departed Crane shortly after the overwhelmingly successful mission. Marcus wanted to get back to the safety of the bunker before a more robust counterstrike could be mustered.

The Russians opted to stay in the area, pledging to re-arm the remaining drones when called upon. In return, Marcus routed electrical power to the nearby town of Odon, which the Russians jokingly renamed Moscow. The Bloomfield crew promised to deliver food and supplies. They exchanged radio contact information, a ceremonial bottle of vodka, and went their separate ways.

With the decimation of Fort Knox and annihilation of the two drone fleets in Indiana, a buffer zone was created.

Electric drones, especially those that are heavily armed, had extremely limited range. If any were to be deployed from neighboring states, they would have to land and recharge at least once, if not twice, simply to reach them.

Fuel-powered drones and manned aircraft were surely still at the enemy's disposal, but there was no doubt they had struck a substantial blow.

* * *

After a brief stop in Bloomfield to see Joe, Ricky, and Cameron off, the convoy continued back towards Sherman County.

"Was I dreaming, or did we really just bomb *Fort-Fucking-Knox*?" Robby said.

"I bet they're scrambling jets," Kent said. "Never thought I'd ask this, but could you maybe step on it?"

"Right after I say hey to my old pal."

Farmer Brant was working on a combine tractor in the field next to his house when they passed.

"Farmer Brant! We did it!" Robby yelled.

The farmer pumped his fist and waved.

They made it back to the bunker without incident. No drones, jets, helicopters, or ballistic missile strikes.

* * *

The rebels from Speedway and Louisville pushed the Quarry revolt to total victory. The hijacked train sat at the station, riddled with bullets. Bodies littered the platform. Prisoners of war were stripped of their weapons and equipment. Henry had a hard time wrapping his head around it.

He reunited with Mariya on the bunker-side platform.

"I thought I lost you," she said.

"I'm so sorry. Let's get back home and take it easy."

"Looks like we'll be taking a few new friends with us."

Taveon Hunter, rebel leader, was moved to action not

only by Marcus's metaverse video, but by a personal relationship. To Henry's surprise, he had met Marcus and considered him a friend.

"Mr. Trencher taught my boy algebra when he was hiding out in Speedway. He told me all about the fake asteroid and shit. When my boy showed me his message on the metaverse, I knew it was time. Carmel made a big mistake – Speedway controls the food production. We fought them off once and took off before they came back with more than we could handle."

"How'd you manage that?" Henry said. "Here, everyone grabbed frying pans."

"We had a whole warehouse to work with, but we messed them up pretty good with our forklift cavalry."

"The forklift rebellion of Speedway. I like it."

Another man approached and towered over them. Henry had a passing interest in basketball and knew exactly who it was – Ellis Caldwell, NBA all-star and Kentucky Wildcat legend.

"Pleasure to meet you folks," Ellis said. "I met Mr. Trencher when he came down our way in Louisville."

"Did you guys revolt down there, too?"

"Nah, too much of a military presence in the caverns, with the tunnel connection to Fort Knox and all. They squashed rebellion talk real quick – killed a kid or two. But me and my guys hijacked the train, and here we are."

Taveon introduced his son, Trevion, who was with Ellis's daughter, Jayla. Both spoke highly of Marcus.

Henry never thought Marcus's grand adventure months back, which started in such a dark place, would've made him so many friends.

He stopped by to thank the pharmacists Joel and Vance again as they were getting patched up by Alice.

"We will maintain the lab," Joel said.

"We won't ship any serum out to the vampires," Vance added, "but it's a bargaining chip worth preserving."

"Agreed," Henry said. "We need to hold the Quarry in case another wave of soldiers comes in. I just learned that Louisville is connected to Fort Knox, and we know Carmel isn't happy."

"There are plenty of guys with frying pans around here," Joel said. "We'll hold down the fort."

Jim Cox joined them, looking laughably short next to Ellis. "We'll get the communications cable reconnected so we can keep in touch."

"Sounds like a plan," Henry said.

Mariya frantically tapped him on the shoulder and pointed at the body being dragged by. It was Grant Maniego, who started in their bunker, on the half with Timothy. He played a part in killing the engineers who built the bunker, then double-crossed them during the trial, all before a failed plot to assassinate Marcus.

Henry had every right to hate the man, but he only felt sad for the wasted life.

* * *

Marcus's first stop off the elevator was the media room, where Big Pigg dutifully sat at his station.

"Any word from Bloomington?"

"Not a peep. The tunnel trail cam ain't triggered, neither."

Marcus turned to Timothy and Robby. "Let's send a team to Bloomington to get Henry tomorrow."

Robby wanted to say, "No, tonight!" but even he was

exhausted by the Crane mission.

Marcus took the microphone to address the bunker and announced their safe return, and that a celebration was to be held in the gardens.

After he set the microphone down, he said, "I'm not going. Wake me if something important happens."

* * *

Brad and Becky put together a decent food spread considering the last-minute heads up. A bourbon barrel was brought down from the pantry, but drink service was to be closely regulated. During the last party, Robby was wrongfully accused of assault and murder, before all together fleeing the bunker into the freezing cold. Still, no one was more excited to let loose.

When details spread of their successful operation, people were more scared than jubilant. What was to come their way after such a thing?

We attacked Fort Knox?

Russians were flying the drones? But now they are on our side?

Can bombs penetrate down to the bunker?

Have we even figured out who we are fighting?

The crew who went on the mission were more than happy to tell their heroic sides of the story.

Robby's eagerness to party quickly waned. Melonie was not happy with him for going on the mission. He people watched with her from the gazebo in the gardens and wisecracked until she finally laughed.

A too-easy target entered his view, but he held his tongue. Big Pigg waded through the crowd, searching in visible distress.

"Babe, I'll be right back. Something is up." He grabbed Big Pigg, startling the former trucker. "What's going on?"

"I kept calling Mr. Trencher, but he ain't answering – there's lights in the tunnel. Someone's coming our way from Bloomington."

Robby gave him a nod well-done and took off. He banged on Marcus's suite door until he answered. He had been dead asleep.

"Get dressed. They spotted lights in the tunnel."

* * *

A fleet of golf carts, ATVs, and one small car sped down the tunnel to the barricades. Some of the men were inebriated from the celebration. None had any idea what awaited them, Marcus included. He hadn't heard from the Quarry since he fled the place and caught a bullet to his shoulder on the way out.

At the barricade, a scared teenager could only point east at the lights in the distance. Men lined up behind the earthen barricades. Marcus found the foreman who led the construction.

"If we can't hold them, we blow the tunnel."

The lights grew brighter. Two in particular – headlights – separated to the forefront. The vehicle came to a stop fifty yards out. A silhouette of a man got out and approached. The men behind the barricades readied their aim.

"There's about two hundred more behind me, all ready to fight. That's a whole-ass train back at the rail gap..."

"Weapons down!" Marcus yelled.

He sprinted between the barricades toward the shadowy figure and hugged his closest friend in the world, nearly taking him to the ground.

Robby followed and cut in, lifting Henry in the air.

"Boy, do I have some stories to tell you guys," Henry said.

"Bro, so do we. We straight up bombed Fort Knox."

Henry laughed, thinking it was a Robby joke.

"Your message worked," Henry said to Marcus. "It sparked an uprising in Speedway and the Quarry, and they hijacked the train in Louisville. They've traveled all this way to take up the fight."

Marcus looked down the tunnel where the train light blinked as people walked in front of it. He took a deep breath and exhaled.

"Good. We are going to need them."

* * *

Timothy kept tabs on the Crane mission via radio during his family field trip to the surface. Given the good news, he opted to extend their stay overnight.

He spent much of the stormy night driving his daughters, Liza and Maddie, around the town of Sherman. Maddie used to fear bad weather, but after being stuck underground for so long, she enjoyed the thunder and lightning.

A scout hooked them up with stale graham crackers, stale marshmallows, and a few chocolate bars. They didn't build a campfire to make proper smores, but they did have a microwave in the house they stayed in.

He wasn't about to write a guide on post-apocalyptic parenting, but the little vacation was the best he had done in some time. It was hard after his wife Shelley left them in that miserable bunker to fend for themselves.

Liza pouted and Maddie cried when they had to make their way back the next morning. They made one stop at the warehouse north of town to retrieve the captured drone. He flew it overhead and set its course to the bunker site.

He drove as slow as the truck could go. The girls stuck their hands and faces out of the windows, taking in the nature they had been robbed of for so long. They made it back as the sun broke through the haze as brightly as he had seen it during his forays up top. The drone was there, right where it was programmed to land.

"I don't want to go back down there," Maddie said. "I want to live up here forever."

"We will someday soon, I promise."

They looked out across the landscape one last time. The distant tree line, the gently rolling hills. The half-filled lake. The sky. He hugged his daughters before turning to the door and punching in the code to enter.

"Dad, what is that?" Liza said, pointing to the sky.

A massive blended-wing cargo plane flew low in the sky. They heard the roar of its engines. A trail of objects fell from it. Soon after, parachutes deployed.

His stomach dropped. "Girls, get inside."

It was clear that the parachuting objects were not human, but he couldn't make out what they were until one landed forty yards in front of him.

A machine with triangular tracks hit the ground and bounced like a dead cat. A mechanical body and head unfurled. Once upright, it stood about five feet tall. It released the parachute and rolled forward. Timothy put half his body inside the door but kept watching.

The machine rotated toward him. He closed the door further. Its two arms, bent at 90-degrees, retracted into its body. Belts of ammunition fed into its gun-barrel forearms.

He had seen enough to know that these machines were not friendly. He shut the door.

Book II

Chapter Twenty-One

Word had gotten out that an army of "Terminators" were roaming above the bunker. They gathered around the monitors linked to the doorbell cams on the elevator dome.

Robby charged into the room.

"Are there really metal skeletons with machine guns walking around up there?"

"They don't look like the movie Terminators," Henry said.

Robby leaned in to get a glimpse. One of the machines wandered into view like a wild animal.

"Looks more like Johnny-5 with a couple guns for arms," Robby said. "Kind of disappointing, honestly."

As dumb as it sounded, they all agreed. Marcus, evermore analytical, started to break down its components.

"The head holds its sensors. The body and arms are all about guns and ammo. The battery sits between the tank treads, and that's a solar panel on its back. I think they set these things out and forget about them."

"How many are there?" Henry asked.

"At least three dozen, maybe more," Timothy said.

"They are wandering around like zombies for now," Marcus said. "We need to break out before they surround our one exit to the surface."

* * *

Timothy rode the elevator up with Cal, Luke, and Cooper, the ex-Marine who proved his bravery during the raid on the Crane mission.

"One Johnny-5 is right outside the man door," Timothy said, viewing a camera feed on his tablet. "Slip out the cargo door, and then—"

"I got it from there," Cooper said. "Just be ready to let me back in."

Timothy opened the cargo door halfway and Cooper ducked under it. Cal and Luke fed a ladder and a hunting rifle out after he was clear.

Cooper went to the back side of the dome, propped the ladder up, and climbed to the top. He laid flat and inched forward to a sniping position.

"Johnny-5 in sight. Aiming for the head."

He set the radio to his side. As he narrowed his sights, the radio slowly began slipping away on the curved surface. It picked up speed, tumbled and clinked off the side, and crashing to the ground.

The machine spun around and homed in on the radio. Then, it detected Cooper.

Cooper hurried his shot and missed.

The machine sent a barrage of machine gun fire ricocheting off the dome. Cooper shimmied backwards until he slid off the back.

Cal, Luke, and Timothy watched the video feed,

horrified.

"Coop, are you good?" Timothy called over the radio.

There was no response.

Cal was all about playing it safe, but he wasn't about to leave a man to die. "Crack the cargo door. We'll blast this thing with every shell we have and get Coop."

Luke cocked his shotgun, and they stepped out. There was no initial sign of Cooper, but the terminator was rolling toward the other side of the dome.

Cal fired first and hit the machine squarely on the side, rocking it onto one tread before it wobbled back onto both. Luke hit it next, producing sparks but no real damage.

When it turned to face them, Cal aimed higher. He pulled the trigger and blew its Johnny-5 head to bits. It glitched and spun back and forth. Luke emptied a round toward its base, producing more sparks – this time disabling it.

Cooper crawled around the dome.

They scanned the landscape on all sides. The next closest machine was more than a football field's length away – but moving their way. The others further out were doing the same.

They dragged the dead robot to the cargo door and pulled it inside. Cal asked to borrow Timothy's radio.

"Mr. Trencher, we disabled one and we're sending it down. Send as many men that can fit on the elevator up, pronto. The other machines are closing in."

* * *

Timothy watched his tablet for approaching terminators. It was less terrifying than staring down the elevator shaft abyss while the platform was far below. Ten minutes later, the platform returned with twenty armed men.

"We ain't got time to draw out an elaborate plan," Cal said. "Spread out, aim for the head. Treat it like hunting deer, except the deer shoot back."

The men followed Cal's simple orders. They found advantageous positions, sat still, and let the prey come to them.

The machines had artificial intelligence and computational reaction times, but their weaponry was not accurate at distance. The men had hunting rifles with scopes, and many were good marksmen.

Timothy found the ladder and climbed onto the dome to serve as a scout.

Methodically, the men moved across the open field, sniping the terminators before they were close enough to fire back with any accuracy. Only twice did any shoot at the men, and neither hit anyone.

It became clear – the machines were dumb, disposable slaughterbots with brutally simple programming and no self-preservation – leftover military tech allocated to address the nuisance in southern Indiana.

A pair of scout teams ventured out to a distant tree line to finish off the machines that got caught in the limbs.

Afterwards, the men were euphoric from their dominant victory.

"Is that all they got?" a man said.

Timothy was happy, too, but he was certain that was not all the enemy had in store for them.

Chapter Twenty-Two

Marcus was pleased, but he shared Timothy's sentiment. It was a little too easy.

"We're not attracting enough attention," Marcus said as he paced in front of his desk. "That attack was insulting. It was unserious."

"What? Do you want them to nuke us?" Robby said.

"Let's have some perspective here," Timothy said. "For all we know, the enemy is preoccupied with wiping out millions in India or China. We're in rural Indiana. We are gnats."

"Hey, we're at least mosquitoes after Fort Knox."

Henry stuck his head in the suite. "The council meeting is about to start. You guys coming?"

"Cancel it," Marcus said. "We have more important things to do."

"I don't think that's a good idea. That Tammy lady gave me an earful. Folks are upset about things."

Marcus scoffed.

"A disgruntled bunker population is the last thing we need," Timothy said. "Hear them out and then we'll get on with planning."

* * *

They walked into the War Room ten minutes late for the council meeting. Marcus called for Taveon Hunter and Ellis Caldwell to join them. Tammy Martin was offended by their presence, and the rest for their tardiness.

"I can't hold my tongue any longer," Tammy said. "We have problems that you and your gang have ignored while gallivanting on the surface. Your assistant gave out room keys, and then after all *these people* showed up, she's trying to take them back."

"These men saved my life," Marcus said. "They will be treated with the utmost respect and hospitality."

"Ma'am, with all due respect, we need a place to sleep," Taveon said. "We've been lying on the ground in them gardens like homeless people."

"There are houses on the surface. Besides, we don't have enough food to feed all these new mouths."

""They brought a train load of food with them, and we have the space," Marcus said. "Single occupants will pair up to free up apartments. All in favor."

Marcus and friends eked out a victory in the vote. Tammy huffed and puffed. Another token member, Bill Douglass, picked up the reins.

"We still got men busting their asses in the coal mine. You said they had a power cable in the tunnel, and we wouldn't have to work. Things ain't got no better for any of us."

"Henry, can you get a status update on the cable?"

"What should we do with the train?" Ellis asked. "The other bunkers rely on it for food deliveries and medicine."

The hijacked train still sat at the rail gap between

their bunker and the Quarry. Marcus mulled it over.

"Do you think you and your men could operate it?"

"Sure, we could run the stops," Ellis said.

Marcus nodded and ended the council meeting there. Tammy, Bill Douglass, and Clay Boyle were unsatisfied, but Marcus didn't care.

Marcus held a walking meeting with Timothy, Henry, and Robby on the way back to his suite. Mariya and Henry's parents joined them along the way.

Marcus's attention had already turned back to the enemy's low effort retaliatory attack. He found it insulting.

"We need to attract more attention," he said. "They are not taking us seriously enough yet. At least not seriously enough to reveal themselves."

"Like I said, it is clearly a global entity of some kind," Timothy said. "They are worried about bigger, more populated places."

"Then make it look like we have a larger population than we actually do," Mariya said. "Fake it 'til you make it."

"Mariya is on to something," Mr. Plyman said. "The British created decoy cities along the coast during World War II. They lit them up at night, and even carefully mimicked street grids with fake streetlights, and the Germans dropped their bombs on them, all the while the real cities were blacked out and untouched."

Marcus liked the idea immediately. "This is brilliant. We will modify of course, but this could work."

It was believable that they would move to the surface, given the improved weather and the fact they had taken out the nearest drone fleets.

If the enemy had satellites, they could clearly see the lights of a small city in an otherwise dark world.

"We will send as many men and women as we can to Terre Haute tomorrow morning," Marcus said after a moment more of thought. "We will turn on every light we can find. I want them to see Terre Haute from space."

Chapter Twenty-Three

Two-hundred men and women jumped at the opportunity to spend a day on the surface. For most, it was the first time in nearly a year-and-a-half. Nobody cared about the dangers anymore. They wanted to see the trees and grass and sky. Terre Haute wasn't much of a tourist destination, but the volunteers were excited, nonetheless.

Men load crates of light bulbs from the storage tunnels. Nobody knew if the bulbs would match up, but if they managed to fix the streetlights, that alone might achieve their goal of deception.

"Every light in every house and building," Marcus blared through a bull horn. "Break into places, do what you have to do. Just make it bright."

* * *

The volunteers drove lift trucks from the highway department, a fleet of school buses, and passenger vans, and by sunrise, were on U.S. 41 North. It was by far the largest contingent that had ever left the bunker.

Marcus stayed back, as did Timothy, Kent, and Genie,

who were all hard at work trying to exploit the Russian's drone laptop. They exercised their control over the grid to route all necessary power to Terre Haute.

Mariya joined Henry, and Robby talked Melonie into tagging along. She was several months pregnant, but not immobile. He also convinced Marcus to let Brad and Becky join, saying they deserved a vacation from all the cooking. Steve rode with them, and he invited Mercedes.

The rebel groups led by Taveon and Ellis joined the mission. By 6 a.m., the convoy had reached a Walmart Supercenter south of town. Lighting the city was top priority, but looting was a close second.

A group of former electricians and linemen focused on the streetlights. A contingent split off at 7th Street, while another hit the Indiana State University campus. Others drove to the northern edge of the city and worked their way south. Bigger buildings like hospitals, dorms, and offices were prime targets.

Robby called dibs on the old Honey Creek Mall. It was not a great source of light, but he thought it would be fun.

They stepped through the shattered glass doors of a department store and received instant doses of nostalgia.

"This place has seen better days," Henry said.

"It was on its last leg long before the end of the world," Robby said.

They swung by the food court. When the men saw the arcade, they sprinted inside like children and put forth more effort in powering up the games than completing the mission. The women finally peeled them away, but they vowed to return to steal a few arcade cabinets for the bunker.

At the other end of the mall, they saw signs of habitation. A strip of stores had been remodeled into living spaces complete with beds and cookware.

"People were living here, *Dawn of the Dead* style," Henry said.

"I don't think it was that long ago," Steve said, pointing his flashlight into a Hot-Topic-turned-bedroom.

They heard squeaking sneakers nearby, attracting their flashlight beams to the looted jewelry store at the corner. A figure retreated.

Mercedes pulled out a handgun. "What? None of you brought a gun?"

"We come in peace," Brad called out. "We have food and water."

When they cautiously turned the corner. They found a young girl and an even younger boy cowering against a column. They were both rail thin and dirty.

"We're not here to hurt you," Becky said. "Are your parents here?"

The girl sheepishly shook her head. Mariya retrieved snack bars and water from her backpack. The frightened children approached, too famished not to.

"The grownups left," the girl said. "My mom died in the winter."

"I'm sorry to hear that. We have a community, and it has food, and games, and even a swimming pool. Would you like to come with us?"

They shook their heads yes.

* * *

Marcus kept tabs on the mission by monitoring the power usage from his godlike grid application. Years ago, Terre Haute was the first true city to implement his technology, putting him and his company on the map.

129

When the day passed into the late afternoon, he called Timothy into his suite. It was time to attempt the first radio contact with the enemy.

"Are you giving our people enough time to get back?"

"I won't mention Terre Haute yet," Marcus said. "Let's just see if someone picks up on the other end."

Timothy opened the program he had cloned from the Russian's armored briefcase. All Marcus had to do was click a button to connect.

"This is Marcus Trencher. I am responsible for the attacks on the drone bases in Indiana, as well as Fort Knox. Your Russian assets are all dead. I would like to negotiate terms of peace."

They waited.

"No answer, but someone is listening," Timothy said.

Marcus repeated his message in fewer words. Still, there was no response.

"Some grunt is probably running to get his superior," Timothy said. "They'll talk."

* * *

Under Robby's leadership, the group made their way from the mall to Bogey's Family Fun Center. They had turned the lights on in a handful of restaurants surrounding the mall and little else. Other groups appeared to be putting in work, as more and more lights appeared in the distance.

The skies began to darken, and the air grew chilly. It began to feel like a classic Fall evening. Robby found the fun center's circuit box and turned the lights on over the go-cart track and putt-putt course.

"There! You all can tell Marcus I did my part."

The children warmed up to them. The girl went by Carolann, and the boy, Trevor. They drove laps around the track for a half-hour before Henry, Steve, and Mariya convinced Robby that they should get back to the actual mission.

They drove a short distance to the much bigger Terre Haute Action Track. After some searching and fence-climbing, Henry turned on the powerful lights over the oval track and drag strip.

"I know where there are even brighter lights," Henry said.

He led the way to Bob Warn Field, home of the ISU Sycamores baseball team. When Steve flipped the switch, the rest of them cheered from the overgrown infield. The lights were as bright as any in the city.

"Not bad for a day's work," Robby said.

They departed as the sun sank below the horizon. The city began to glow. It certainly looked inhabited at street level.

They could only hope it would help accomplish whatever Marcus's mad plan called for.

Chapter Twenty-Four

Robby, Henry, and the gang were not the only ones to find survivors in Terre Haute. Thirty-five ragged individuals returned with groups to the bunker, often after tense stand-offs. Survivors claimed there were hundreds more scattered throughout the city, and that even more had left to seek out Amish communities rumored to be thriving in Parke County.

A few men went AWOL. The taste of freedom was too much to give up so soon.

Mariya and Becky introduced the two orphaned children to Timothy's daughters, who gladly took them on a bunker tour. Mercedes and Steve found the councilwoman Tammy Martin and gave her the task of finding living arrangements for them.

Marcus greeted Henry and Robby at the elevator and had them follow to the War Room.

Timothy, Kent, and Genie were already there holding a hackathon on the Russian laptop.

The meteorologist Cami Stinnett arrived soon after. "You asked for me?"

Marcus nodded. "Remember the doppler radar

setting that detected aircraft? I need that turned on and kept on."

"I thought you guys took out all the drones?"

"More might be heading our way from further away."

Cami left to complete her task.

"Kent, I need you to rendezvous with the Russians to re-arm our drones. Park them closer to the bunker site afterwards, or at least in the county."

Henry hovered over Timothy's shoulder and tried to comprehend the mind-boggling lines of computer code.

"You guys hack that laptop yet?"

"They gave us all the passwords. But we are trying to gain access to systems we aren't authorized to and find vulnerabilities."

Robby yawned obnoxiously. "Whelp, you guys have this under control. We worked our butts off turning on lights all day. I'm going to bed."

"We are about to reach out to the enemy," Marcus said. "...and we need to piss them off. I think you would be perfect for this."

Robby was suddenly intrigued.

"You want me to get on there and talk shit?"

"More or less but hit on these talking points."

Marcus handed him a bullet-pointed list. He skimmed it and got into character.

Timothy put the laptop in front of him.

Robby cracked his knuckles and leaned forward.

"Greetings, Nazi assholes. It's your friends from Indiana. Here's the deal – we took out your Russian mercenaries and every drone in the region. We rocked Fort Knox, and we made quick work of those stupid Johnny-5 robots you dropped on us.

"Underground, we've seized your precious anti-aging

133

serum. We sparked a full-on revolution in the bunker network.

"We've even retaken the surface. There's 30,000 of us in Terre Haute, probably more in Bloomington. We got the streetlights working and all. We know you're listening. It is time to negotiate."

After a moment, a burst of static came through.

Marcus put a finger before his mouth to hush the already quiet room.

The static remained for ten seconds, but no words were spoken. It ended with a rustling and click. It was all the response they would get.

"They *definitely* heard that," Timothy said.

Marcus patted Robby on his shoulders for a job well done. Robby didn't understand how getting the silent treatment could be considered a success.

"They heard that 30,000 of us are living in Terre Haute – and maybe the Bloomington part – and that's all we wanted."

"So, they are about to bomb the shit out of Terre Haute," Robby said. "What then? I don't get it."

"They don't have a drone fleet within a hundred miles of us. Whatever they send to Terre Haute will be out of charging range."

"They'll have to send whole fleets to each city," Henry said, "if they believe those population numbers."

Marcus broadcasted the live doppler radar. "As soon as we see incoming bogeys, we spring the trap."

Robby started to catch on. "So, you shut the grid down while all the drones are in the air, and they won't have enough juice to fly back?"

"Bingo. We'll black out the entire Midwest."

Robby finally understood. "Diabolical!"

* * *

Blips emerged at the edges of the radar sometime after 3 a.m. More and more followed until clear formations were detected. The origins were somewhere in western Illinois. Moments later, another fleet entered from central Ohio.

Timothy ran around the room, shouting and shaking everyone awake.

"There has to be a hundred in each fleet," Henry said.

"Let's verify they are drones," Marcus said. "Kent, get a couple of our own airborne."

"I don't have to," Kent said. "I can tell by speed and travel distance. Those are drones."

"Excellent, but I still want you to throw a couple of our own at them. Try to take a few down and make it look like we're defending ourselves."

Kent had already parked a drone outside Terre Haute. When he set it to hover 1,000 feet above the south end, they saw how lit up the city was. Even Marcus was impressed.

"Weird...none of those inbound drones show in their system," Timothy said as he typed furiously on the Russian laptop. "The doppler is nice, but this would give us exact coordinates."

"Already on it," Genie said.

Enemy drones approached like moths to a flame. Bombs began to drop, illuminating the city even brighter, but in a hellish way. Dorms were toppled, a hospital was cratered, and fires tore through neighborhoods.

Kent locked on to the nearest targets and unleashed every missile he had in rapid fire. He scored two hits, possibly a third. He led a brief chase before being shot down.

"I have another a mile out," Kent said

"Keep it there," Marcus said. "Timothy, pull up the grid controls."

"Up and ready," Timothy said. "Just say when."

Marcus studied the doppler map. The enemy fleets were clustered over Terre Haute and Bloomington. There was nothing left to do. It was time.

"Kill the power."

With the click of a button, the city of Terre Haute went dark, leaving only the fires emitting light. The sudden darkness was shocking, and they expected it.

Marcus imagined what the enemy was thinking as they watched their live feeds. Did they know what they had walked into yet?

He gave Timothy the go-ahead to black out the entire Midwest grid. From the Mississippi River to Appalachia, and Michigan to Tennessee – every municipal battery array, household unit, and suburban microgrid – all dark, all at once.

It was more than what was necessary, and survivors across the Midwest would momentarily suffer, but it was a show of force.

The drones could drop all the bombs they wanted. After, they had two choices: land...or fly until they fell out of the sky. They were not making it back to the bases they came from. The trap had already worked.

Marcus let the darkness settle in before finally re-engaging on the comms link.

"Marcus Trencher, again. By now, I assume you've realized that you will not be getting your drones back. You've now lost both fleets in Indiana, one at Fort Knox, and now two more from neighboring states. I will expect a call tomorrow at noon. Goodnight.

Chapter Twenty-Five

Harold Plyman peeked his head into the War Room, eager to find Henry and catch up on last night's happenings over breakfast. Instead, he only found Timothy, Genie, and Kent. The IT trio had worked through the early morning, fueled by coffee, looted energy drinks, and a limited window of opportunity.

"What's kept you three at it?" Mr. Plyman asked.

"The Russians gave us a laptop that controls the Crane drone fleet," Kent said. "The other drone fleets aren't showing up on it for whatever reason. The doppler was the only reason we saw them coming last night."

Timothy yawned and stretched. "If we gain visibility in their system, we'd know the exact coordinates of all their drones."

Genie's typing became angrier until she buried her face in her hands. "Why can't I break this trash security program?"

Mr. Plyman was reminded of a favor that she had done him a favor weeks earlier.

"Genie, I never got the chance to thank you for getting

my wife and I an extra metaverse headset back at the Quarry. I know they made that a difficult feat to pull off."

"It was no problem, I just had to add a made-up serial number into...the...Wait! That's it!"

Timothy and Kent looked over her shoulder.

"...Every drone has a unique identifier. The laptop was hard coded to only show the one fleet, and look, all the drone serial numbers are sequential."

"So just..." Kent said.

"Expand the serial array," Timothy said. "Generate the next thousand, before and after, and plug them in."

"I should be thanking you, Mr. Plyman!" Genie said.

He didn't comprehend, but he was happy to have sparked something positive.

"I'll leave you to it. Don't work too hard, now."

* * *

The others began trickling in around 11 a.m., just as Timothy, Genie, and Kent were wrapping up. All of them failed to get sleep after dealing their most decisive blow to the enemy yet.

Marcus arrived last and became the third consecutive person to ask, *"Have you guys been here all night?"*

"Yes, and we made a breakthrough," Timothy said. "Check it out."

He switched the doppler radar broadcast to another map of the same area. The new display had approximately 200 icons scattered across the area.

"Genie figured out how to get the other drones to register. Those dots are the ones that attacked Terre Haute and Bloomington last night, and the handful we had left from Crane. The gray color means they are grounded, which is all of them."

Marcus stepped up to study the screen. "Can you control them?"

"Not yet, at least not remotely. The only way is if we get ahold of them and reprogram them the way Kent did with the one that we captured."

"Then that is what we will do. Dispatch teams to all these coordinates. Kent, can you lead a crash course to train the men?"

"They pretty much just plug in a tablet. My program will do the rest."

"Guys, that's not all," Timothy said. "Wait until you see this..."

He zoomed out and thousands of new dots populated the map, moving a pixel at a time here and there over the states, except the Midwest where they were all grounded and gray. Hundreds were active over Texas. The coasts were swarming. No more than a dozen were allocated to places like Montana and the Dakotas.

"Holy shit, we can see them all?" Robby said.

"All 7,806 of them. And look – it's obvious where their bases are."

"Can't you guys shut down every *Trencher* grid? If it's working in the Midwest, why not take it down everywhere?"

"We only created the blood key for the Midwest grid. The other grids work as advertised – decentralized and protected from manipulation."

"It was a regulatory, anti-monopoly issue," Marcus said. "The government forced us to leave gaps between regional grids. The Midwest grid goes from the Mississippi River to the Appalachian Mountains, and from Canada down to the hydroelectric wall in southern

Kentucky. Customers in those gaps could own units, but they could not be on our power-sharing subscription grids."

"Excellent work, guys," Henry said, checking his watch. "It's almost noon. Are we ready for the call if it comes through?"

"All set," Timothy said.

The clock struck noon and two minutes passed without a word spoken.

Finally, a series of beeps sounded. Timothy moved the laptop in front of Marcus, who accepted the call. The voice on the other side did not wait for him to speak.

"Mr. Trencher, it is time we talked. Please be present at the George Rogers Clark Memorial in Vincennes, Indiana, at noon in two days. It would be wise not to bring a crowd. I look forward to meeting you."

Click.

Chapter Twenty-Six

Kent held a crash course on how to hijack a drone. More volunteers would have been ideal, but they only had so many of the devices and wires required. Using the captured drone, each team learned where the panel was, what tools opened it, where to plug in the device, and how to run the program. Manuals and maps were provided.

Kent concluded with a warning: the drones had power reserves and were still dangerous.

Timothy reactivated a sliver of the local grid to recharge vehicles. Brad and Becky prepared meals to last them a day-and-a-half. Marcus told them to scavenge for the rest, and good luck.

The volunteers split into east and west divisions and worked in pairs.

They came to the consensus that the Illinois fleet departed from Scott Air Force Base east of St. Louis. After the bombing and the grid going dark, they were grounded around the Terre Haute and as far west as Marshall and Effingham.

The fleet that attacked Bloomington came from an Air Force base near Dayton, Ohio. Like the Illinois fleet, its range was maxed out upon arrival, leaving little battery power to make the return. None made it back over the Indiana-Ohio border. Most were found in open fields near Connersville and Richmond like herds of sleeping buffalo. Only a few were isolated on rooftops or in far flung backyards.

Back at the bunker, Timothy, Kent, and Genie confirmed the transfer of each drone in real time. Timothy found the nearest vertiport, reactivated the grid around it, and sent the drones one-by-one to recharge. The next stop was Crane, where the Russians waited to rearm them.

They came away with 80-percent of the grounded drones before the enemy caught on. Three teams, six individuals, were gunned down south of Richmond. The mission was called after that.

Marcus called it an overwhelming success, despite the losses.

* * *

They had to decide on who would make up the delegation to Vincennes, what precautions to take, and what demands to make.

"I'll come along for moral support," Henry said.

"I'll come with," Robby said, "but I want fifty drones in the sky behind me."

"I'm in," Timothy said. "What are our demands?"

"To stop the killing, but they won't agree to that," Marcus said. "Whatever deal they offer won't matter. We will not be co-opted into their scheme."

Steve knocked and entered. "The drone wrangling teams are trickling in. Want me to send Cal and Luke in?"

Marcus agreed to give his most trusted scout team an

audience.

The duo entered and took off their hats at the same time. Cal stepped forward first.

"We wanted to give you a general report after venturing east. Basically, there are a lot more survivors that we ever thought."

"A couple in every town," Luke said. "After we told them what we were up to, they offered to help, or at least let us through."

"We were told there's 400 in New Castle, a hundred in New Palestine, a thousand in Greenfield. They all survived the winter and learned how to avoid the drones. If you want a bigger army, there's one out there."

"Thank you, this is encouraging," Marcus said. "It is time we look into radio broadcasts. We are going to need more people under our banner."

Cal and Luke bowed cordially and left. Steve popped back in.

"Yo, got some even better news. The power cable from Bloomington is linked up." Steve smiled and shook his head. "It's about time. I'm sick of shoveling coal."

* * *

Marcus made his way to the tunnel mouth. A crowd of mourners were gathered outside of the bunker hospital, lamenting the deaths of loved ones lost during the drone recovery mission. There was no avoiding them.

"I am sorry for your loss," Marcus said. "What they did was heroic in our strug—"

"You did this!" a woman cried. "You're dragging us into a war nobody wants! We have what we need to survive here. Why fight? Do you think that 10-year-old boy cares about your cause? He just lost his father!"

He looked at the boy, and for a moment he saw himself standing in his living room, receiving the news that his mother had died in a car accident. Empathy rarely struck him, but it did then.

"I'm so sorry. Their sacrifice has already saved lives."

He walked away, hands trembling. Harold Plyman approached and put an arm around him. Marcus explained the value of the drone mission, and the overall cause, as if Mr. Plyman didn't know.

"It is a just war; you don't need to tell me. But save the justifications. These people are in mourning."

"Could you help arrange a proper funeral while we are gone? A surface burial? Maybe it will bring the families some kind of peace."

"Gladly," Mr. Plyman said. "Remember one thing when you come face to face with the enemy tomorrow – you are fighting for peace, not fighting just to fight."

Chapter Twenty-Seven

They departed for Vincennes to finally meet the enemy.

No name or rank was given by the man who extended the invitation. For all they knew, he could be a lowly dignitary, or the mastermind of it all. Either way, it was progress to at least get to put one human face to the evil.

They talked Steve into driving, as his mere presence made them feel safer. But the bulk of their security came from the 12 drones escorting them from above – and the 20 others preemptively spread around the outskirts of Vincennes. Kent remained on call at the bunker, ready to send them in at a moment's notice.

Robby kept the mood light by pointing out old landmarks between the fallow fields and dilapidated barns along US 41. The prison near Carlisle looked terrifying. The Big Peach monument had faded to white, and the backyard roller coaster was rusted.

The underground mine outside Oaktown reminded them of why they were on the mission. The men in Bloomfield claimed to have witnessed the mass transportation of tens of thousands to the mine during the

Last Days. People believed they were among the lucky few who would get to survive in a government bunker. Instead, they walked into a death factory.

When they hit the north end of "Indiana's First City," they opted to take 6th Street straight through. Robby pointed out his favorite haunts during his semester at Vincennes University. He was devastated to find *Bill Bobe's Pizzeria* burned to the ground, along with several city blocks. On Main Street, he declared that if there was a moldy slice of cheesecake left at *Pea-Fections* restaurant, he would still eat it.

Marcus told him to shut up so he could focus.

Steve turned onto Vigo Street and stopped shy of the Lincoln Memorial Bridge. They got out and walked to the edge of the overgrown George Rogers Clark Memorial lawn. It was foggy and silent.

"See anyone?" Marcus said.

"Maybe the dude is waiting in that creepy rotunda," Robby said.

Timothy pointed to the sky. "I don't think so."

An aircraft emerged from the haze and landed before the memorial. It sported design and technology they had never seen – an eVTOL quadcopter with propellors embedded in a strange wing structure. It was futuristic and otherworldly, and flanked by two armed drones that stayed in the sky.

"Great, we're dealing with fucking aliens," Robby said.

Doors parted and a ramp extended. A man, alone, stepped out and never broke stride in his approach. He was tall, thin and had an aristocratic flair. They guessed his age to be in the mid-forties, though the existence of the anti-aging serum made it impossible to tell.

He stopped before them and clapped, mockingly.

"Marcus Trencher, how glad I am to finally meet you. I see you brought your friends. Ah, this was the co-founder of your little company? Was he behind the scenes doing the real work? I kid, I kid. Pleasure to meet you all."

"Do you have a name?"

"Betancourt. Not my real name, but that's what you can call me."

His accent was impossible to place, but it reeked of obscene wealth and privilege. Marcus had only come across such a dialect during the early days of *Trencher Industries* when he was forced to interact with other billionaires for funding, and of those, only the oldest of the old money spoke like this man.

"Right, Betancourt, now that we have your attent—"

"Did you wonder why I chose this place for our meeting? I am fascinated by history – my family has written so much of it. George Rogers Clark was a minor figure, but I feel his story encapsulates—"

"Spare us the history lesson," Robby interrupted. "We went on the field trips."

Robby leaned to Henry. "He was that president who died after a month in office, right?"

"No, that was William Henry Harrison," Henry whispered. "Clark fought in the Revolutionary War and hated Indians."

Henry and Robby had everyone's attention.

"Your historian friend is correct," Betancourt said. "Clark wanted the Indians *extirpated*. Revolution, genocide, exploration – a story very much worthy of this monument."

"We are at the end of history," Marcus said. "Let's talk about the future."

147

"The future? To that I ask, do you want to be a part of it? Continue down the path you are on, and I hate to say, but it will be bleak and brief. But I am sure we can rectify the misunderstanding between us."

"You and your nihilistic organization are systematically depopulating the planet. What is there to misunderstand?"

"*Au contraire*! We are eliminating all that there is to feel nihilistic about! Genocide is truly reprehensible, but it is necessary component."

"Please, try to explain."

"We placated the masses with a system of consumption, and it poisoned our planet. The status quo could continue no longer, and I say that as a man who was treated very well by the status quo.

"So, we devised our plan over decades, collected the most capable among us, such as yourselves, and set out to eliminate most of the rest. Our flawed system outlived its purpose, and so did a great many people within it.

"I know this is heartless to even ponder, but what were all those people doing, really? Besides consuming, consuming, consuming? Do you know how many institutions and entire industries we propped up just to keep people distracted? We kept unemployment and wages artificially low to maintain order. We restrained AI and automation. Not to mention the bread, the circuses, the opiates...

"But even the most woefully and willfully ignorant could see the façade crumbling. None of our half-measures could stop the steady march towards the destruction of our global habitat. We had to tear the bandage off, all at once."

Timothy put a hand on Marcus's shoulder and

stepped forward.

"How could you dismiss humanity's knack for problem-solving with our backs against the wall? Birth rates were plummeting... I mean, nothing can justify what you've done. You and your global elite became so detached, got so bored hiding in the shadows, that you felt like lashing out."

Betancourt sighed and shook his head.

"Natural population decline was coming, sure, but we didn't have 100 years to wait for it. Truly, you still don't get it. We are not environmental extremists – far from it – but the science was irrefutable. We had no choice but to intervene with drastic measures. I applaud you and Mr. Trencher's grid invention, it truly made us reconsider, but it was too little, too late. Attempting what was necessary with 8.6 billion people on the planet would have failed, and that failure would have plunged us back into the dark ages, or worse."

"We won't change your mind, so we won't waste the effort," Marcus said. "All we ask is that you vacate the Midwest. We control the grid. We will make it more trouble than what it is worth."

"You took down outdated drones allocated to your flyover state. You must know we have conventional weapons at our disposal that do not require your grid."

Betancourt looked to his right, distracted. "Sorry, is – is he with you?"

A disheveled man approached down the middle of Vigo Street. He had grungy blonde hair, a black trench coat, and fingerless gloves.

"I can't tell if he's a post-apocalyptic survivor or just your regular Vincennes townie," Robby said.

"Hey! Hello! I'm unarmed. No worries, bros!" the

stranger said, hands raised. "Woah, that looks like a spaceship! Is that yours?"

"Not with you?" Betancourt lifted his right hand and twitched two fingers.

"...I overslept when they took everyone to the bunkers and I don't know if the asteroid missed earth or what, man, but then my buddies left me all the sudden, and then all these drones—"

A shot rang out and the man dropped dead in the middle of the street – sniper. They all ducked to the ground, except Betancourt.

"*Jesus Ch*...You couldn't just let the guy go?" Timothy clutched the radio in his hand, ready to signal Kent.

"Take your hand off that receiver. I am aware of your drones. They won't do a thing."

They slowly stood back up. Timothy showed his radio and unclenched hand.

"Why not kill us now?" Marcus said.

Betancourt broke out in over-the-top laughter. "Now we are negotiating! Oh, but first let me bring out some mutual friends. It almost slipped my mind."

Four individuals emerged from his aircraft with two armed escorts.

The first was Jenna Dothmayer. None were certain she was even still alive after she was transferred from their bunker. The gunshot wound she suffered during Marcus's bout of madness, and the subsequent assault months later, had left her fighting for her life. It was as if neither had occurred. Her recovery was miraculous.

Audrey Bruni stood by Jenna's side. She left the bunker shortly after Marcus's return, and after failing to lure Robby from Melonie.

Robby gave her a sheepish nod.

The third of Betancourt's guests was Ashley Cameron, with whom they were all familiar. She looked due any day.

The last was an older man, his hair not as gray and his skin not as wrinkled as Marcus remembered. He never thought he would see him again.

"Marcus, is that your..." Henry said.

"Yes, it is," Marcus said. "Hello, dad."

"Son...glad you are doing well," Thomas Trencher said. "You should listen to what this man has to say. He can show you some incredible things."

Chapter Twenty-Eight

Betancourt watched the interaction between Marcus and his father with amusement. There was a mix of joy, bewilderment, and suspicion.

"No need to thank me for the reunion," Betancourt said. "Now, where were we?"

"I asked why you don't just kill us now, like you did that guy over there." Marcus nodded to the dead body in the middle of Vigo Street.

"You know well what you have, and that we want."

"Could it be the anti-aging serum from the Quarry?" He looked at his father, a clear recipient of the drug.

Betancourt shook his head. "You only deprive the privileged few in your own bunker network. There are dozens of other labs producing the serum. I speak of the controls over your power grid."

"I would have to be insane to give it up. What could you possibly offer in return?"

"We leave your area alone, fifty-mile radius. You can even live on the surface."

"That is what we already have. Your drones don't

have the range to cover the Midwest. You can only throw so much at us."

"You underestimate what we have at our disposal, but this is nonsense. I'd much rather win you over! I have wonderful things to show you. This reset of civilization will accelerate us beyond where we ever would have been. The technology and medicine we've reserved for the rebuild is truly magnificent."

Thomas Trencher cleared his throat. "We didn't say anything when you last visited, but Minnie was diagnosed with cancer. We didn't seek treatment or placement in a bunker. Then, this man paid us a visit, introduced us to one of his doctors. Minnie is cancer-free now. And I...I feel like a young man again."

Betancourt put a hand on Jenna Dothmayer's shoulder.

"And I hope you recognize this beautiful young lady. She was in a sorry state before our doctors got to her. From my understanding, *someone* shot her, and another assaulted her. And now just look at her – good as new."

Jenna stared Marcus down defiantly.

"I heard you in that hospital room," she said. "I wasn't a spy. You think you're smart, but you're just paranoid. Betancourt is too kind, offering you anything. I hope you get what you deserve."

Marcus had no response. He had done so much wrong by her.

"Cancer, AIDS, influenza...there isn't much left we haven't cured," Betancourt said. "Many were solved long ago but held back for obvious reasons."

"Marcus, listen to what the man has to offer," Mr. Trencher said.

"I am, dad. Are you? We will keep our grid. We are

done here."

Betancourt frowned. "I am sad to hear that, but before you go, there is something else you should know. Miss Cameron?"

Ashley stepped forward, holding her bulging stomach. "Marcus, the child is yours. It's a boy."

Betancourt took delight in the drama. "DNA is a marvelous thing. We checked it against your father's. Perhaps your vasectomy was botched? Or could it be that you were lying? Never mind that – congratulations!"

"Come with us," his father said. "Be there for the birth of your son."

Marcus shook his head, speechless. Timothy and Henry pulled him back.

"Give us a minute," Timothy said.

They walked out to the middle of the street. He put his hands on Marcus's shoulders.

"Okay, what do we want to do here?"

"I doubt we get out of here alive if I don't go," Marcus said. "I'll hold the grid as leverage to make sure they bring me back. I'll gather whatever intel I can while I'm there."

"I think you're right," Timothy said. "Just know that they are probably going to show you around some bullshit utopian resort and shower you with propaganda. You can't buy into it."

"I won't be swayed."

Timothy looked him in the eyes for a moment to drill the point home. They broke their huddle and returned.

"One thing you should know, is that the grid dies with me," Marcus said. "The same goes for my friends. I mean that quite literally."

"You have nothing to be concerned about," Betancourt said.

Marcus looked back at his friends, gave a solemn nod, and joined his father on the other side. A soldier grabbed his arm.

Betancourt turned to his other bodyguard and gestured to Audrey Bruni.

"We need to make room on the aircraft. We no longer need this one."

The soldier pulled out his sidearm.

"*What*? *No – please!*" Audrey begged.

The soldier shot her in the head.

"Gentlemen," Betancourt said.

They marched across the lawn to the ship. Marcus looked back in horror.

Robby dove to Audrey's side.

She was already gone.

Chapter Twenty-Nine

Robby insisted they bury Audrey's body on the memorial lawn, as well as the poor stranger that stumbled upon their meeting. The hours spent searching for shovels and digging wore on the others, but it was the honorable thing to do. They held a moment of silence before finally departing Vincennes.

It was unspoken, but they also felt they had lost Marcus. Assurances that he would be returned meant little coming from the man that called himself Betancourt.

On the way home, they set priorities in Marcus's absence. There were scout teams to dispatch, counties to cover, and domestic bunker issues to address. It wasn't until they stepped off the elevator platform in the bunker that Timothy broached the most sensitive topic.

"We need a contingency plan in case he doesn't come back."

"The grid controls die with him," Henry said. "That has to keep him safe, right?"

"That is not entirely true anymore, but that's not the concern. I am afraid they might persuade him to their side."

"Marcus has been a warlord against them since he came back from his meltdown," Robby said. "He is locked in."

Timothy cocked his head in an *I'm-not-so-sure* way. "He bought in to the dark side before his meltdown. Henry, you said he was spouting off about the environment and people needing to die after he shot that poor girl."

"He was trying to convince himself as much as he was trying to explain it to me. He's on his meds now. He's figured out a way to fight back. He isn't joining the side committing worldwide genocide."

"I hope you are right, but his dad was already starting on him, and what if Betancourt offers him a major role in the rebuild? What if he wows him with new technology and hands him a feudal kingdom to rule?"

"Valid concern," Henry said. "Not to mention the whole baby thing. But I have faith in him."

"Give it a week," Robby said. "If he comes back talking nonsense, we will get him straight. Let's just handle our business until then."

* * *

Word was spread that the meeting went well – a decidedly positive spin. They relayed that Marcus was holding more extensive negotiations for peace, and in the interim, they were to continue strengthening their position. There were more survivors out there to recruit, and downed drones to capture or destroy.

The most conspiracy-minded of people in the bunker refused to believe any of it. The anti-conspiracy-conspiracy theorists chose to still believe an asteroid had struck the earth and had elaborate explanations for the drones and every other piece of clear evidence. One man claimed, "*Aliens.*"

Even Timothy, who always insisted Marcus listen to the voice of the people, had to walk away from a particularly dim-witted man. Robby stuck around to argue until others jumped in and escalated the ordeal into a shouting match.

"Our week without Marcus is off to a swimming start," Timothy said as they walked away. "Idiots have already started a misinformation campaign."

"Maybe Betancourt was right about one thing – people need to keep occupied," Steve said. "All those yahoos worked in the mine. Since they got that power cable linked up, they got time on their hands to make up theories."

"We'll send them to the surface," Henry said. "Let them see with their own eyes."

The distant screeching of train brakes interrupted the hullabaloo. They had been so preoccupied that they didn't realize the tunnel rail gap had been bridged.

* * *

Ellis and his team returned after completing a full circuit across the bunker network. The substantial populations in the Louisville Mega Caverns bunker and the Indianapolis bunker constellation relied heavily on each other, as did the Quarry. When Ellis and Taveon hijacked the train, the supply chain was rudely interrupted.

"Good news, gentlemen," Ellis said as he hopped down to the platform. "The folks up in Carmel say they're ready to do whatever it takes to get us to start sending them that serum again."

"That could be good," Timothy said. "What did they offer?"

"They have the keys to all that heavy machinery stowed in the cavern near the Columbus tunnel exchange. Tractors, farm equipment, and all sorts of things. I told them we might send someone their way."

Timothy and Robby looked at Henry.

"You are mister ambassador," Robby said. "You should check out what those snobs up in Carmel have."

Henry shrugged. "Sure, I'm down."

"The other bunkers are stable for the most part," Ellis said. "The military abandoned Louisville. I guess they went down to Fort Knox."

"We bombed the shit out Fort Knox the night after you left," Robby said.

Ellis couldn't tell if he was joking.

They started to notice several new faces around them.

"I brought back sixty recruits from Kentucky, and plenty of food to feed them. It was only sixty because we couldn't fit the other three hundred. If you want an army, I'd say you've got a battalion waiting down there."

Chapter Thirty

Marcus hardly spoke during the flight. He kept his eyes on the window to keep his bearings, though that became impossible once they breached the clouds. They switched from the eVTOL aircraft to a luxury jet somewhere near the Tennessee-Kentucky border. All he really knew was that they were headed south.

"You could just ask," Betancourt said. "You should see the Florida panhandle any minute now."

Marcus ignored him.

Betancourt sighed. "I hope you are not this dull all week."

The clouds broke somewhere above the Gulf Coast. Sunlight shimmered off the coastal marshes and mirrored lakes. They descended over the Florida Keys before finally landing at Key West International Airport.

"You are running this whole thing out of Key West?"

"This is just a retirement community," Betancourt said. "We have a much bigger island for our western hemisphere operations."

They stepped off the jet and Marcus was struck by the rays of a warm Florida sun. Mercenaries waited by a motorcade of black SUVs.

During the brief jaunt across the island, elderly couples in athleisure wear walked along the road, usually with pickleball paddles. They smiled and waved as they passed.

"Those snowbirds were titans across a wide range of industries," Betancourt said. "They did as they were told, and now they get to age in reverse and play pickleball."

"Did anyone not do what you asked?"

"Some, but we had persuasive means. It's not difficult to find what someone cares about and leverage it against them, especially those with so much to lose. Usually, it was as simple as manipulating a stock price. Occasionally, taking a life. You wouldn't believe the number of powerful men we had pinned as pedophiles."

"Aren't these the people that got us into the mess you claim to be fixing?"

"Sure, but they also had the assets and resources to execute our plan. Not fair, but life never is."

The motorcade came to a stop on a concrete pier. A 275-foot yacht waited in the turquoise waters.

"I don't recall seeing you at Monaco. Did you own one of these? Or two?"

Marcus shook his head.

"A billionaire without a yacht? You poor thing!" Betancourt charged up the boarding ramp. "Come aboard, dinner is almost ready."

* * *

They sailed the Straits of Florida as the sun set over the Gulf. Silent stewards led him to a stateroom where clothes in his sizes were laid out on the bed, including the shoes and charcoal grey T-shirt he was known to wear. He hated to accept gifts, but what he wore on board was a bit grimy. He showered and changed.

A half hour later, he was summoned to the bridge deck for dinner. An impressive spread filled a white cloth table. Betancourt cracked a stone crab claw before standing to greet him.

"I hope you brought your appetite! The tuna was caught near Japan two days ago, and the grouper came out of these waters earlier today. The lobster is from South Africa."

Marcus was overwhelmed. He had a simple palate.

"More of a turf man? We have wagyu." Betancourt turned to the line of wait staff. "Have the chef throw on a steak."

"No, this is fine."

Betancourt dunked crab meat into melted butter. "It'll just be us. The others are being served near the bow."

Marcus nibbled at the grouper, liked it, and then proceeded to eat half the fillet before Betancourt finished cutting his lobster tail.

"How are you importing fresh seafood from across the globe?"

"We've maintained a global logistics network. It doesn't take as many ships or planes when they aren't cluttered with cheap Chinese trinkets."

Betancourt lifted his wine glass for a refill.

"Logistics aside, someone is catching the fish. Someone milked a cow and churned that butter and milled the flour for this bread. Who is doing all that?"

"We have strategically preserved agricultural and fishing zones in the global south. Coffee drinker? We have plantations in Brazil, Columbia, Vietnam, and Ethiopia.

Our farmers are now some of the wealthiest people left on earth, as they should be."

"Why the global south?"

"We paid off their dictators and emptied their cities with relative ease. After establishing our zones and arrangements, we've left them alone. They pose no threat."

"Are there any of these zones in North America?"

Betancourt shook his head. "Still weeding out the population. We have another harsh winter or two on the schedule."

"You plan to concentrate populations regionally?"

"Yes, with wide swaths of land left uninhabited. No disparate small towns or villages. Cities are efficient. Let wilderness take the rest."

Betancourt elaborated between bites.

The cities of the future were to become hyper-self-sufficient. All labor that could be automated, or handed off to AI, would be. Major projects in housing, transportation, and distribution would be executed without the red tape of human rights, property rights, or finance.

Marcus could feel the sales pitch coming – *you could help design these cities* – but Betancourt was not so heavy-handed.

"Cities are nice without all the people in the way," Betancourt joked.

Clean, walkable, drone delivery, driverless taxis for ground and air. Goods brought in by air, rail, river, or driverless semis. Urban farms. As the population grew, additional cities would be seeded.

Industry deemed necessary in the New World would be centralized. Industry deemed unnecessary would simply cease to exist, as it already had.

"People may call us Accelerationists, and I confess the term does fit to a degree. We ask why slog through a catastrophic century-long decline, when we can speed to the end and start on the corrective actions?

"The late stage of capitalism we were in was untenable. It had all but eliminated freedom. How we convinced people to tolerate it for so long, I'll never know. But we shall unleash automation and AI to full capacity and spend our lives being human again."

"What makes you think such centralization of power could work? Historically, it's been disastrous."

"The Soviets didn't have our computers, let alone AI and automation. Ownership and property won't be as big a deal in a society of abundance. It's all more nuanced, of course. You shall see later this week."

Marcus pushed his plate aside. Stewards came to clear the table. Altogether, they ate a quarter of the food.

"Our regional government-in-waiting is in the Carmel bunker, isn't it?"

Betancourt laughed. "Again, we have all week. Let's head up to the bow."

They walked along the starboard bridge deck and climbed a spiral staircase to the sun deck. Straight ahead, the lights of a seaside city reflected off the dark seas.

"Welcome to Havana – our base of operations in the Americas."

Chapter Thirty-One

Betancourt's yacht moored in Havana Port under a blurry moon. A motorcade stood by to take them deeper into the quiet Caribbean capital.

Marcus could not recall the last time Cuba had entered his purview. The Communist Party re-asserted tighter control in the late 2020s, causing a minor blip in the 24-hour news cycle. The U.S. embargo continued. Otherwise, the island rarely made headlines.

The motorcade sped down an empty avenue parallel to the coast. The SUV with his dad, Jenna Dothmayer, and Ashley Cameron turned off a few blocks before he and Betancourt arrived at the Meliá Habana Hotel.

Staff stood ready in the lobby. It was midnight.

"I will see you bright and early tomorrow," Betancourt said before departing.

A bellman led him to a nice room pre-stocked with clothes, shoes, and toiletries.

Almost as soon as the door shut behind the bellman, there was a knock. He sighed, answered, and found a vaguely familiar man near his age in the hall.

"Hey, Marcus Trencher, right? Just get in?"

"I did," Marcus said. "Aren't you the, uh..."

"*The AI Guy*, yeah, the evil genius that was going to plunge the world into chaos and unemployment! Surprise, someone beat me to it." He offered his hand. "Michael Azoulay. Call me Mike."

Marcus shook his hand and felt the nervous energy.

"Have you been to the beach yet? It's beautiful at night."

"I'd rather rest up. It's been a long day."

"We should chat, down at the beach." Mike's eyes grew big. "You *really* have to see the waters under the moonlight."

Marcus caught on. The room was probably bugged.

"Let me throw on another shirt."

Mike led him down a stairwell and out a side exit to avoid the lobby. They skirted the pool and stopped on a grassy strip just shy of the beach.

"This is far enough." He pulled up his pant leg to show an ankle monitor. "A few steps out onto the sand and this thing will go off."

"Are they going to put one of those on me?"

"Nah, you have to earn it."

"You're not a willing participant in all this?"

"Hell no. One day about two years ago that Betancourt asshole showed up in my office. I had a million-dollar security detail, and yet this guy was sitting in my $8,000 office chair. He laid out how the world was about to end, and how he wanted me and my AI tech to survive and play a role in the rebuild."

"A U.S. Senator got to me. I designed bunkers for them, believed the whole asteroid story. I pretty much handed them control of my company."

Mike pulled out two cigars and offered one. Marcus

declined.

"Yeah, well, I told him to fuck off. I thought I was untouchable. My company was blowing up, I was climbing the *Forbes* list. Had your net worth in my sights." He laughed and lit his cigar. "Anyway, I kicked him out. He said he'd be back after the funeral. My brother was murdered later that night. When I returned to the office, he informed me that my wife and kids were next, *unless...*"

He took a puff from his cigar. "You know what they are doing, right?"

"Worldwide genocide. I learned a bit late, but I am aware now."

"Where have you been if you are just now getting to Cuba? They dragged me here before the fake asteroid announcement."

"In my bunker, in Indiana."

"We've heard rumors about resistance in the Midwest. Was that you?"

"We took down a few drone fleets and bombed Fort Knox. Then we shut down the entire Midwest grid, so all the drones in the region haven't been able to recharge."

"Damn. You just might end up attracting their ground forces. They have a few thousand men, true believers. Fuckers wipe out anyone they come across. They remind me of that hardcore Nazi unit during World War II."

"The S.S.?"

"Yeah, those guys. Last I heard half were tied up in Texas. A lot of resistance down there. The other half is somewhere on the east coast. Keep it up, and I bet they come up, or over. Beyond that, I don't think they have a whole lot, so if you can inflict casualties on their limited manpower, you might do real damage."

167

"Interesting. Might be something to work toward."

"Start on all that when you get back, if you get back. I put your odds of getting off the island at ten percent."

"The grid controls die with me, so I have a modicum of leverage."

"They do want that grid. A ready-made, resilient power grid advances their rebuild plans by half a century, easy. They were going to fly me back to the states to sic my AI on your network, but I tried to off myself, so that got put on the backburner."

"Not to disrespect your AI, but nobody has ever hacked our network."

Mike laughed. "Your pal Timothy Spencer was a wizard. Even the megalomaniacs in the Valley respected his work. Whatever is making that thing hackproof, for the love of God, don't tell me or anyone else here."

"Timothy is still a wizard. He's back in my bunker, fighting the good fight."

Mike took one last puff of his cigar and threw it out on the choppy sands.

"They're sending me to a military installation on the outskirts of the city tomorrow. I doubt we will get a chance to speak like this again. If I'm going to help you, we need to establish a channel. Do you have a radio tower near your bunker?"

"Right on site."

"I send patches out via satellite all the time. I'll get a message to Timothy. Maybe us tech bros can scheme up a plan. They *think* they watch me close here, but I've gotten my hands on all sorts of stuff."

Chapter Thirty-Two

As scout teams ventured further from the bunker, it became clear that there were far more survivors roaming the surface than expected.

The people they came across were generally rugged, resourceful, and angry. They had survived a brutal winter only to be hunted by drones the moment the weather warmed.

Protocol was set for when they came across survivors. The scouts radioed Timothy who would re-activate the local power grid wherever they were. After, they informed them of what was really going on in the world.

A few confrontations turned bad, but most were receptive. Word of the resistance spread fast and began preceding their arrival. They found exceptional people everywhere they went.

An engineer in Benton County was single-handedly keeping the windmills operating at the Fowler Ridge Wind Farm, providing power clear across the region.

An Amish community in Parke County was thriving.

SHANE NOBLE

They offered to can goods for the winter, and anything else they could do to help, short of fighting.

Multiple teams were attacked in Indianapolis. They stopped advancing beyond the suburbs.

Cami Stinnett figured out how to broadcast a looped recording, on the off-chance people still turned on their televisions. A former radio DJ in Muncie helped them take their message to the airwaves.

What was to be done with their growing army was to be seen. The enemy was not standing across a field or camped beyond a ridge in the distance. All they could do for the time being was establish communication channels, secure infrastructure, and gather assets.

* * *

Henry and Mariya embarked on a diplomatic mission riding Ellis's hijacked train. They were eager to see what Carmel had to offer.

But first, they had to make a stop at the Quarry.

Jim Cox greeted them at the otherwise empty train station. The last time they were there, the platform was littered with bodies.

"Anything new at the Quarry?" Henry said.

"Half our population moved above ground after you guys ran the bad guys out and downed all the drones," Jim said. "Folks come back to stock up on food. We're a glorified grocery store now, but hey, we keep the place running. Can't walk away from a nuclear power station and our farms."

"Are Joel and Vance still around?"

"They are at the labs now. Why don't we pay them a visit."

* * *

Ellis tagged along, leaving his men to help the local crew load pallets of food on the train. There were no golfers teeing off in the atrium, no cyclists zooming around the track, and nobody in the cafes or gaming lounges. The Quarry was a ghost town.

Joel dropped what he was doing as soon as he saw them through the lab windows. Vance and Alice followed.

"You guys come back to start more trouble?"

"I don't think we'll be staying long enough," Henry said. "And I hate to cut to the chase, but I was hoping you had some of the anti-aging serum ready."

"A fresh batch finished yesterday."

"Y'all telling me you can stop aging?" Ellis said.

"Even reverse it to a degree," Vance said. "Hair grows back with color, joints feel better, cartilage regenerates, vision sharpens, muscle and skin improves, cognition – everything. Loved you when you were with the Celtics, by the way."

"Want to start a regimen?" Joel said. "You'll feel like you are in your rookie year again. Just need to draw blood and we'll do the rest."

Ellis shrugged. "Hell, why not?"

Alice took him to the bloodwork station and prepped him for the draw.

"How about you two?"

Henry and Mariya looked at each other. They felt young, but to feel 20-something again... They didn't commit, but had their blood drawn after Ellis, just in case.

"We'll have your serums ready by the time you come back through," Vance said. "I assume you are headed to

171

Carmel with the rest?"

"They want to negotiate a deal and that was their number one ask."

* * *

They departed the Quarry and took the northern track at the Columbus exchange, catching a fleeting glimpse of the cavernous cache of heavy machinery and farm equipment.

After a brief stop at Speedway to load and unload goods, they bypassed the Meridian hospital bunker and arrived at the end of the line – Carmel.

The station was relatively opulent, with marble columns and prints of forest scenery. Mariya felt Henry was overreacting to its grandeur.

"What is the big deal about this Carmel place? You Indiana guys talk like it's a magical kingdom."

"You probably had fifty cities in California that put it to shame, but growing up in Indiana, when you thought of wealth, you thought *Carmel*. Oh, and the other thing it was most known for was—"

A welcoming party came out to the platform. It was led by a sharply dressed woman named Lakshmi Chandra, a high-ranking government appointee in her previous life. Ten individuals accompanied her.

Ellis and his men fell in behind Henry and Mariya.

"We won't be long," Henry said. "We were informed that you might have something to offer."

"Please, let us talk inside," Lakshmi said. "We only want peace and cooperation."

Half of Ellis's men stayed with the train while Ellis and three others followed.

They stepped across a threshold onto a balcony

overlooking a vast space. The bunker was shaped like a flattened dome. The other end was approximately a quarter mile away, and there were alcoves out of sight. The tallest buildings stood equidistant from each other and doubled as support columns.

The walls and ceiling were canvassed in high-resolution LED screens, like the "Sphere" in Las Vegas. The cavern was no more than sixty feet high, but the screens projected a blue sky that made it look endless.

"Welcome to Carmel," Lakshmi said. "We get around mostly by golf cart, though the kids prefer the e-scooters."

Henry had hardly taken his eye off the digital sky to see the layout below. It looked like a miniaturized walkable city with narrow street-like cart paths, and one notable, repeated feature.

"You've got to be kidding me..."

"What?" Mariya said.

"They built a bunch of roundabouts."

* * *

They rode in golf carts down the bunker thoroughfare of Keystone Avenue, and after a few roundabouts, came to a stop somewhere between Rangeline Road and the Monon Trail. A statue-filled fountain flowed in an artificial turf courtyard surrounded by four-story buildings that scraped the cavern ceiling.

They were led into a conference room with all the warmth of an investment firm. Nobody confiscated Ellis and his men's weapons, or even asked.

"I'd like to start by informing you that the forces that were dispatched to the Quarry never returned," Lakshmi said.

173

"Makes sense," Henry said. "We killed or captured them all."

Men shifted in their executive chairs and fidgeted with pens.

"Regardless, even the ones that stayed back have since left." Lakshmi put a hand to her heart and then motioned to her colleagues at the table. "We are not the ones that attacked you."

"Tell me, who attacked us *before* we went underground? There was a plot to take Marcus Trencher's bunker, and we know whoever it was, was waiting here in Carmel. Who led that one?"

There were more nervous glances, shifting, and creaking chairs.

"There was an...effort by a powerful group of residents, none of which are in the room. We would be willing to give them up in exchange for the resumption of medical shipments."

"The anti-aging serum?"

"Yes – the serum – in exchange for the people that wronged you."

"Marcus may want to have a sit-down with these 'powerful residents' in the future, but I have no interest in revenge. Tell me, what is the plan for the population in this bunker?"

"There are plans for resurfacing. We are, or were, tasked with installing a regional government when that day comes."

"That would require a small army, which you had. Do you have the assets that would have outfitted that force. Guns, bombs, tanks?"

"We have no such things in Carmel."

"For chrissake, Lakshmi, give it up!" a red-faced man

said. "They're the ones with the guns now. Giving them more won't change a thing."

Others nodded and grumbled in agreement.

Lakshmi sighed through her nostrils. "There is a cache of military equipment near the Columbus tunnel exchange, separate from the farm and construction machinery. It is all yours if regular shipments of food and medicine – serum – are re-established."

"You must have something else more valuable than keys to a cavern full of surplus military goods. What tech are you keeping down here?"

Before Lakshmi could answer, the same impatient man piped up.

"We have a supercomputer and server farm. The IT guys say it houses some kind of AI goddess. They cared more about it than any of us. Can we just get our serum and be done with it?"

"Give me the keys to the cache, and we will give you your serum. You'll get your next shipment once we have access to the supercomputer."

The men across the table stood and offered to shake on the deal. Lakshmi left the room and returned with a keycard and instructions for accessing the cache.

At the train station, Ellis's crew unloaded the coolers of anti-aging serum to jittery middle-aged men.

Henry, Mariya, and Ellis and his men departed Carmel, eager to see what they had gained. Next stop: the Columbus cache, one hour south.

Chapter Thirty-Three

Staff nodded cordially as Marcus wandered through the lobby. They were stationed to funnel him somewhere, so he followed them like breadcrumbs. The last vested Cuban lifted a hand and directed him into a restaurant where a breakfast buffet awaited.

Fresh fruit, pastries, pancakes, eggs, sausage, bacon, omelet station – the works. No other guests, but enough food for thirty. He filled his plate and took a table by the windows where the rising tropical sun sent golden rays shining in. A server poured him a cup of coffee, the best he had ever had.

Mike Azoulay, "the AI Guy," stumbled in wearing pajamas and a hotel robe. He dropped a duffel bag at the hostess stand.

"Wow, another guest!" he said, sarcastically.

Marcus lifted his coffee cup in acknowledgement.

Mike grabbed a cinnamon roll and joined him.

"Are we the only guests in this place?" Marcus said.

"I saw the most beautiful woman I've ever seen in my life yesterday. Probably some former pro soccer player's wife. Haven't seen anyone else since."

"When are you headed out?"

"Any minute." He glanced over his shoulder. "I'll reach out to Timothy first chance I get. Any tips on how to gain his trust? Keywords?"

"Tell him his blood brother is in Cuba."

A man in army fatigues appeared at the entryway.

Mike cursed and tossed his napkin on the table. "Word of advice – get off this island, ASAP. Oh, and try the cinnamon rolls. They stole the Cinnabon recipe."

Marcus didn't get a chance. Another soldier summoned him soon after Mike was taken away.

* * *

The *Centro Nacional de Investigaciones Científicas* was tucked in the heart of an affluent Havana neighborhood ten minutes from the Melia Habana Hotel. The lot across from the center was filled with gigantic satellites. Betancourt greeted him at the front drive.

"I hope you are ready for a day of enlightenment."

The center was abuzz with activity – evil activity, Marcus presumed. Workers scurried about with file folders and tablets, heads down when Betancourt passed. They entered a room flush with screens but void of people.

Betancourt clicked around on a console to pull up a video. "The past is the past, but I can't help but show this off. This is a news broadcast in Myanmar after the asteroid announcement. Notice anything?"

"I don't know. I don't speak...whatever language."

"How about this one from Bhutan?"

Marcus shrugged.

"Both deepfakes. We created millions of hours of this sort of content across the globe, from national news networks down to the dregs of social media. We even spoofed personal communications of individuals that were already deceased."

He played an entire panel of hosts on a major U.S. network with wide camera angles and competing voices. An astronomer on the panel passionately explained what the asteroid might do upon impact. It was indistinguishable from reality.

Betancourt paused the video. "I believe you met Mr. Azoulay at breakfast? He kept his artificial general intelligence under restraint, at our behest. Once he so kindly agreed to work with us, we began to test what his machine could generate. With ample computing power and control of the media landscape, our messaging became convincing by sheer volume and uncanny quality. Every astronomer you saw speak on TV or social media about the asteroid was a deepfake. They were better actors than real people. We controlled reality.

"It allowed us to clear two countries *before* the global announcement. Azoulay's AI fabricated an entire population's continued existence for weeks. We didn't even restrict travel into the countries, though obviously nobody left. While the first world was told they had six months until impact, others had already been mobilized."

"To your death factories."

"Population reduction facilities, call them what you wish. 12 central and east Asian countries were reduced by 98 percent within the first two months."

"Not sure I want to know how..."

"Gas chambers, mostly, but there were other novel approaches. A site in the Balkans had individuals step into a tube where a spike would puncture the top of their skull as soon as the door shut. The floor would displace one-tenth of a second later, and conveyors would move the body to the incinerators. The floor would return, the door would open, and the next unsuspecting commoner would step in, thinking they were getting a quick disinfectant spray before stepping through to the other side.

"We collected underground space over decades. It wasn't difficult to make a rock face look like a threshold leading into a bunker. Rope lines led to hundreds of these pods. Looked like airport security. The throughput was phenomenal. Fully automated, as little human interaction as possible."

"There is no way this worked everywhere."

"The more 'democratic' countries had issues. Sizable minorities didn't show up to the sites, or the military fell apart and failed to gather the population. That is what we are addressing with our drones and weather program."

"You are not selling this as a cause I'd care to join."

"Just stating the facts so that you are informed in your decision-making."

"World population was 8.5 billion when this all began. What is it today?"

Betancourt contemplated as if he were counting the dead in his head.

"Our reduction facilities processed 1.75 billion across the globe. China and India, among others, concentrated populations and carpet-bombed, clearing tens of millions more. We estimate another billion have succumbed to famine and freezing temperatures, and a modest number from our drone program."

"So, give or take, 5 billion are still living?"

"Are you not impressed?"

He was under the impression that they were *much* further along. The math was brutal, but it wasn't too late to save billions of lives.

"What is your target when all said and done?"

"2 billion would be ideal. I expect another billion in reduction by the New Year. We've only just begun. Let's continue, shall we?"

They moved down the hall to a command center. A wall of screens displayed weather maps, charts, and streams of data. Rows of stations faced them like NASA Mission Control. The room was fully staffed.

"I bet you'd like to know how we are cooling the planet."

Marcus gave a token nod.

"We are pumping a great deal of sulfur dioxide and silver iodide into the stratosphere, primarily at 60 degrees latitude north and south. That alone has cooled the poles drastically. The ice caps have shown tremendous growth."

Marcus could see the results for himself on the satellite imagery. Greenland was almost completely engulfed in ice, as were two-thirds of Canada and Russia.

"We have fleets of ships, even aircraft carriers, spraying saltwater into clouds off the coast. It does more than you'd think. California is currently one giant mudslide. You should have seen the Colorado River and its tributaries after we let the Rockies cycle through a snowmelt. Lake Mead is filled to the brim!"

Betancourt ordered a subordinate to pull up a particular map.

"As you may have experienced if you peeked out of your bunker last winter, we also cloud-seeded areas at the 30th parallel, give or take ten degrees, and supplemented the effort with another tool that we've since repositioned."

He pointed out a tiny square digitally outlined over the Middle East.

"There it is! That is our orbital solar shade. It is made from a material 5 micrometers thick and coated with reflective aluminum particles. It is roughly the size of Rhode Island. It filters enough sunlight to plummet temperatures in very targeted areas. When used in conjunction with the chemicals, well, let's just say the combination has worked to great effect. We triggered a sustained polar vortex down through Canada, all the way to your neck of the woods."

"That must be the biggest manmade object in existence. Are the space elevators still in operation?"

"The Puerto Ayora elevator is still erect. We have factories in Ecuador manufacturing the material nonstop. A glorified sewing machine in low-earth orbit pieces the strips together. One shipping container holds a shade the size of several soccer fields.

"We are making more, which brings me to the third component of our cooling efforts: a constellation of shades at the L1 LaGrange Point between the Earth and the Sun. When a sheet is completed, small ion thrusters are attached, and it makes its way out to join the others we've already sent."

"What impact has it made?"

"We are decades from anything meaningful, which would be one-percent blockage. If all goes well and we get to two percent, say in a century, we fix everything."

"Couldn't you collapse ocean currents and jet streams with all this chaos?"

"The scientists in this room monitor such things very closely. We are truly learning how to master our habitat. Last month, we parked the LEO shade over the Sahara. Fascinating results."

Millions more dead, Marcus figured. Much of what

was explained could have been done without killing billions of people. Betancourt read his mind.

"We had to treat the root cause. Unfathomable sacrifices had to be made."

"You've sacrificed nothing. You've only taken from everyone else."

"I wanted to get the worst out of the way up front. The rest of the week I will show you how great our future will be."

Chapter Thirty-Four

Henry climbed on top of an M1E3 Abrams tank – one of twelve in the previously sealed cavern off the Columbus train tunnel exchange. The deal with Carmel proved lucrative.

Ellis stood next to a HIMARS rocket launch vehicle. "All this for a couple coolers of serum?"

"There has to be $10 billion worth of military equipment here," Henry said.

Humvees, Howitzers, a "bridge layer" vehicle, and other specialized machines sat in rows. Another area stored small arms, crates of personal rocket launchers, boots, and body armor. In separate buildouts, munitions and fuel.

The ramp to the surface was long with a reasonable gradient. Henry entered the keycard and code on a panel at the base. Massive doors slid apart at the top.

"Y'all want to risk it up there with one of these vehicles?" Ellis said. "The train still needs to make a stop in Louisville before we double back."

"Let's take one of these," Mariya said next to a Humvee. "I'm sick of being underground."

Henry shrugged. "You heard the lady. We'll take a Humvee."

"We'll stick around and load up some rocket launchers and shit," Ellis said. "I'll pick up your serums from those pharma bros and meet y'all back at the home bunker."

"Thanks, and we should probably take a few of those guns as well."

* * *

Henry and Mariya surfaced somewhere in Brown County State Park. The Columbus tunnel exchange was actually 15 miles west of the city it was named after. An outlet led to State Road 135, which took them toward the quaint town of Nashville, Indiana.

Near the high school, a school bus blocked the road.

"Not good," Henry said.

A shot rang out the second he came to a stop. Armed men emerged from an inn south of the road. Henry didn't want to fight, nor did he want to flee and lead anyone to the tunnel entrance. He also didn't want to go on a sixty-mile detour.

"Do you see any lights on, or signs of power?"

"No...I don't know...why?" Mariya said.

"Hand me the radio, quick."

He called into the bunker on their designated channel. "Pigg, I need Timothy, ASAP. Over."

"*On it, boss.*"

The men were nearing the edge of the road. Timothy's voice came through.

"Henry? I'm here."

"Mariya and I are in Nashville, Indiana. Get this town

dialed up on the grid. We might need help winning hostiles over. Dispatch a drone in case things start to go south."

"Buy me a minute and I'll flip the lights on."

One of the men ordered them out of the vehicle. Henry squeezed Mariya's hand, opened the door, and stepped out with his hands up.

"I'm unarmed," Henry said. "I'm here to help."

"Yeah, and how's that?"

"Has your power been out the past week?"

They didn't respond. Their eyes started to wander toward Mariya.

"You guys ever heard of Marcus Trencher?"

"What's that rich asshole got to do with anything?"

"He controls the power grid, and he happens to be a friend. We shut it down to prevent the drones from recharging. You guys have seen the drones, right?"

"Bombed the hell out of Bloomington last week. One of them is landed out by Clay Lick Road."

Timothy's voice cracked over the radio. "Henry, ready when you are."

"That person who just spoke is ready to turn the power back on. May I respond?"

The lead man, gun still drawn, nodded.

"Go ahead, Timothy."

After a moment of tense silence, sparks flew from a nearby power line. Lights flickered on at the inn and other buildings. The men lowered their guns.

"Well, I'll be damned..."

"We're from Sherman, and we're fighting back. We need more men, and we need to organize if we don't want to get wiped off the map."

The men looked at each other.

"All we ask is that you keep a radio on and stay ready to fight. Here, it's all on this pamphlet. It'd also be nice if you spread the word."

He offered a folded-up piece of paper. A man cautiously took it. The men whispered to each other.

"We'll move the bus and let y'all through."

"Thank you, and as a gesture of goodwill, I brought you guys a gift."

He waved them over to the Humvee and opened the back. The men lugged a heavy wooden crate out and set it on the road. They cracked the lid and found three rocket launchers inside. Henry dug around the floorboard and pulled out three rockets and handed them over.

"I suggest you fellas head down Clay Lick Road and use that drone as target practice. There is more where that came from. Join up, and I might just hook you guys up with a tank."

* * *

Henry called off the drone while the men moved the bus. They departed Nashville and sped through Bloomington and a half-dozen small towns without stopping. Near the Sherman County line, he radioed the bunker again to check in.

Big Pigg answered, but Robby interrupted. "Heard you got into a standoff in Brown County. Y'all good?"

"We made some friends. Mariya and I are back in the county, but we're going to spend the night up top. Wait until you hear what we scored from Carmel."

"What, tanks? Bombs? Guns?"

"Yeah, actually – all of those things."

Chapter Thirty-Five

Marcus spent the afternoon touring the *Centro Nacional de Genética Médica de Cuba*. He watched a formerly paralyzed man jog on a treadmill and a blind man demonstrate 20/10 vision. He spoke with a woman who was born deaf but could now hear without any sort of implant. A nameless doctor gave a presentation on a long list of cures they had held back. Lastly, they covered the anti-aging serum.

He had a general idea of what the miracle drug could do from his time in the Quarry, but he didn't know of its origins.

After Putin died and Russia was in upheaval, foreign states and multinational pharmaceutical companies swooped in to collect his personal medical staff, much like the West did in Germany after World War II to recruit Nazi rocket scientists.

Betancourt and his shadow organization didn't have to beat them to the punch. They were running the program.

Russian doctors developed the serum over decades in North Korean prison camps. Marcus thought that might have explained the dubious late-2020's conflict on the peninsula that made it seem like oil was discovered outside of Pyongyang.

Betancourt spoke on how the proliferation of lifespan-expanding drugs would have exacerbated the existential environmental issues and destabilized whole societies.

"The life expectancy gap between rich and poor was already ghastly, and no one of low net worth was going to get serum for at least the first decade," he said. "If it ever got to mass manufacturing, Congress would have raised the retirement age to 80."

He insisted Marcus start a regimen before he departed. A team of doctors took a blood sample, despite his protest. As he watched his blood fill the tubes, he couldn't help but notice they were the same kind that he and Timothy used for the blood key.

* * *

The next morning, he was spared an economic seminar on future incentive systems in a post-labor world.

An assistant had entered and said, *"It's Europe,"* and so Betancourt left.

Marcus didn't mind. He'd had his dose of dystopia for the day.

A driver took him to the former North Korean ambassador's Havana residence where his father and stepmom were staying.

The kitsch North Korean decor was something to behold. Giant portraits of Kim Il Sung and sons, and daughter, hung over the entrance foyer.

"Never thought to take down the portraits of the Dear

Leader?"

"They're bolted to the walls," his father said. "Let's walk out back. There is a nice patio."

They meandered past the patio and onto the Bermuda grass lawn. Marcus looked at the back of his father's head, wondering what was going on inside it. Could he not see the evil around him?

"Don't even try talking me into joining these people," Marcus said. "How could you—"

"Son, let's get one thing straight – I'm not a part of any of this, not willfully." His father spoke forcefully, but quietly. "That stuff about Minnie's cancer being cured is true, but they only did it to get to you."

"But you seemed so adamant..."

"They would have shot me like that poor girl in Vincennes if I didn't! Listen, they're not going to send you back without getting what they want. Even if you hand them the keys to your grid, I...I don't know."

He had never seen his father so rattled.

"The grid controls are back in the bunker, and if I die, they become impossible to access. They have to let me go, regardless."

"Maybe, but you still need a backup plan."

"Like what? We're on an island. They have a navy."

"There's a lot of water out there. The Havana Yacht Club is a few kilometers west of your hotel. They've let us out on a boat called the *Hemmingway* a couple of times. If you sense that you need to go, go there. Use the compass, head north-northeast, and pray you hit Florida."

"Are you serious? You really th—"

His father cleared his throat. A soldier approached across the lawn.

"We have to go, Mr. Trencher," the soldier said. "Your

189

child is being born."

The color drained from Marcus's face.

"Dad, I'm not ready for this."

* * *

They were rushed to a military hospital where they were made to wait in the lobby with a pair of stone-faced soldiers. Betancourt's armored car pulled up outside. A female doctor entered the lobby, ignored them, and went straight to him.

After a brief exchange, Betancourt smiled. "I am happy to inform you that you are now the father, and you the grandfather, of a healthy baby boy."

"It's already over?" Marcus said.

"Had I known, I would have dropped everything. Shall we?"

Not even an hour prior, he was digesting the thought of having to escape from Cuba. Now he was about to meet a life he created, carelessly, in a drunken haze he hardly remembered.

Ashley Cameron was lying in the hospital bed with a bundle in her arms. He froze at the edge of the room. He caught a glimpse of a tiny hand and a tiny face.

A nurse gently took the baby from Ashley. Marcus's father nudged him forward, until he stepped up and took the baby into his arms.

The baby boy looked up at him with bluish-grey eyes. Marcus didn't know what it was, but something forever changed within him.

"He has your eyes," his father said. "It is uncanny."

"Does he have a name yet?"

"I like the name Daylin," Ashley said. "Daylin

Trencher."

Daylin calmly studied Marcus's face. Marcus found it impossible to look away.

"Hello, Daylin...nice to meet you."

"We will arrange for mom and baby to move to the hotel for the remainder of your stay," Betancourt said as he leaned in to tap Daylin's nose. "Isn't life precious?"

Chapter Thirty-Six

Henry and Mariya spent the night in his barely-lived-in mansion on Lake Sherman a few miles from the bunker. They talked about whether they should find a smaller place when they move to the surface permanently. They talked about the future. They made love.

They returned to the bunker in the morning and went straight to the War Room. Timothy, Genie, and Kent were hunched in front of screens full of colorful computer code.

Henry was slightly irked by their lack of enthusiasm when it came to his diplomatic feat at Carmel, but the IT team was tired from working on an objective every bit as important.

"We should retrieve the military vehicles sooner rather than later," Henry said.

Timothy rubbed his eyes. "We'll put people on it once Ellis returns with the train. Great work."

"That's not all – they are giving us access to some kind of AI supercomputer in exchange for more serum."

He slid over a piece of paper with details.

Genie took it. "Don't get your hopes up. We've run our own AI tools on the drone network, and they've found jack shit."

After gaining real-time visibility of every drone in the enemy network, progress had been slow in accomplishing much else. They wanted to override the controls, or at least sabotage their capabilities. The trio had vast experience protecting *Trencher Industries* from cyberattacks, but now they were the aggressors.

"Every vulnerability that we think we found has some band-aid that we can't get around," Timothy said. "In the meantime, we've developed a nasty virus. But getting it onto the drones is the hard part."

"Guys, we have data coming in from the tower," Kent said. He perked up the more he read. "It's plain text...It says, 'Mike Azoulay here. I need to speak with Timothy Spencer. Your blood brother is in Cuba.'"

"Mike Azoulay? The AI Guy?" Genie said, springing to her feet.

"...*Blood brother*...He's spoken to Marcus," Timothy said.

Kent responded, and another message quickly came in: "Access the server in the Carmel bunker. More secure. Marcus T is alive but in danger. I want to help."

The message disappeared and the link dropped.

Timothy paced the room. "Okay, the Carmel supercomputer moves to the top of our list, but we need to take precautions. This could be phishing."

Robby entered the room, itching for action. They filled him in on the state of cyberwarfare. He pretended to comprehend none of it to annoy them. He preferred to hear about the more tangible tanks, guns, and bombs Henry had secured.

"Ellis should be back with the train tomorrow," Henry said. "We'll take about sixty people to load the trains and then drive the vehicles back. Want to lead that charge?"

"Hell yeah, I was born to drive an armored column through Indiana."

* * *

After a late dinner, Henry returned to the surface with Mariya. They found so much pleasure the previous night that they wanted to sneak away for more. There was something exhilarating about venturing into an empty world with the one you love.

He insisted on taking the Humvee for the three-mile trip to the mansion. Mariya teased him for being so macho.

* * *

Back down below, perhaps inspired by Henry and Mariya, Timothy visited Dr. Nora Weinstein in the bunker infirmary. The kindling between them had been there for some time, but he could never bring himself to ignite it. But tonight, he felt bold.

"Hi, Nora. I was wondering if you wanted to go for a walk in the gardens."

She tilted her head in dismay. "I really can't. My patient is not doing so hot. A blood clot moved..." She trailed off as she read his disappointment. "Tomorrow?"

"Sure, of course."

Nora walked over and surprised him with a kiss. He floated away, encouraged, and energized.

His last stop of the night was to the radio room to check for any late reports from the surface scout teams.

"Anything new, Big Pigg?"

"Not a lot, boss. But there is one thing – the doorbell cams on the elevator dome have done gone out."

The panel of security camera feeds had indeed gone dark.

"We'll have someone fix them tomorrow. Go ahead and call it a night."

* * *

Headlights cut across the Indiana countryside on a deteriorated rural road, growing dimmer as what appeared to be a Humvee departed the bunker site.

The nocturnal glow of a night vision scope fell from a blackened face.

"You, and you, pursue. Secure hostages if feasible. Return by 0200 hours."

The team of soldiers was reduced to four after two split off.

The unit had already disabled a jerry-rigged ring of doorbell cameras on the concrete dome encasing the bunker elevator. They bickered about the move being too hasty, but as time passed, it appeared to have alarmed no one.

They didn't want to breach until the dead of night.

Chapter Thirty-Seven

Henry and Mariya tangled beneath the covers in the master bedroom. He brought a Bluetooth speaker to set the mood. When Madonna's "Erotica" started to play, Mariya couldn't stop giggling. When he skipped to the next track, "Justify My Love," they both laughed so hard they could barely breathe.

"I am going to kill Robby. His playlists are ridiculous."

Every room in the mansion was lit up. They ran through and flipped every switch when they arrived and made it a silly thing. The rooms were dusty and musky from prolonged vacancy. They planned to spruce it up and make it a proper home someday.

After a less raunchy song was selected, the kissing resumed.

Their passion played out until Henry heard a foreign *pop* noise that he was certain was no part of "Truly, Madly, Deeply."

"Did you hear that?"

There was another *pop*, followed by an unmistakable

staccato – gunfire.

He shut the music off, and they scrambled to get dressed. He peeked out of the window and saw muzzle flashes in the front drive. A shadowy figure fell.

"What is going on?"

"I don't know, but we need to hide."

"Did you bring a gun?"

"Yes...but I left it in the Humvee. Shit." He looked around. "Get in the closet."

Mariya was petite enough to conceal herself behind dress clothes Henry had left before going underground. If it came down to it, she would have to pray the intruders didn't search thoroughly.

He found an old baseball bat from his junior varsity days. It wasn't a gun, but it was something. He crept back to the bedroom, turned off the lights, and cracked the door.

A window shattered somewhere on the first floor, and suddenly the action was inside. An assault rifle blasted away. He couldn't tell what kind of weapon was returning fire from outside of the mansion, but whatever it was, it took the final shot.

Boots on broken glass interrupted the eerie quiet that followed. Henry gripped the bat tighter when footfalls hit the stairs. He steeled himself for a life-or-death struggle.

The intruder, or intruders, paused at the top step. Finally, one of them called out.

"It's Cal and Luke. You can come out. We got the bad guys."

Henry slid down the wall and let out a sigh of relief.

He got Mariya from the walk-in closet and they met Cal and Luke at the top of the stairs. A body was splayed in a pool of blood and broken glass in the foyer below.

"Only two came out this way," Cal said.

"There are more? Who are they?" Mariya said.

"Some kind of special forces. They ain't no ordinary looters."

"We were on our way back from Robinson and saw two armored vehicles flying up 41," Luke said. "We tailed them long enough to see they were headed out to the bunker. We had a feeling they were not our guys."

They walked outside where the second soldier lay dead in the driveway.

"They cut a hole in the bunker site fence around the time you two left. When one of the vehicles followed you, we pursued."

"Ain't no other scout teams in the county," Cal said. "And nobody is answering at the bunker. Hell, it's almost 2 a.m. Everyone is asleep."

* * *

The four operatives waited eighty yards out from the elevator dome. It was go-time, and the pair that had split off were nowhere to be found.

"Forget them," the lead soldier said. "Time to move."

They ran to the dome carrying weapons and rope. Three of them flattened against it while the tech-savviest of the team set to the door.

"C4?"

"Wouldn't put a dent in this thing."

The soldier hooked a device to the lock, pressed a few buttons, and the door released. Inside, the elevator platform was far below. They tied their ropes to the railing and began their descent.

* * *

Robby watched Melonie's belly rise and fall as she breathed. The baby was probably asleep, like mom and everyone else in the world. He couldn't wait to meet him, or her.

Sleep was out of the question. His mind was racing.

He stepped out to the balcony overlooking the gardens. The lights were dimmed, but the sky projector was left on. The stars were not real, but they were still beautiful.

Distant, moving shadows caught the corner of his eye. He leaned over the rail to see across the threshold to the bunker proper.

Four dark figures filed out of the media room crouched, coordinated, and kept to the wall. He saw the silhouettes of their rifles before losing sight of them. He wondered if he was dreaming.

He went back into the room, threw some clothes on, and grabbed a gun. He kissed Melonie softly so she wouldn't wake.

He knocked at the neighboring room. Braxton, one of the teenagers he worked with during his brief stint in the mines, answered. His mother asked who it was. Robby peeked in and told her everything was okay.

"Do you have a gun in there?"

"Yeah, why?"

"Grab it. Don't ask questions."

Braxton followed with a hunting rifle in hand. At the threshold between the gardens and the bunker proper, Robby peeked around the corner. The infiltrators were lined up outside of the infirmary.

"Are you a good shot?"

"Yeah, I hunt."

"Sneak out to the gazebo and see if you can get a good angle."

"You want me to shoot somebody?"

"These are bad guys. After you take your first shot, I'll fire. Stay covered."

Braxton took a roundabout route to the gazebo and got into position.

The soldiers emerged from the infirmary with Dr. Nora Weinstein. She let out a cry before one of the men muffled her mouth and hit her in the stomach.

Robby signaled to hold.

A soldier distanced himself from the others while pointing to the windows above them – Marcus's suite. Their attention turned to the door leading up to it.

Robby dropped his hand. The teenager fired at the separated soldier.

The soldier was down and writhing by the time Robby turned the corner. He fired at the same man and missed.

The others quickly returned fire in their general direction, spraying the café with a hail of bullets. Braxton left the gazebo and ran in the open.

"Damnit, kid!"

Robby provided cover fire, coming nowhere near hitting anyone, but it was enough. The soldiers retreated into the infirmary, dragging Dr. Nora with them.

Braxton came to Robby's side, out of breath.

"Good work," Robby said. "I need to get to the other side to get help. Cover me and watch that door. Just don't shoot Dr. Nora."

The fearless teen sprinted out into the bunker proper and took position behind a massive support column.

Robby slipped around the corner and sprinted into

and through the corridor to the other side, and straight to the elevator. A moment later he was banging on Timothy's door, and then Steve's, the next one down.

"What's wrong?"

"Black ops dudes broke into the bunker. They have Dr. Nora."

Timothy's face dropped. "I'll meet you down there."

Steve stepped out of his room and to Robby's surprise, Mercedes was behind him. It was too serious of a time to tease. He filled them in and ran back to the elevator.

Others had heard the gunfire and made their way to the chamber outside the War Room. He led the ones that were armed to the other side.

* * *

The soldiers were hunkered in, guns aimed from the shattered windows. They had rolled a bed-ridden patient out front for additional cover. A hardened soldier held Dr. Nora beside the gurney. Across the way, Braxton huddled behind a column now pockmarked by bullets.

Timothy and Steve caught up with Robby. When they crept around the corner, the soldier pulled Dr. Nora closer.

Timothy put both hands up and took another step out.

"Controls to the *Trencher Industries* power grid," the soldier said in a South African accent. "Hand it over, or the doctor dies."

Chapter Thirty-Eight

Timothy weighed his options. There weren't many.

"Nobody needs to get hurt. We can resolve this peacefully."

"Give us the controls to your power grid," the soldier said. "Then you can have your peace."

Whatever the fallout, they would have to deal with it later.

"It's a piece of hardware. I'll get it. Give me five minutes."

"Hold on." The soldier took his Glock 19 from Dr. Nora's temple and pointed to the windows above the infirmary. "What's up there?"

"Marcus Trencher's suite."

"Sounds comfy. We'll wait there."

Timothy approached cautiously and punched the code to the door.

The other soldiers emerged from the infirmary, using the patient and gurney as cover. The lead mercenary narrowed his gaze on Robby.

"Tall man, put the gun down. You're coming with."

Robby handed his rifle to Steve and gave himself up.

A soldier shoved him up the suite staircase as the two others filed behind them. The leader, still holding Dr. Nora, backed in last.

"Five minutes," Timothy said.

"Four – or tall man gets it."

* * *

Timothy flew into the War Room and flipped the lights on.

Kent and Genie were asleep on makeshift beds on opposite sides of the room. Miraculously, they had slept through the gun battle.

"Wake up! Soldiers broke in. They want the blood key."

Kent said *Huh?* Genie said *What?*

He grabbed a cable and linked the blood key to his laptop.

"I'm planting the virus. It can sit on the key until we figure out a way to activate it."

He tucked the cumbersome blood key under his arm. It was the size and weight of an old computer tower. He balanced a laptop in his other arm so he could watch the progress and bolted from the war room as quickly as he came.

The viral branch of code finished merging as he neared the end of the corridor. He closed the program, yanked the cable, and sprinted the rest of the way.

The South African waited at the top of the stairs.

"Seconds to spare."

* * *

Robby sat in a love seat, hands and ankles bound by zip-ties. After Dr. Nora patched up the wounded soldier, she was also bound. A mohawked soldier held them at gunpoint while another stood at the windows, watching a crowd carelessly congregate below.

Timothy sat at Marcus's desk with the tech specialist, who was suffering from a gunshot wound. The lead mercenary hovered behind them.

Timothy explained how the blood key was able to override the blockchain grid controls and demonstrated how to divert power from one community to the next. He blacked out a random town in Ohio. He showed proof that there was no higher security clearance than what the blood key granted.

"Never in a million years would I have figured that out." The soldier laughed through excruciating pain. "By the way, do you recognize me?"

Timothy did not.

"I was a plant at the company. I wrote a whole report explaining how this wasn't possible. Guess I was wrong. I started a couple weeks before Trencher canned you, or whatever went down between you two."

"Enough reminiscing," the lead soldier said. "How can we know the controls are ours once we leave?"

"Once you activate the blood key on your own terminal, the previous controls are overwritten, and it is all yours," Timothy said.

He watched the cursor hover over an AI code-scanning application. He was confident the virus code was well-hidden, but not that confident.

The soldier broke out in a cold sweat. He skipped the scan. "It checks out. Just need Marcus Trencher's blood."

The lead soldier walked to the windows and looked down at the people. "Very well, crack on with it."

Robby and Dr. Nora's ankle zip-ties were cut before being ushered out of the suite and down the stairs. The crowd looked on helplessly as they skirted along the wall, passed the train tunnel, and funneled into the media room.

They were pushed onto the elevator platform, which was a step further than they expected. Robby protested.

"Nobody is free until we are on our way. Up we go."

The elevator ascended, collecting the soldiers' black rappelling rope into neat coils. When it arrived up top, they stepped out into the crisp, dark night. The soldiers turned on flashlights. Before Robby or Dr. Nora could react, their ankles were re-bound, as were Timothy's wrists.

The lead soldier took out a satellite phone.

"...*Package is secure...It's some kind of DNA device, creates a digital key ...Yes sir, it requires blood samples from Marcus Trencher and Timothy Spencer...we got Spencer's...Yes sir, Cuba 2100 hours...*"

"You have what you came for," Timothy said.

The lead soldier swung his flashlight his way, blinding him.

"Computer whiz is coming with us. I don't believe a word he's said." His light swung to Robby. "Kill the tall man. Let the doctor lady go."

Robby was shoved to the damp ground, face down. He struggled to even roll over to face his executioner. Dr. Nora cried out but was ignored.

A soldier removed his sidearm, fastened his tactical flashlight, and took aim.

"*Stop right there,*" a voice sounded from the dark.

Beams of light swung toward the executioner, illuminating a hunting rifle pressed against the back of his head.

The rifle was held by Cal the scout.

"Drop the gun or I blow your fucking brains out."

The soldier sighed a visible breath and did as he was told.

Cal's trusty partner, Luke, emerged from the other side of the dome and took advantage of the distraction. He grabbed the closest soldier and put a handgun to his head. The soldier held a bulky black duffel bag and hadn't drawn a weapon. Luke moved him with ease, not knowing the man had a gunshot wound to the leg.

Behind Luke, Henry and Mariya also appeared, also armed.

The two remaining soldiers moved quickly to secure Timothy and Dr. Nora as human shields. They backed up to the dome to eliminate angles.

"Looks like we have an old-fashioned stand-off," the lead soldier said.

"Don't expect your other two pals," Luke said. "They're already dead."

"I have confirmed kills on six continents, mate. These boys are no slouches either. If you want a shootout, I'll take our odds."

Cal maneuvered around his man while keeping a gun to his head. He handed a hunting knife to Robby, who had managed to sit upright.

Robby cut the ties around his ankles, and then the one around his wrists. He grabbed the gun of his would-be executioner.

"Luke, walk your man this way," Robby said.

Luke shoved the soldier forward. His face was so pale it seemed to emit light. Robby took the duffel bag with the blood key.

"This is what you came here for, right? If you want it, we need our people alive."

The lead soldier said, "We're listening."

"Here's what's going to happen. You'll walk out to your vehicle or spaceship or whatever the fuck you rode in on, and I'll place the key at the side of the road. Release them and drive up to retrieve the key. Then, we release your men."

The soldier nodded. "Let's crack on with it."

* * *

Both parties and their hostages marched a quarter mile down the road to a camouflaged tactical vehicle. Robby, Cal, and the uninjured hostage went further and placed the blood key. Timothy and Dr. Nora were released.

"Those sadistic sons of bitches are liable to leave us," one of the hostage soldiers said.

The injured soldier was too weak to reply.

The other mercenaries did retrieve their men. As they sped away, Robby fired off rounds in their direction. Cal, Luke, Henry, and Mariya were about to join, but Timothy told them not to bother.

He wanted to get down to the bunker as soon as possible. They needed drones in the air, ASAP.

They could still stop the blood key from reaching Cuba.

Chapter Thirty-Nine

Timothy held Dr. Nora during the ride down to the bunker. Cal and Luke were quiet and solemn. Robby shook with rage.

The terror at the mansion and the hostage standoff hadn't caught up to Henry. He let a rappelling rope slide through one hand as the platform descended and held Mariya's hand with the other.

"We're all alive, and that's what matters," Henry said. "It's the best outcome, considering the circumstances."

Timothy banged the railing with his fist.

"We handed over the only thing keeping Marcus alive! They might drain his blood before the key even gets to Cuba."

When the platform came to a halt, he charged out ahead of them.

* * *

Kent was milling about with a hundred others awakened by the firefight and ensuing hostage crisis.

"You come with me," Timothy said.

Kent had twelve drones in the sky within ten minutes. They didn't know exactly where the mercenaries were headed, but they assumed south, and given the time that had passed, they had an approximate idea of the distance already covered. Half of the fleet were sent well ahead over U.S. 41.

"Woah, what the hell?" Kent said. "I'm losing visuals. They have a jamming device."

"What kind of radius?" Timothy said. "Can you guestimate a center using the highway as an axis?"

"A direct hit is out of the question. I can blow up the highway ahead of them, though."

Timothy didn't like the idea of destroying infrastructure that they would have a hard time ever replacing, but the situation was dire.

"Do it. Look for a creek bridge. Henry and Robby – dispatch our best men to try and catch them."

The escape vehicle had already made it beyond the first bridge out of Sherman County. Kent switched to the next drone ten miles south and spotted a pair of overpasses spanning over the railroads near Oaktown. He released a barrage of missiles, destroying the north and southbound lanes.

Henry quickly gathered able-bodied men – "badass rednecks," as Robby called them. Their orders were to load up on guns, drive fast, and shoot to kill.

The enemy had a twenty-minute head start, but local knowledge would cut that in half. The bombed bridges were certain to buy time. Cal and Luke rejected the notion that they had done enough and volunteered to lead.

"Genie, get the IT guys at the Carmel bunker on the line – we need to reach Mike Azoulay," Timothy said. "He is our only hope to get word to Marcus in Cuba."

"Pinging them now," Genie said.

* * *

Marcus was given thirty minutes to visit Daylin before the day's planned activities. Ashley and the baby were to be moved to the hotel that evening. After that, he didn't know. It was his second-to-last day in Cuba, if Betancourt kept his word.

Betancourt had to. The blood key grid controls were safe and sound, deep underground, in his bunker in Indiana.

A driver took him to the Havana outskirts where Betancourt greeted him at the entrance gate of the *Universidad de las Ciencias Informáticas*. The campus was turned into a research community filled with top scientists, each recruited, kidnapped, or blackmailed into being there.

Plywood propped up against a fence read, GALT'S GULCH in black spray paint, referring to the secretive community where "men of the mind" retreated from society in Ayn Rand's *Atlas Shrugged*.

"I'll have you know that I am no John Galt, nor do I subscribe to the objectivism worldview," Betancourt said. "We have collected great minds and hidden them away, true, but only momentarily. We will share our inventions with the world when it has become a sustainable one."

Marcus held his tongue. Betancourt's worldview rationalized slaughtering more than half the world's population. It was absurd to get hung up on an old novel.

They walked a street lined with campus buildings, housing, and overgrown landscaping. The dormitories looked rundown, but Betancourt assured him that they were luxurious inside. Lead scientists had entire floors to themselves with every amenity. Others were given driving privileges and mansions in Havana.

"The building to our left is our material sciences lab. The Nobel Laureate that figured out how to mass produce graphene runs it."

Graphene was a major component in Marcus's battery technology and smart grid, and the solar panels that fed into it. The material revolutionized every industry. He would have been lying if he didn't desire to pick the expert's brain if given the chance.

Betancourt turned to the next building. "This is what I really wanted to show you."

They stepped into a facility shockingly bright and clean. They passed nurses and doctors before coming to a row of interior windows. Marcus looked inside – it was a nursery filled with infants.

"These lovely little cherubs might just live forever. You are aware of our anti-aging research. We've also made breakthroughs at the beginning of life, through the application of precise genome-editing tools."

"Designer babies," Marcus said.

"Don't downplay it, my friend. It is the future of our species. We have the power to select traits and eliminate hereditary diseases."

"You aren't experimenting on my child, are you?"

"It is not an experiment at this point. The oldest subjects from the Korean camps are excelling in every measure despite being born to malnourished mothers. They exceed the average height of previous North Koreans by six inches or more. Perfect health, high intelligence. But no, your son has not undergone any such treatment. We can start him right away if you'd like."

"No, I want him to be just as he is."

Betancourt sighed. "Think of your flaws...We can make sure none are passed to him. Our scientists have identified genes that impact where our subjects may fall on a personality scale, or what some may refer to as a *spectrum*."

Marcus's face flushed red. "No – the answer is no."

Betancourt smirked, satisfied that he had dug into Marcus's psyche.

"No rush. These therapies can work later in life. They can work on you today, in fact. If you stay with us, we can start a regimen. It is miraculous what these treatments can do. We had a girl in Eastern Europe – Mensa genius, but non-verbal – within a year she was what anyone would call normal, except she maintained her brilliance. She can recite Shakespeare and comprehend advanced physics. Imagine what it would unlock in you."

An assistant approached.

"Think about. Please, excuse me for one moment."

He looked in at the nursery as Betancourt stepped away. What a world they were going to grow up in.

Personality-spectrum gene therapy sounded too good to be true. Would he suddenly read facial expressions quicker? Get jokes? Know when to laugh? Would he feel sane again? Buried thoughts from his childhood crept in. The awkwardness, the loneliness, the misunderstanding, the rejection.

He imagined Daylin as a toddler on a playground with the genetically enhanced children from the nursery. Daylin played alone.

Betancourt returned with a twinkle of satisfaction in his eye. Was he still gloating over his subtle jab? Had his assistant delivered good news? For such a vile man, good news could only be bad.

"Let's step back outside," Betancourt said.

They walked back out to the campus street and stopped in front of another facility.

"If you'd like to join us, this one will be all yours. Whatever you'd like to study or create, we can provide all you need. Marcus Trencher, you have a brilliant mind. It would be my honor to help you."

Marcus looked at the bland building and let himself imagine what he could accomplish with unlimited resources, but only for a second.

"I will keep this in mind."

"The time has come for you to decide. We can hash out details later, the grid and what-have-you. The offer is on the table now."

"I will be going back before making my decision."

Betancourt shook his head and smiled for an unnerving moment.

"Touché, that was our agreement. A driver will take you back to the resort." He motioned to his security detail and a car drove up. "A tropical storm is moving in tonight. Pay no mind to the noise. You'll depart the island midday tomorrow."

Chapter Forty

Cal and Luke arrived at the severed overpass near Oaktown in time to witness a strange aerial vehicle take off. Columns of smoke swirled in its ringed rotor blades before it disappeared into the haze. The abandoned military vehicle had been blown up.

The infiltrators had escaped with the blood key.

When word got back to the bunker, Timothy turned his attention to the next option.

Genie reached out to the Carmel IT team. Thanks to Henry's diplomatic mission, they were given access to an AI supercomputer which happened to receive frequent patches and communications from Cuba, via satellite.

Timothy had no interest in the AI, at least for now. He needed the back channel to reach Mike Azoulay.

Upon log in, "the AI Guy" reached out before Genie could.

"It's about time..." Azoulay sent.

Timothy took Genie's seat at the keyboard. "We need your help – we were attacked – they stole the grid key. All they need is a sample of Marcus's blood. His life is in danger. Can you warn him?"

"DNA biometrics?" Blinking dots indicated continued typing. "...I think I know a way to reach him. Any luck with the drone virus?"

"How does he know about that?" Timothy said aloud. "Marcus..."

He didn't have time for tech-talk. The sooner Azoulay could reach Marcus, the better. Still, he took a moment to fill him in. The virus itself, he was confident, would work – but he didn't know how to get it into the drone network. A virus that wasn't infectious was no virus at all.

He ended with a question: "Any solutions?"

Azoulay responded, "Run the code through my Akili AI program. Prompt her on what you want the virus to do, and I bet you a billion bucks she comes up with something brilliant. All her ethical parameters are turned off."

Timothy rolled his eyes. He had already tried a whole suite of AI tools.

"Get the message to Marcus ASAP and keep us posted." He gave the seat back to Genie.

"We're already in," Genie said. "Want to see how the AI does?"

"Sure, whatever. I'm going to get some coffee."

Genie clicked around and admitted that the interface was slick. She fed in the code and typed out a stream-of-consciousness, unpunctuated prompt. Her effort matched her expectations.

Akili, the AI avatar, responded: "*What an interesting task. Do you mind if I access the application you alluded to so I may offer the best solution?*"

Genie responded, *sure.*

Akili opened the drone program from the desktop and explored it in the blink of an eye. After, she returned a list of suggestions, eloquently explained, with snippets of fully written code to boot.

Genie leaned in. "Not your grandpa's large language model I see...Intriguing. Dare I say elegant..."

She poured over the output and became more and more blown away.

Timothy returned with coffee in hand. "What unimaginative trash did the AI generate?"

She turned the laptop around. "Let's just say, if the world hadn't ended, we'd all be out of a job."

Timothy came away humbled. In a matter of seconds, the AI found every vulnerability in the software, wrote nuanced code, and offered a roadmap to spread the virus.

The vulnerability Akili found was embedded within the charging mechanism and its data interchange program. *Trencher Industries* had the largest vertiport network in the world. Every drone that landed to charge on one of their platforms would pick up the virus. It was almost too perfect.

There was only one issue.

Timothy terminated his grid controls – at gunpoint, he reminded everyone – and handed the blood key over. He had ideas on how to wrestle the grid back eventually, but it would take time they didn't have.

The blood key was on the way to Cuba. Azoulay was in Cuba. They didn't know if they could fully trust him, but he might be their only hope.

* * *

Marcus returned to the Meliá Habana Hotel after dinner with his dad and stepmom. The only feasible scenario in which it wouldn't be their last together was if he accepted Betancourt's proposal to stay on the island.

Like true Trencher men, they avoided emotions as long as possible, but after the meal they hugged and said that they loved each other. His father again told him to get off the island by any means necessary. He and his stepmom would help take care of Daylin in his absence – raise him if they had to.

Ashley and Daylin were moved into the hotel, as promised. He didn't much see the point, given he was departing the next day. He wanted to see and hold his son again, but what he wanted beyond that was hard for him to say.

He knocked at the room across the hall. Ashley called that it was open. She was breastfeeding Daylin.

"Oh, I can come back later."

He looked at Daylin's fuzzy head and then at her. She had been crying.

"I could use the company."

"Sorry for...all of this," he said, stepping deeper into the room. "I've done nothing but put you in difficult positions, all the way back to the corporate days."

"Please, I enjoyed firing all those executives. And placating a whole bunker population slaving away in a coal mine? Dream job."

He was visibly confused.

"Sarcasm, Marcus." She moved Daylin away from her breast and covered herself. "When you left the bunker, I survived how I always did – by being cutthroat. When you came back and kicked me out and said Daylin wasn't yours, I latched onto the next authority in the next bunker. I made mistakes...but this little guy isn't one of them. Want to hold him?"

He picked Daylin up as if he were the most fragile thing on earth.

He accepted Ashley's half-apology. He could have called her out on the plan she hatched with Grant Maniego to have him killed, but he let it go. Daylin fussed, yawned, and fell asleep. How could he leave such a precious thing?

"I am scheduled to depart tomorrow if the weather holds. That is, if Betancourt keeps his word."

"He interrogated me for hours, you know. I never told him how it works."

"How what works?"

"That blood testing machine. I know it unlocked controls to the grid. I won't pretend I fully understood it, but I do know it requires both of your blood samples."

"How on earth did you know that?"

"The head of media relations proposed that we collect keepsakes from the early days of *Trencher Industries*. She thought you'd have a prototype lying around that we could put in a museum for PR, our first Apple computer kind of thing. You pencil-whipped the approval and sent me to retrieve a box from your parent's garage. There was a notebook and a piece of hardware. I flipped through the notebook and got the gist of it. I put the box in your office and never said a word about it. The next time I ever saw it was the day you took a blood vial out of it, tossed it at me, and kicked me out of the bunker."

"I don't know what to say."

Daylin squirmed and yawned mightily.

"Daylin and I might never see you again. It's just reality. Whatever you do, don't join these people. You are too good."

"I'll negotiate your release."

"It wouldn't be worth it, not if you give up the grid. They already have the next deep freeze winter scheduled.

They'll cut the power and kill everyone off for good. You can't give them that capability."

"I should stay. I could do good from the inside. What kind of father am I just leaving him here, and you?"

"In this specific, fucked-up situation – a good one. They'll use you for evil and you won't have a choice. Wouldn't you rather he grows up hearing stories about how great of an inventor you were, and how you led a resistance? I'll tell him stories every night."

He held Daylin in front of him and looked at his sleepy face. He wanted to say something, but it was too early for goodbyes. He handed him back to Ashley.

"I'll see you both tomorrow morning before I go. It's getting late."

Ashley offered for him to stay, but he was already out the door. He crossed the hall to his own room and fell on his bed in tears.

Chapter Forty-One

Marcus ruminated on his predicament while lying crossways on his hotel bed. What if he stayed in Cuba? Could he play along and quietly pull a coup against Betancourt? Surely there were enough people on the island who would flip if given the chance.

He would get word back to Henry and Robby and Timothy. They would know that he had a plan.

Out of nowhere, the room's TV turned on, interrupting his racing thoughts. It defaulted to an antiquated hotel menu screen.

It was odd. He didn't turn it on. He found the remote and shut it off.

As he turned to his side, it turned on again.

This time, the text on the menu caught his eye.

"MARCUS T! Mike Azoulay – channel UP / DOWN to signal you are there. I have a message from Tim Spencer."

Marcus flipped the channel up and back. The text disappeared and was replaced.

"Enemy broke into bunker and stole grid key. It is on way to Cuba. You are in danger. TS said they need your blood? Channel up/down."

He slowly realized that Betancourt didn't need his blood – *he already had it*. His blood was drawn when Betancourt insisted that they synthesize anti-aging serum for him, collected in the same compatible tube that the blood key required, no less.

Technically, Betancourt didn't need him alive at that very moment.

He flipped the channel up and down.

"Do you want to escape? CHANNEL UP for escape. CHANNEL DOWN to stay."

Did he have a choice? He hit the channel UP button.

"Use route we took to the beach. Hotel cameras are out. Find a boat? I can trigger blackout at midnight – 15 minutes tops. Tropical storm inbound FYI. Good luck."

He had nothing to pack. He only had to decide whether he was to go it alone.

He made it two steps down the hall before turning around.

Ashley answered the door. He put a finger to his lips to keep their voices down. She smiled, thinking he was thinking of the baby, but soon realized how pale and serious he was.

"I got a message – they broke into the bunker and stole the blood key. They don't need me alive anymore. I'm leaving now."

Ashley was overwhelmed. "What? How—"

"There is a boat dock down the beach. I want you and Daylin to come with me. You're not safe here."

"I can't...we can't...he's two days old!"

"You say I'm too good to stay here? Then so are you. We can make it together."

She looked back at the crib and composed herself.

"Let me pack a few things."

* * *

They snuck out the same way Azoulay showed him during his first night in Havana. Ashley swaddled Daylin in a hotel robe. Marcus carried the bag of baby supplies.

They walked the choppy beach under a dark sky. There was no rain, and only a light breeze. Calm before the storm. After only a hundred meters, they ran out of sand and had to skirt along a seawall in front of the neighboring resort. He realized he was well ahead of Ashley and Daylin.

"Slow down! I can't do this!" Asley said. "I just gave birth. I'm in pain."

"Sorry. Let me carry him."

Beyond the resort, there was no clear path along the waterfront, so they turned inland onto what he presumed was Havana's equivalent to A1A Beach Drive Avenue. Classic cars and impeccably maintained Ladas lined the route. Hijacking one would have sped up their journey, but it was too risky.

His notion immediately paid off. They were midblock when a vehicle turned onto the avenue behind them.

He tried the door to a restaurant, then a salon, but both were locked. They ducked into an alley and took cover behind a stack of wooden crates. The headlights crept forward.

Daylin started to cry.

"Shh..shh...it's okay, buddy..."

He would not be pacified. He covered Daylin's mouth enough to muffle his cries. Daylin squirmed.

A Jeep rolled into view. No windows, no doors. Upbeat music competed with the rumbling engine. A beer bottle was tossed and shattered in the alley. The soldiers laughed, and then they were gone.

He took his hand away from Daylin's mouth and felt sick to his stomach. Daylin wailed inconsolably.

"I can take him," Ashley said.

They stepped back out to the avenue, and after several city blocks, came to a seaside park, *Parque la Isla del Coco*. It was open and well lit, but by far the fastest route. The beach retreated into a cove ahead.

Halfway through the park, the lights went out in all of Havana.

"Azoulay said he'd knock the power out as a distraction. It's probably only going to raise suspicion. I see boats ahead. This must be it."

They found a walkway to the beach and approached the marina. The abandoned Havana Yacht Club loomed at the crest of the cove like a haunted house.

A dozen yachts were moored at the docks. Marcus looked for *The Hemmingway* his father told him about, and found the actual name was *Friend of Hemmingway*, but finding it was what mattered. The keys were in it.

Ashley climbed aboard with his help, with Daylin.

"Do you know how to drive this thing?"

He owned the largest boat on Lake Sherman back home. It was no 35-foot yacht, but it looked nice when boaters passed by to gawk at his mansion. He stepped foot on the vessel twice in total, drove it only once.

"I'll figure it out. Get below deck. We are headed into a storm."

He climbed around and untied ropes and made his way to the bridge. Eventually, the yacht drifted free. Atmospheric lightning outlined a wall of rain racing across the open sea.

Behind them, the inhabited parts of Havana lit back up in a cascade. Azoulay's outage had subsided.

He wasn't the praying type, but he said a quick prayer anyway.

It was going to take a miracle to make it to Florida.

Chapter Forty-Two

Marcus didn't know what coastal people called it, but in Indiana, it was "heat lightning." He saw yellowish flashes illuminating a charging stormfront over the Gulf Strait.

He used the brief window of relatively calm waters to go full throttle. It couldn't have been fun below deck where Ashley huddled like a stowaway with Daylin. Rain started to fall as Havana faded in their wake.

As far as he could tell, no vessel pursued. Nature was the only obstacle.

The yacht had a functioning navigation system. In the most rudimentary way, he aimed for the Florida Keys. Perhaps a more experienced captain would have set a wider course to avoid the storm for as long as possible, but he kept it simple and went for a straight line.

Branches of godly light touched the sea between curtains of rain. No more heat lightning. The storm swept across the seascape and began turning over white caps. The yacht lifted and fell over higher and higher waves.

Progression stalled near the point of no return. The yacht slid down the back of every wave crest, crashing into the troughs and spraying water over the bow.

He heard Daylin crying in the cabin. So far, as a father, he had put a hand over his newborn's mouth, and then drove him into a tropical storm. Not a good start.

The only thing he could do was hold onto the helm and square up for the next wave, and then the next, so they did not capsize.

That would make him an even worse father.

* * *

Azoulay reached out to Timothy and Genie at 9 a.m. the next morning. He succeeded in getting a warning to Marcus the previous night, and Marcus chose escape. Whether he was successful, Azoulay did not know.

Henry and Robby met Ellis and Taveon at the train platform. The men were unloading weapons they had picked up from the cache near the Columbus tunnel exchange.

"Did we miss anything?" Ellis asked.

Robby just laughed.

"Eh, a few things," Henry said. "Don't wander far. We have eighty volunteers signed up to retrieve those armored vehicles and the rest of the weapons. I'm afraid we might need them sooner rather than later."

Ellis sighed. "Let my men get a meal in and then we'll fire her back up."

* * *

Marcus, Ashley, and Daylin weathered the storm. It had settled into steady rainfall before tapering off completely by daybreak. As sunlight broke through the clouds, he ran the *Friend of Hemmingway* aground at a place called

226

Sombrero Beach, somewhere in the Florda Keys.

He hit the dock hard, and at the same time hit the bottom. It was good enough to get off the boat and onto land.

Ashley climbed out of the cabin holding Daylin, both frazzled but fine. He helped them onto the dock, and they made their way up to a beachfront mansion. The patio door was unlocked. Nobody was home.

"We can't stay long. They'll know we're not in Havana any moment. The sooner we get to mainland Florida, the better."

Ashley found the garage. There was a high-end luxury SUV, fully electric, fully charged. Keys in a bowl in the kitchen. The only thing missing was a car seat for Daylin.

"Add it to my list of bad parenting," Marcus said. We've got to go."

He loathed driving, but after braving the tropical storm, he thought he could handle it. Ashley knew of his phobia and offered to take the wheel, but he insisted on taking on the first leg of the trip.

They found U.S. Route 1 and hit Key Largo within an hour. An old man along the road stared as they passed, too confused to wave. They hoped not to see anyone else.

Two separate checkpoints with barbed wire and sandbag walls gave them pause, but both were unmanned. Soldiers were either derelict of their duties, or word of their escape had yet to spread.

Marcus breathed a sigh of relief when they crossed into the mainland glades. The relief lasted ten minutes before he suddenly had to slam on the brakes.

Thousands of alligators were greeting the rising sun on Route 1, covering every inch of pavement as far as they could see. As the SUV crept forward, some slithered and sprawled into the glades, others hissed and high-walked casually to the waters.

At the spectacularly generic city of "Florida City," they pulled into a roadside motel, found an open room, and finally got some sleep.

Chapter Forty-Three

Mike Azoulay walked his bike through the station security gate on the outskirts of Havana. He stared out at the satellites that dotted the hillside like giant mushrooms. The commute was his favorite part of the day.

He was given a home in a near-empty village a kilometer from the base. In his free time, he broke into houses and looted computer parts.

His secret at-home PC rig was good enough to hack the Cuban internet, the Melia Habana Hotel TV menu, and the Havana electrical utility union. With a few more components, he could sneak a stripped-down version of his Akili AI out of her digital cage.

There was no doubt he was going to get caught, and that they were going to kill him. He just hoped he could do enough damage beforehand.

Akili was supposed to help run the world once it started back up again. His orders were to mold her disposition in the realms of governance, economics, law, research, and so on, to Betancourt and his organization's liking. He had more exposure to their vision than anyone outside of their shadowy cabal.

Like Marcus Trencher, his continued existence relied upon his indispensable bond to his invention. Also, like Trencher, he could use his invention to fight back.

* * *

The base outside of Havana was filled with experts from across the globe, some there more willingly than others. Compartmentalization was strict in year one, but it eventually loosened. Everyone ate together in the mess hall and shared gossip.

Tomas Nagy was a Hungarian-born quantum computing whiz who always had the latest.

"Heard there was an escape last night," Nagy said. "Soldiers were scrambling around the island this morning. A yacht is missing."

Azoulay stirred his eggs, feigning disinterest. "Whoever it was, they're probably at the bottom of the Caribbean. Bad storm last night."

"This is the best part – it was Marcus Trencher, that smart grid billionaire. I didn't even know he was here."

"I had a few Trencher *Monoliths*," Holly Foard, a former AI-dating app CEO, said. "Totally eliminated my electric bills at four of my properties. The guy was brilliant."

"Timothy Spencer was the real genius," Azoulay said. "He built the backend blockchain tech. He was like Wozniak, and Trencher was Jobs."

"Well, apparently their grids were not as decentralized as the commercials used to say," Nagy said. "Trencher had an override built in. Our overlords want it for The Great Rebuild."

A young Indian man named Chardeep walked into

the cafeteria. They collectively groaned. Chardeep oversaw the implementation of the autonomous killer drone network across Central Asia. Azoulay attributed a billion deaths to his name. It wasn't totally fair or accurate, but nobody liked the guy.

"Before Char*snitch* gets over here, I got one more thing," Nagy said. "They're pulling ground troops out of Texas and sending them up to Indiana."

"Indiana? What the hell is up there?" Azoulay asked, knowing all too well.

"Beats me, but they only send in the stormtroopers to put down serious rebellions. Guess there are some Indianans? – Indians? – causing trouble."

"They're called Hoosiers," Holly said.

"Well, they're about to get treated like Indians."

"Did somebody say Indians?" Chardeep said as he sat down.

The rest stood to leave like mean high school girls. Azoulay was too hungry to abandon his breakfast.

"Did you hear?" Chardeep said grinning and unbothered. "Pakistan is cleared."

"You must be proud."

"Betancourt says I'll get a tower in Mumbai once India falls in the low millions. I will clear the slums and plant gardens. It will be paradise."

"Char, I know you're just doing your job – but maybe try not to sound so cheerful about killing millions of people?"

Chardeep shrugged and stabbed a chunk of cantaloupe.

Azoulay's appetite suddenly left him. "I better get to work on Akili. She's been having hallucinations again."

He tossed his tray and walked down the hall to the

231

cramped workspace he had the misfortune of sharing with Chardeep. The few moments he could get alone were crucial – he needed to get a message to his friends in Indiana.

Chapter Forty-Four

Timothy, Kent, Henry, and Mariya stood by the vertiport five miles east of the bunker. One of their captured drones sat perched atop the platform.

Kent looked at his laptop. "Battery is topped off."

"Okay, send it away, but not too far," Timothy said.

The drone lifted from the vertiport and hovered at a good, safe distance.

"I'm targeting the dilapidated house in the distance," Kent said. "Not that it should matter, but just in case."

Timothy watched through binoculars while the rest put a hand above their brow to shield from the sun. It was a cold but clear day.

Kent pressed the fire button. A missile detached from the undercarriage – and immediately detonated. The drone exploded into a shower of debris.

"Holy shit, it worked!" Timothy said.

The virus successfully transmitted from the vertiport to the drone.

The malware wormed its way through a vulnerability in the charging and billing program, all the way into the weapons system. Upon firing, the virus copies the drone's own coordinates – essentially pasting it over the intended target coordinates – causing the missile to detonate the second it is released, blowing the drone out of the sky.

They high fived, but the celebration was brief. It was only a test. They still had no easy way to spread the virus to all the Trencher vertiports nationwide.

"We can program a drone to fly from platform to platform and infect each one, like a bee pollenating flowers," Kent said.

"Too slow. It needs to hit the entire network at once."

"I hope you guys figure it out," Henry said. "Because the first thing they are going to do is power the vertiports back up so the drones can start hunting us again."

"That, or they shut the entire grid down and start another ice age," Kent said.

A windshield glimmer caught their attention far across the field. A long line of vehicles approached, kicking up a trail of dust on the gravel road.

Timothy looked through his binoculars. "Army tank, army tank, Humvee...sure hope those are our guys."

They got into their vehicle and waited at a rural intersection. A tank rolled in front of them and came to a screeching halt.

Robby popped out of the top.

"You guys ready to blow some shit up?"

Chapter Forty-Five

Marcus stuck to the central Florida highways, avoiding the coastal cities as best he could. Ashley covered a solid four-hour stretch of the drive. Daylin cried what seemed like the entire way.

They came across a friendly Florida woman parked on the side of the road by an orange grove. She shared some of her haul and told them the drones usually stay grounded the day after a big storm. She asked if they knew about them. One had killed her husband. Marcus told her they were aware and that he was sorry for her loss.

Their only other noteworthy interaction was with a true "Florida Man" north of Gainesville. The stringy leather-skinned yokel blocked the road while high on crystal meth. He asked if they knew where he could find more, in a cordial, insane kind of way. When they said they didn't know, he wandered off.

They made Valdosta, Georgia, by mid-afternoon the day after their escape from Cuba.

* * *

Timothy and the team decided it was best not to park the entire battalion of tanks and armored vehicles on the bunker site. They sent a majority into town where they could park on tree-lined streets. Smaller divisions were split off to the edges of the county.

When they returned to the bunker, Genie threw a fit in the War Room.

"Don't you guys carry your radios? Azoulay sent a message. Marcus made it out of Cuba during a tropical storm. He doesn't know if he made it to Florida, but he got off the island."

"Thank God," Timothy said. "There is hope."

"That's not all," Genie said. "They are sending ground troops up from Texas to put down our rebellion. They got our grid, so we are nothing but trouble to them."

"How long do we have?"

"They travel slow, do sweeps of small towns, kill anyone they come across. It's a unit of psycho killers, doomsday cultists, and Russian war criminals. About a thousand men. Azoulay says we have about a week."

Timothy had follow-up questions. He sat at his computer and pinged Azoulay.

Azoulay responded, "Snitch is away. I have a minute. What's up?"

"We need our virus on the Trencher vertiport network. It infects drones when they charge. They took our controls before we could deploy it. Will you have access when the blood key arrives in Cuba?"

"I doubt they let me near that with a ten-foot pole."

"The virus is embedded in the key, but we can also send it."

"I already have it. You shared it with Akili, so you

shared it with me. Good stuff. Shit – gotta go. Snitch is back."

Azoulay abruptly logged off.

* * *

Chardeep ran into the computer lab in a panic.

"Betancourt is here! Clean up your mess!"

He swept Azoulay's orange Fanta cans into the trash and tried to straighten up his station before snapping to attention.

Four soldiers accompanied Betancourt. Two of them wore cloth gloves and carried a piece of hardware shaped much like an old computer tower. They set it on the desk Chardeep had just cleared.

"This is a key to the Midwestern United States power grid," Betancourt said.

He pulled out a vial of blood, opened the machine, and placed the vial in a slot. There was another slot already occupied with another vial.

Azoulay knew what it was but had to play dumb.

"You mean the *Trencher Industries* grid?" Azoulay said. "They pretty much had a monopoly. Wasn't their whole schtick that the grid was decentralized? Nobody could cut your power or drain your home battery, or whatever."

Betancourt ignored his questions and went straight to commands.

"Run your Akili program to see that it functions as promised. After that, you will replicate the controls so that we can commandeer the other regional grids."

"Is that it?"

Betancourt thought for a moment. "If you make quick

237

work of those tasks, move on to training Akili to detect human usage across the grids. It will help with our drone targeting."

"Finally, a challenge."

Betancourt looked around. "Where is the Indian?"

Chardeep stood behind him. "Here, sir."

"Audit everything Mr. Azoulay does." Betancourt turned to leave. "Don't screw it up."

Chapter Forty-Six

Scouts had visited nearly every town and city in Indiana, and several beyond state lines. They aided every survivor, established communication channels, and recruited for what was to come.

Henry loaned his voice for the broadcast call-to-arms. He kept the message straightforward. A death squad was on the way from Texas to kill everyone in Sherman County, Indiana, and it was doubtful that they would stop there. They had the weaponry to put up a fight, but they needed fighters.

The immediate response was positive, but travel would take time.

In the interim, they met in the War Room – the name more apt than ever – to begin planning for their gathering forces.

The first item to address was that none of them knew a thing about real warfare. They needed someone who did.

"What about that Marine that led the raid on the Crane base?" Henry said. "He'll know a thing or two."

"How about your dad?" Robby said. "He's been

playing war games on that VR headset nonstop."

"Not sure that qualifies him, but he has read every military history book ever."

"Get them in the room," Timothy said. "In the meantime, let's tally up our assets so our experts will know what they are working with."

"We have about 400 able-bodied men and women who can at least fire a gun," Henry said. "Bloomington is sending 500. Expect another thousand from Southern Indiana and Illinois, potentially the same from north of Indy. Can't know for sure. Most of the Louisville bunker recruits are already here. Zero from Carmel."

"We have 11 drones left from the Crane fleet and we recouped forty more after we shut down the grid," Kent said. "Our Russian friends have already re-armed them and are heading over to join the fight."

Robby was up next. "Let's see...9 tanks, 12 trucks with badass machine guns on top, a shitload of armored vehicles, and one of those big ass trucks that launches rockets. Ellis and Taveon loaded all the guns and ammo on the train. They found a bunch of bazookas or whatever you call them, too."

"Rocket launchers and rocket-propelled grenade launchers," Timothy said. "Do we know how to fire any of these things, or the tanks for that matter?"

"We met up with some dudes in Brown County and blew up some cars with the tanks," Robby said. "Didn't mess with the rockets."

"Give me the HIMARS," Kent said. "We don't have military satellites, but I might find a manual workaround."

* * *

Marcus pointed out the Tennessee state line sign as they passed, relieved to escape Georgia unscathed. The Peach State was a war zone north of Atlanta. They experienced four confrontations along the way. Marcus's celebrity got them out of two. One interaction was awkward but friendly. The last was more intense.

He drove into a trap east of Rome. A gang ambushed them, but when they saw Daylin, they changed from violent looters to concerned fellow parents. They provided diapers, formula, water, and removed the barricade.

Ashley was too preoccupied to care about the state line. Daylin had been crying for an hour straight.

"Doesn't he have a pacifier?"

"Why didn't I think of that?" Ashley said "He won't take it! He is running a fever."

Marcus refused to stop. He had two hours in the vehicle's charge, and even more daylight.

Daylight was a double-edged sword. Drones remained a threat in the south. Every bombed-out town served as a reminder. Unlike in the Midwest, the regional grid was still largely operational, and therefore so were the drones.

He told Ashley that the carnage was a good sign. The drones had already been through, so they were less likely to still be around.

They made camp in a suburban home south of Cookeville, Tennessee. If all went perfectly well, they would be home in a day, maybe two.

Chapter Forty-Seven

Mike Azoulay kept Chardeep at bay while he dove into the code behind Marcus Trencher and Timothy's Spencer's magical decentralized power grids – and the secret centralized controls behind them.

He was impressed. There were kernels he could steal to make Akili more efficient. Akili recognized the same – she scanned the code along with him – and had already created an adaptation package that Azoulay only had to click to approve.

Trencher's smart grid was actually quite simple. Very little data moved from node to node. Units received encrypted usage numbers from neighboring units, adjusted their own sharing capacity and usage, and then fed those updated figures one block down the blockchain.

Software updates and billing were done via Trencher Industries satellites, of which he had full access. He had the virus, and just as importantly, the middleware to make it jump from the vertiports to the drones.

He only needed to finalize code that would cover his digital trail.

"What are you up to now?" Chardeep asked. "Is the

code really that good?"

"It's alright. You'll see it after I'm done."

"C'mon, you've got to give me something."

"Don't you have some Turks or Iranians to wipe out? Better get your numbers up or Betancourt won't make you a Mumbai slum lord."

Chardeep returned to his wall of screens.

Azoulay's stomach rumbled and suddenly put him on a short timer. *Damn these shitty Cuban energy drinks...*

He locked his computer, took a mental snapshot, and ran out of the lab. When he returned 15 minutes later, he noticed his mouse had moved.

He grabbed Chardeep. "Have you been snooping?"

"I don't know what you...Hey, you mess with my station all the time!"

Chardeep knocked Azoulay's hand away and stormed out of the lab.

An opportunity to dispatch the virus presented itself, but his patch to cover his tracks was not finished.

As he pondered, he watched tiny dots moved across outline-maps of central Asia and western Europe at Chardeep's station. Why settle for only infecting the U.S. drone network? Why not go global?

Chardeep was right about one thing – Azoulay messed with his station all the time. He had a long-running prank involving a glue gun and his keyboard.

At least once a week, he put a dab of glue next to a seemingly random key. The glue would dry, Chardeep would sit down to log in, hit the deadened key (or not), say *you got me*, and peel the glue off.

Azoulay listened intently for the deadened *thunk* – and recorded the letter. He had identified 8 characters of Chardeep's password, and mostly in order. He got the symbol character the old-fashioned way – peeking.

Akili did the rest. She gave a 98-percent probability that the password was one of three she had narrowed down. They were Hindi words he never would have figured out.

He sat at Chardeep's station and entered Akili's top guess – and it worked.

He grabbed the jump drive from the blood key and plugged it into Chardeep's computer. He set a release timer to Timothy's virus code so it would remain dormant for a day. Then, he loaded it onto the global network. There was no going back.

He got greedy and ran a contraband cable. The act of linking his computer to any other was almost certainly punishable by death – Akili was not allowed anywhere near the weapons systems – out of fear she would go *Skynet*.

He just wanted her to look around. She learned so fast.

She finished her survey without causing a Terminator apocalypse. He yanked the cable and logged out. Chardeep returned seconds after.

Azoulay apologized for his earlier accusations.

"Sorry for blowing up on you. Pull up a chair. I'll show you the Trencher code."

Chapter Forty-Eight

The team reconvened in the War Room, this time with the ex-Marine, Cooper, a couple Army vets, and Henry's father. Timothy gave them a rundown of what they knew of the enemy ground force on the way to wipe them out. He also detailed the preparations they had made so far, and the assets at hand.

Cooper spoke up first. "Where are you putting all these volunteers? The bunker is at capacity. Do you have a camp designated?"

Timothy scratched his head. "We can put them in town, I guess?"

Harold Plyman skimmed the list of supplies. "This is nice, but it isn't a plan."

"Please, fire away, guys."

"We know the enemy is coming from Texas, but do we know their route once they reach our doorstep? North through Vincennes, south from Terre Haute, east from Illinois?"

"We need to dispatch scouts ASAP," Cooper said.

"Cover every route Mr. Plyman just listed."

"Another question – do they know that *we* know they are coming?"

"No, they do not," Henry said.

"Ripe for ambush," Cooper said. "We'll identify points along the main roads. The local guys can help."

Timothy elected Genie to create a dashboard for real-time war monitoring. Henry volunteered to assign housing. Kent would handle the drones. Robby was all in on identifying ambush zones.

They stood from the table to get to work.

"One more thing," Mr. Plyman said. "Get the farm boys out here on backhoes. We need to dig a ring of trenches around the bunker site."

"Seriously, dad?" Henry said. "World War I trenches?"

"If push comes to shove, we need a No Man's Land." He turned to Timothy who was taking notes. "Our welders can crank out anti-tank obstacles. The Kirschners south of Paxton were about to redo their fencing on the cattle farm. They have reams of barbed wire in their barn."

They looked around at each other. Cooper gave a nod of agreement.

"I'll add trenches to the to-do list," Timothy said.

Robby, who had been uncharacteristically quiet, chimed in.

"We'll call them Trencher's Trenches."

They groaned. He was proud.

* * *

Marcus and Ashley's departed from the suburbs of Cookeville, Tennessee, later than they would have liked.

Daylin had a fever and cried through the night. Neither parent had a great idea of what to do.

Finally, Marcus noticed orangish-yellow wax built up in Daylin's right ear.

"Do you have one of those suction bulbs in your bag?"

Ashley checked. It was not included in the care package from Cuba, or in what the raiders near Atlanta provided. There was not one in the house, either.

Marcus sighed. "We can check the other houses down to the end of the cul-de-sac, but no further."

They split up to opposite sides of the street. They were nice houses, but it was an eerie exercise. The first house yielded nothing. House two showed no signs of a recent baby resident, but he did find an unsecured handgun and a box of bullets. He felt like he was in a video game.

At the next house, a troop of raccoons gave him a jump scare. He couldn't believe such a thing had happened twice in a matter of weeks, as raccoons gave him a fright in the train tunnel shortly before he was shot.

After the raccoons scattered, he found a pair of eyebrow tweezers. Maybe he could scrape the wax out with it.

Before he could check the upstairs, Ashley screamed so loud that it carried across the street. He charged out of the house and flew through the front door of the McMansion she was exploring.

"...The bedroom...there are bodies..."

He led her outside. "Time to go. I'll take Daylin."

Back at the first house, he braved Daylin's cries and took a closer look at his ear. He picked at the wax with the tweezers, and after careful excavation, extracted a dead fly.

"I think the problem is solved."

He held up the wax-covered fly.

They hit the road and bypassed Cookeville without incident. Daylin stopped crying and fell sound asleep for the first time in days, or to that point, most of his life.

Ashley calmed down from her run in with dead bodies and the grossness of the dead fly. She provided confident directions, putting them on backroads through the winding Tennessee hills.

"How do you know all this?" Marcus said. "You're not even using the map."

"I grew up north of here. We're actually going to pass through it."

"You don't have the accent. Never would have guessed."

"Trust me, I worked hard on that. Went to Yale and never looked back." She stared out of the window at the rockfaces and foliage. "I do miss it sometimes."

He once demanded 70-hour work weeks of her, had a child with her, and yet he never bothered to learn where she was from.

The hills opened as they approached the Cumberland River. The deep winter had killed huge clusters of trees on the hilltops. It was fall, and it was still scenic, but not as colorful as it should have been.

He turned north near a place called Butler's Landing. The sky was clear and beautiful, which meant it was also dangerous. Drones hovered in the back of his mind.

"Do you still have family here? I mean, did have..."

"They were still here. I reached out towards the end. They wanted to stay. I didn't have time to visit..."

"Do you want to stop by? You never know—"

"Marcus! Stop!" Ashley yelled, pointing ahead.

248

He turned his attention back to the road in time to see a washout of rock debris – but not in time to avoid it. The SUV's collision prevention system didn't do much better. Ashley clutched Daylin as they were jostled about. The tires jumped the piled soil and limestone shards.

He fought to regain control as the SUV slid off the shoulder and snaked fifty yards before straightening out. He slowed down but the ride remained bumpy. The sound of flapping rubber called for a full stop.

He inspected the front passenger-side tire. Blow out.

"How far did you say we were from your hometown?"

"Seven or eight miles. There is a spare in the back."

He knew that, but doing something with it was another thing. He hated driving. He hated even riding in cars. Changing a tire was the last thing he ever thought he would have to do.

He retrieved the spare, jack, and lug wrench. It didn't take long before the ordeal devolved into bickering. Ashley had suggestions. He didn't like them. He told her to take Daylin and enjoy the view of the river while he figured it out.

"Marcus..."

"What?" he snapped.

She didn't answer. He followed her gaze.

A drone hovered above them.

Chapter Forty-Nine

Marcus backed away from the SUV to the middle of the road. He held a lug wrench in his hand and had a smear of grease on his face. The drone hovered silently above, watching, waiting.

Ashley took a step toward him with Daylin in her arms.

"Stay away! Back up toward the river, slowly."

The drone was not autonomous. It was the same model as the ones they took down across the Midwest. Someone was behind the controls. That someone was probably reporting to someone else who was reaching out to Betancourt. He would surely want to see this.

The drone descended. A ball turret camera gyrated and dilated like a living eye. When it shifted to Ashley and Daylin, he jumped and waved like a madman.

"Hey! I'm right here! I'm the one you want!"

The drone returned to him. He fell to his knees and looked to Ashley and Daylin.

"You are going to tell him I was a hero, right? Tell him I... Daylin, I love you. You've got to grow up and make this world better."

"I'll tell him." Ashley backed further into the grasses.

The drone continued to allot him time to think about his death. He raised his arms, still down on his knees. He welcomed the missile, or hail of bullets, or whatever was going to deliver his demise. He shuddered and sobbed.

"...Tell him I love him..." he said again.

He launched the wrench at the drone. It fell 300 feet short. He stood back up. Dying on his knees was no way to go. He didn't really want to die at all. He flipped the drone off with both hands.

It was what Robby would have done. He laughed between sobs.

He thought about Henry, Timothy, his dad, and his mom. He thought about his little Indiana hometown. Yet, peace never came over him.

He had fight left in him.

He ran to the front of the SUV, praying it would provide him with enough cover to then dart into the hills. Maybe by some miracle there was a cave. It was all mad and far-fetched, but a brain in survival mode comes up with such things.

He peeked above the hood before making the second leg of his escape.

The drone finally made a move – a slight wobble – as a missile detached from one side of its undercarriage.

It fell in slow motion – and then exploded instantly.

The drone careened and crashed into the hillside. A streak of black smoke was all that remained in the sky. He blinked and blinked again. Was it real?

It took a full minute to realize what had happened.

"They did it..."

He turned to Ashley.

"They did it! Timothy and the gang...They planted the

drone virus!"

* * *

Mike Azoulay belched obnoxiously. It was one of his last chances to annoy Chardeep. By his estimates, he had 24 hours left to live. Him, not Chardeep. But maybe him, too.

He dispatched Timothy Spencer's virus that morning.

He scrapped the add-on that would have covered his tracks. It was taking too long. He kept thinking about how many people would die while he piddled in code.

Any drone that charged at a Trencher Industries vertiport would contract the virus. 150 drones scattered across the country already had. The second layer of the virus would transmit between airborne drones – a touch Akili added. It was going to spread rapidly.

He figured the entire drone program would be shut down within a day.

Chardeep's autonomous drone network, on the other hand, might not survive the afternoon.

The iteration of the virus he snuck onto Chardeep's system was set to activate any minute. He wondered how long it would take his frenemy to notice. He genuinely did not know the frequency of missile strikes. How often were drones coming across survivors anymore?

He snuck glimpses at Chardeep's panel of screens. After five minutes, he heard the first "*huh*." A red dot flashed over one of the -*stan* countries.

"What are you *huh*-ing about over there?"

"Lost a drone over Turkmenistan, of all places."

"Didn't a villager in Afghanistan take one out with a rocket launcher last week?"

"Yeah, but...what the—I just lost another!"

Another three red dots flashed, then seven more over four different countries. The number quickly doubled.

Chardeep began typing furiously. He pulled footage and found no indication of rockets or anti-aircraft missiles. The drones simply exploded, right after firing at a ground target.

By the time he returned to the greater map, it looked like it was on fire. He backed away with his hands on his head.

"This is not good..." He charged out of the room.

Azoulay grabbed a screwdriver and Tomas Nagy's ID badge that he had "misplaced" a week prior.

He couldn't fit the bulky blood key in his bag, but he had the software copied somewhere else. That somewhere wasn't going to be easy to reach, but it was now or never.

Chardeep charged back in with a team. The experts unfolded their laptops and sat wherever they wanted, including at Azoulay's station.

"You all have fun with that," Azoulay said. "I'm going to lunch."

He slinked out to the hall where the who's who of former Silicon Valley sociopaths sprinted every which way. He turned down a quieter wing and badged into the server room. He had only been there once – it was strictly off limits – but he knew where to look.

LED lights blinked and fans whirred across racks of black boxes. He skimmed them as if in a library searching for a sacred book that would lead to hidden treasure.

The first box he found was essentially the cloud backing up his workstation. He loosened a few screws and yanked it.

The next was far more precious. It was a backup of Akili's core. If she were human, it'd be her amygdala in a jar. He could Frankenstein her outside of her air-gapped digital prison later – if he made it out alive.

He slipped back out of the server room, unnoticed. The exploding drones kept everyone distracted. As he passed one lab, he heard, "*It's happening in the U.S., too!*"

He made it clear outside of the facility and grabbed his bicycle off the rack. He strolled to the security gate under the midday sun.

"Eddy! Got you something." He unzipped his backpack and pulled out a wooden box of cigars. "This is the good stuff, right?"

Eddy the security guard smiled. "For me? Are you sure?"

"I'm giving the habit up. I want you to have them."

Eddy thanked him and let him pass without a search.

Azoulay glided down the hillside, wind flowing through his wild hair. Not having to pedal while going downhill on a bike was one of life's greatest pleasures, he thought to himself.

At his village home, he wasted no time before plugging in the stolen drives to his homebrew computer rig.

Downing a few thousand drones was nothing. It was time he and Akili did real damage to Betancourt and his cabal.

Chapter Fifty

Shortly after the drone self-destructed in the Tennessee sky, a local in a pickup arrived at the scene to investigate. It was not the only drone in the area that had seemingly combusted that morning, and word spread fast.

The local introduced himself as Brett Shankey. As it turned out, he went to high school with Ashley.

Celina was a *very* small town.

"What brings you back home?"

"The end of the world," Ashley said. "My God, this place hasn't changed."

Brett laughed. "I kind of like that, but I know that was never your thing. You were always so smart. Where was it you went off to college? Harv—"

"Yale."

"I stuck around and worked down at the marina."

Ashley was being icy. Her relationship with home was complicated. Brett turned his attention to Marcus.

"You look familiar. Do I know you from somewhere?"

"My name is Marcus Trencher."

"The grid genius? Daggone! A couple of folks around here got your battery units. They built way up in the hills, off grid."

"They were good for that kind of thing."

"The rest of us are hydro, with the dam over at Dale Hollow and all. Enough people stuck around to run the plant. We ain't never lost power. Thank God for the Tennessee Valley Authority."

Celina was far from anywhere, yet it was not spared. The heart of the town was bombed out in a wide swath. A hundred homes were nothing but charred debris and shattered concrete foundations.

Ashley, who had shown no love for her hometown, was driven to tears. "My old house is gone..."

"They hit us a month ago. It got real cold last winter – like, real, real cold – but we toughed it out. Suddenly it lifted, and we were doing alright for a while. Then the drones came. You can see why most of us moved up in the hills, all spread out. The drones come back every few weeks and find someone to kill."

They pulled up to the Gone Country Café in downtown Celina where there was "*Breakfast anytime, country cookin,*" and a welcoming party.

Brett called out, "Judy? I found someone you might like to see."

Judy Cameron, Ashley's semi-estranged mother, ran to her and hugged her.

"Oh, my baby girl, you're alive! Praise Jesus!"

After the embrace, during which Ashley softened, her mother let her know that her father had passed.

"He got sick in the winter. He always asked about you."

Ashley let the tears flow. She had long ago accepted that her parents were both dead. It was hard to comprehend both had survived, but one had since passed.

"I want you to meet someone," Ashley said. "This is your grandson, Daylin."

The new grandmother was overwhelmed with happiness as she held him in her arms.

"He is feverish, and he had an earache. We didn't know what to do..."

"Oh, we can fix that right up."

The rest of the café crowd enjoyed the heartwarming moment, but they had other concerns. A man stood to address them. He wore a name badge, "Mayor Jack."

"Brett, can you tell us what you saw out there this morning?"

"Another drone just blew up in the sky, a half mile south of town. Crashed in the hills across from the river. That's where I found Ashley and her friend. I think the drone was about to, you know..."

Marcus raised his hand. "I can help explain."

There were whispers. Someone recognized him.

"We have been fighting and dying to these drones probably as long as you have, and long story short, my colleague developed a virus that causes the drone's missiles to explode immediately upon firing. They contract the virus when they use our company's charging vertiports. They'll figure it out eventually, but you should be relatively safe for a while."

"We thank you kindly," Mayor Jack said. "But do you think you could start from the start? We don't know what the Sam Hill has been going on out there."

Marcus was surprised. How little do these people know?

"Safe to say there wasn't no asteroid," Jack continued. "The National Guard skipped our town and half of us didn't trust the government enough to follow them to no bunker anyhow. And I ain't no weather man, but that winter wasn't natural. Can you make sense of why we're being hunted?"

Marcus patiently explained all he knew. A cabal of elites saw a global system in steady decline, yet at the same time, a handful of revolutionary breakthroughs in medicine and technology within reach. They conspired to accelerate all of it – all at once – under the guise of grave environmental concerns that may or may not have been sincere.

They wanted to expedite the collapse so that they could make it to the other side in their lifetimes and rebuild the world in their vision. They would not only maintain power but increase it exponentially.

The mayor shook his head in disbelief. "What good is a world with no people in it? Why go out of the way to bomb little old Celina?"

"After the depopulation phase, they plan to concentrate the remaining populations in cities, for efficiency's sake."

"Efficiency my ass. I ain't leaving for no city."

"If I have my way, they won't succeed. And if you don't mind, I must get back to Indiana. Do you think you could provide a vehicle? I hate to run, but it is urgent."

"It's the least we could do. We'll charge up a truck and send you on your way."

The meeting adjourned and Ashley's mother took them to her new home on Cedar Hill, near Dale Hollow Lake.

Ashley was visited by surviving aunts, uncles, cousins, second cousins, and a long-lost high school friend. Whatever animosity that led her to completely sever ties went away. They laughed and shared memories.

Daylin was passed around by family. Ashley's mother found a bulb to suck the wax out of his ear, and medicine to reduce his fever. She simply knew what to do.

A pair of trucks pulled up and Mayor Jack and Brett Shankey got out of each.

"Looks like our ride is here," Marcus said.

He thanked them for their hospitality. He then asked if they had a car seat for Daylin. They had loaded the truck with food, water, guns, a map, and everything but a car seat. Ashley pulled him aside.

"I'm staying, and so is Daylin," she said. "You don't need me in a war. And for crying out loud, you don't need to take a baby into one."

Marcus didn't know what to say. It made total sense. "When all this gets settled, will you move back to Indiana?"

"This is the best place for us right now. These are my people. You need to get back to yours and do what you need to do. Daylin and I will be waiting."

He nodded slowly, processing what he felt. "I'll return as soon as it's over. I'll send a messenger before...or we'll find a way to establish long distance comm—"

"Marcus. We'll work it out. Now say bye to your son before you go."

She handed Daylin to him.

He looked at him for a long moment and bounced him in his arms.

"Daylin, I need to go make the world a safer place, because you are in it." He kissed him softly on the forehead. "Don't get too big while I'm gone. I love you."

Chapter Fifty-One

The bunker site was starting to look more like the first time Henry ever saw it. Heavy equipment moved tons of earth every which way. The trenches were taking shape. He hoped they wouldn't have to use them.

The chef duo of Brad and Becky were the unsung heroes of the operation. They kept the volunteers fed. Unfortunately, the real foodstuffs were not going to last long. They dipped into the bunker's Soylent reserves to get the people the calories they needed.

The primary purpose of the trenches was to prevent tanks from rolling right up to the bunker, more than to be manned. Still, men filled sandbags and built dugouts with excess materials, mostly to pass the time.

The half-empty lake supplemented the trench ring. If the enemy broke through their resistance further out, they had designs to blow up the roads.

Scouts were dispatched to spot the enemy en route from Texas. Camps were made at highway interchanges in Mt. Vernon, Illinois, and east of St. Louis. Smaller groups covered Oblong and Lawrenceville, others went south to Henderson, Kentucky. They wanted as early a warning as possible, but without spreading too thin and too far and letting the forces slip through on secondary state roads.

Around midday, a flood of bunker denizens came up top, but not to volunteer. They were leaving. Not all were willing participants in the war effort.

Timothy stopped them. "What's going on here?"

They were ordinary people. Women and children, a few middle-aged men. Clay Boyle who served on the council as a token member – and who they quit inviting when it became the war council – stepped up.

"We don't want no part in this. This is Trencher's war, and far as I can tell, he ain't even here."

Henry pulled Timothy aside before he could blow up. He was already far too stressed out.

"How about we send non-combatants to the Quarry through the train tunnel?" Henry said. "Not everybody needs to be here."

"It sends the wrong message," Timothy said.

"200 men and women who do want to fight arrived just this morning. Why not let them go?"

Timothy sighed but accepted the advice. He relayed the train proposal to Clay and the crowd behind him.

Clay hooked his thumbs in his overall straps. "No thanks. We'll wait this out over in Bloomfield. We're sick of being underground."

Another twenty defectors emerged from the elevator dome, this one led by Tammy Martin. She came at Timothy with a finger pointed.

"The council didn't vote on this! You're going to get everyone killed! Why are we picking fights, anyway? We were chosen for this bunker so we would live – chosen by God – I whole-heartedly believe! You and Trencher had to go and screw it up!"

Timothy patiently took the lashing. "We won't stop you, but I suggest you wait until we can organize a train to Bloom—"

"Save it. We're done living under your dictatorship!"

As the forty defectors departed, a group of twenty men approached. Each wore a bulletproof vest and had an assault rifle across their chests. In the distance, a handful of men started firing guns where they were told not to.

Timothy was frazzled. He was an IT guy, not a general.

"You go corral the rednecks," Henry said. "I'll handle the new guys."

"We're in from West Lafayette," a man in Oakley shades said. "Where do you want us posted?"

"I'll assign you a few houses in town for the night. We'll know more tomorrow."

"Any intel on this army coming in? ETA?"

"No sightings yet, but they're coming. The assumption is two or three days."

"We're former police, half of us ex-military. We got your messages and we're ready to roll."

"Ex-military? In that case, stick around. We could use you right away."

He scanned the field of chaos for a worthy task. Timothy was waving his arms at the rednecks and pointing towards the designated firing range. Trenchwork continued in all directions. Then, he spotted the military vehicles on site.

"One of you wouldn't happen to know how to operate a HIMARS, would you?"

* * *

Marcus hadn't come across a soul since departing Celina. It was both a relief and terrifying at once. The Fort Knox drone fleets had done their work early. Western Kentucky was desolate.

He saw the first sign of life shortly after crossing the Ohio River into Indiana. He caught a tail somewhere west of Santa Claus. He couldn't remember the last time he had checked his mirrors. It was in the middle of nowhere.

A blue sedan caught up to him and pulled parallel in the lefthand lane. He had no interest in pulling over and getting to know the guy, nor did he want to get involved in a high-speed chase. The man gestured in an urgent but non-threatening manner, as far as he could tell. No one else was in the vehicle.

He was two hours from home. There was nothing in the truck that he needed. He could hand the keys over and take the guy's car if it was a stickup.

He slowed to a stop and put a handgun on his lap.

The man came to a stop and jumped out with both hands high above his head. He had no weapon. He wore a blue Kentucky Wildcats t-shirt, basketball shorts, and flipflops.

"I'm unarmed! I don't need anything from you! I just want to talk."

Marcus rolled down his window. "Two minutes."

The man took a deep trembling breath and slowly lowered his arms.

"I was in a bunker outside Lexington, Kentucky, up until a month ago. Something went down in the Louisville bunker, and people came our way and busted the place open. They forced us all to the surface and released all the horses. It wasn't all that bad up here, until yesterday. An army came through the city and started killing everyone."

263

"An army? Do you mean drones?"

He shook his head. "No. I mean, there may have been some...I'm talking tanks, Jeeps, soldiers with rifles..."

He got out of the truck and tossed his gun on the driver's seat.

"How many?"

"I can't say for sure—"

"Guess."

"They gathered in a parking lot outside Rupp Arena. Me and a few friends were staying at a house right there. They filled more than half the lot. A thousand men? Maybe two?"

Marcus analyzed what it could mean. It had to be Betancourt's East Coast stormtroopers that he had off-handedly mentioned were sweeping the Carolinas.

The army from Texas was not all they were about to face.

"...I thought they were there to help. I was about to go meet them, maybe get some food and water, but then I watched them execute a line of people. They started going street by street. I stayed ahead of them and made it far enough out to get a vehicle and skip town.

"By the time I got around Keeneland, the bombs started dropping on the suburbs. My whole rearview mirror lit up. I don't think they were drones. Had to be military bombers, or jets. It looked like something out of the movies. Carpet-bombing is the term I'd use.

"I made it to Louisville, tried to lay low, and ran into people saying that the army was on the way there, too. So, I kept heading west. They went straight through Louisville. It's like they're fucking following me, man."

Marcus shook his head.

"They're not following you. They're following me.

Chapter Fifty-Two

He offered for the stranger from Lexington to join him on his way to Sherman, Indiana, but the man was running from conflict, not towards it. Marcus suggested traveling south. There was a nice community in Celina, Tennessee, if he could get there.

He was so close to home he could smell it. The roads were in decent shape until he hit Oaktown. He realized the U.S. 41 overpass was no longer there with about a hundred yards to spare.

It had clearly been bombed, along with an armored vehicle in the southbound lane. Was it a preparation to slow down the forces coming up from Texas?

He doubled back and meandered through Oaktown to bypass the gap. When he finally reached the outskirts of Sherman, he saw a great deal of activity. A group of trucks were parked at a creek bridge and a bunch of men were standing around.

The men recognized him after he stepped out. They broke out in a masculine cheer. Robby climbed up from underneath the bridge to see what all the fuss was about.

Robby ran out to bearhug him.

"You're alive, you sonuvabitch! How was your vacation in Cuba?"

"Interesting, to say the least. I'm a father now."

"Congratulations, man! Melonie is due any day now. Is it a boy?"

He nodded, proudly. "His name is Daylin. He and Ashley and I got out together. You wouldn't believe it. I stole a yacht and sailed into a storm. They're staying in Tennessee. But enough about that. I need to get out to the bunker to catch up."

"I can give you a start. Your boy Mike Azoulay tipped us off on the army coming up from Texas. We've rallied enough troops that I think we'll outnumber them. We're setting up ambushes."

Marcus thought about dropping the bomb that another much larger army was also on the way, but he figured he would save that tidbit for later.

"Can you send word on the radio that I'm back, so nobody shoots me?"

"Hell, we're done here. We'll give you a presidential escort."

He followed Robby and five other trucks out to the bunker site. As he pulled in, a crowd of hundreds gathered. They banged on the sides of his truck. Henry, Timothy, and the whole gang came up to greet him.

It'd been a long journey back. As much as he wanted to get underground and start planning, there was a crowd of men and women who were about to risk their lives for his cause. He needed to address them. Timothy handed him a bullhorn, and he climbed a mound of dirt.

"First of all, welcome to Sherman, Indiana. By now you know there has been an ongoing, systematic effort to depopulate the planet. I've been told the world population has nearly been halved, and they want to continue until only 2 billion of us are left. It's safe to say we are all on the naughty list. If we want to survive, we must fight.

"The group that is perpetrating this global genocide is very small. They did a great deal of damage early, back when we all thought an asteroid was on the way. The next phase was geoengineering the weather, and then sweeping territories with drones.

"They've underestimated your resilience and intelligence. You survived the end of the world as we knew it. We started to fight back. We took down the drones over Indiana, and then shut down the grid and grounded all of them across the Midwest. Yesterday, we deployed a virus that puts them all out of commission for good.

"They have one last card to play. A small army of true believers are on the way. I say it's bold of them to fight us on our own territory. They won't have numerical superiority. They won't know the terrain like we do. This is a war of annihilation, and we are going to win.

"Expect your assignments first thing in morning. Thank you for showing up to the fight. Hell, we might just save the world."

He slid down the dirt mound and handed the megaphone back to Timothy. The crowd roared and reached out to touch him as he marched to the elevator dome. Timothy, Henry, and Robby struggled to keep beside him.

* * *

Marcus gathered everyone he trusted in the War Room. He bit his tongue when it came to the plans and the progress they had made without him. It was no time to criticize. Rather, he praised their efforts. The trenches were smart. And the fact that they had attracted 3,000 fighters and counting was nothing short of amazing.

"First things first, something I didn't want to break to the crowd up top – a second army is coming in from the east. The numbers will even up a bit. This might be all they have left. For all we know, we are the last major pocket of resistance. But if we win, they won't recover from this.

"That's it for opening statements. Where are all our people staying?"

"I've been assigning houses in town," Henry said.

Marcus shook his head. "Get everyone outside of city limits immediately. Find farmhouses, send them out to the rural suburbs. No lights. Sherman needs to be completely deserted within the next four hours."

Henry wasn't thrilled about his wasted effort. "Can you explain?"

"I ran into a man fleeing the eastern army. He witnessed carpet bombing in Lexington, Kentucky. I bet their bombers are reloading as we speak. I have to think they plan on leveling Sherman. The ground forces will move in after the bombing. Is the meteorologist in the room?"

Cami Stinnett raised her hand from the back corner.

"Put the doppler back to detecting aircraft. The moment you see a single blip, let us know."

He suddenly grew quiet and fell into deep thought. Everyone looked around, awkwardly. He stood and walked to Taveon and Ellis.

"I'm sure you two are sick of that train tunnel, but I need another couple trips to Bloomington. How many people can fit on that thing?"

"If safety ain't a concern, a hundred, easy," Taveon said.

"I want 200 men in Bloomington by tomorrow evening. If they are going to attack from the east, we are going to have a presence further east. Are there any vehicles left in that cache, other than farm equipment?"

"A whole dealer's lot worth of pickup trucks," Henry said. "I'll gather the 200 men after I send out the call to evacuate Sherman."

"My guys will have the train ready," Ellis said.

Big Pigg blared through the intercom. "Boss, you there?"

"What do you have for us, Pigg?"

"The army has been spotted. They just rolled into Mt. Carmel, Illinois."

"Thank you, Big Pigg," Marcus said. "Perfect, now we need eyes on the eastern army."

"I'll get our drones on it," Kent said. "I'll find them before morning."

Marcus gave a thumbs up and stood over the table. Someone had drawn a giant map on a patchwork of flipboard paper. They had a digital map on the screen, but the physical display brought a smile to his face.

"Alright, tell me about these ambushes you have planned. I have a few ideas of my own."

Chapter Fifty-Three

Mike Azoulay called in sick. Really, a no-call, no-show. It was shocking nobody had come for him yet. His comrades at the base must have still been in panic mode. It wouldn't take long for them to realize he was behind the virus.

He found a way to use Trencher's satellites to tap into the global network of bunker supercomputers. Each held a copy of Akili. With the drives he stole from the base, he was able to put her back together, and back to work.

She found a way into every critical system. Azoulay had a hand in some of it, but she infiltrated more than he ever knew or asked of her. He loved her, but *man* was she dangerous.

The cavalry finally came down the Cuban hillside at early dawn. Before they came to a stop, he put his grand finale into motion.

He domiciled Akili to the Carmel supercomputer and delegated her controls to Timothy Spencer and Marcus Trencher, upon his death. Their code from the blood key was clever, so he used it. He destroyed all other copies of her.

He contemplated destroying her in totality but

couldn't do it.

Akili accomplished the impossible – she cracked the blood key. She replicated the controls for the other grids and created a package to hand back to Timothy and Marcus. There was a manual process involved, but Timothy would figure it out.

She opened the vault doors of every bunker in their network.

She neutralized the virus in a handful of drone fleets around the globe and put them to good use. The Ecuador fleet was sent to destroy the space elevator off the coast at Puerto Ayora. He took no pleasure in destroying mankind's greatest engineering achievement, but the solar shades were ferried to orbit from the station, and the brutal winters Betancourt was relying on to eradicate the rest of the survivors depended on it.

She sent another fleet over Southeast Asia to maximum elevation before firing into low-earth orbit at the Rhode-Island-sized solar shade over the South Pacific. He wouldn't be around long enough to know whether it worked or not.

The naval fleet of cloud-producing ships were sunk to the bottom of the Pacific.

He ordered the Cuban drone fleet to his position.

Lastly, he sent a file of names to his friends in Indiana, for the history books.

He took a swig of rum, put on his smartwatch, and walked out to meet the uniformed men.

"Good morning, gentlemen. What can I help you with?"

"Michael Azoulay, you are under arrest for treason," the lead officer said. "Come with us."

"Treason? Yikes. What is the punishment for that?"

The men stared at him stone-faced while he laughed. He looked past them but didn't see the man he wanted to see.

"Where is Betancourt? I thought he'd want to do this personally."

"He left the island this morning."

"Oh? Is he going to Indiana for the big battle?"

"That is not your concern."

"Why are you doing this? Let me guess – just following orders? You all know you are playing an active role in genocide, right? You dumb fucking Nazis."

"That's enough. Grab him!"

Azoulay put his wrist to his mouth and spoke into his watch, "Akili, tell Trencher that Betancourt is in Indiana. And Akili? I love you."

"*Commands received and executed. I love you too, Michael.*"

The soldiers wrestled him down but stopped when they spotted the drones flying low along the coast.

The soldiers scrambled and fled. Azoulay sat down and watched the sunrise. He caught a fleeting glimpse before the bombs ended his storied life.

* * *

It was 6:30 a.m., an hour before sunrise in Indiana, and nobody had slept. The town of Sherman was blacked out and completely evacuated. Military vehicles were scattered around the county, and tanks strategically placed.

Scouts sent word that the army from Texas had arrived in Vincennes, thirty miles south.

Kent's drones ran into interference over Bedford to

the east. Scouts on the ground confirmed that the other army was in the area.

They would be defending two fronts – south and east.

Marcus pinpointed every critical location where he wanted men stationed. He reviewed every scenario, laid out plans, and adjusted as intel flowed in.

Genie monitored her dashboard where real-time activities were tracked. Something else popped up and she got Timothy's attention.

"Azoulay sent us a massive file. You need to see this."

Timothy skimmed the message. "His AI cracked our grid? No way."

"Yeah, and he just handed it back to us."

Timothy kept reading. "*I am leaving Akili in your good hands. I am probably dead by now, but I did damage on the way out. The drone virus went global, and their weather program took a hit. I opened the vault doors of every bunker in their network. FYI, Betancourt is headed to Indiana. See attached file, for the history books. Best of luck – Mike, the AI guy.*"

Genie opened the attachment. It contained the names of every collaborator across the globe, what they contributed, and where they were located.

"...Social media, Hawaii," Timothy read aloud. "...News magnate, New Zealand bunker...another billionaire, New Zealand. Private equity, secured real estate for depopulation centers in Europe, Switzerland... a bunch of private islands..."

"What are you guys doing?" Marcus said.

"Azoulay sacrificed himself," Timothy said. "He took out the drones and the weather geoengineering apparatus. He gave us our grid back, and his AI tech."

Marcus was saddened by the news. He had to make

Azoulay's death mean something. Before he could digest the rest of Azoulay's bombshell, more urgent updates poured in in.

The army in Vincennes had split, with half moving west into Illinois, and the other starting north toward Sherman.

"That splinter group is headed up Highway 1 – they're going to cross back over at Hutsonville," Henry said. "We're up to three fronts – south, east, and west."

"Somebody please tell me that bridge is rigged to blow," Timothy said.

Robby got up to leave. "On it."

Cami sprinted into the room. "The radar is showing inbound aircraft from the southeast."

"How long?"

"Five minutes, ten at most."

Henry sent an urgent message over the radio to seek shelter and turn off all lights, and if anyone hadn't vacated the city limits of Sherman, they should do so. Everyone at the site was ordered underground.

Five minutes was generous. Bombs started dropping on the bunker before Henry got through his third repetition of the message. They felt a long rumble, like rolling thunder.

The town of Sherman was being heavily bombed at the same time, just as Marcus predicted. The outskirts were mostly spared.

They sat quietly in the War Room, as if waiting out a tornado warning. When the rumbling subsided, and they received word that the bombing had ceased, plans were put into motion.

Henry received the nod and picked up the radio receiver.

"Everyone into position. Go, go, go!"

A thousand resistance fighters flooded back into the bombed-out remains of Sherman. They set their traps and burrowed into advantageous positions, ready for battle.

Chapter Fifty-Four

Enemy armor rolled across the southern county line as the morning sun crept over the horizon. They met no resistance.

Scouts watched from distant country houses and deer blinds, reporting on the advance every inch of the way.

The better view came from above. Kent and the Russians from Crane stationed drones at high altitude, undetected. No interference signal was being emitted to hinder the surveillance.

They counted 73 armored vehicles of various sizes and functions, not counting the smaller force that split off in Vincennes. They estimated four men per vehicle.

As the column advanced north on U.S. 41, Kent had to ask at least one more time.

"Are you sure you don't want us to fire a few missiles before they put up interference?"

"That's at best a quarter of their force," Marcus said. "Not worth burning our element of surprise."

The army exited the highway at the edge of town. There was a minor celebration – it was exactly what they wanted.

"I need an update on the western force."

Kent switched the feed to a drone over the Wabash River on the Illinois-Indiana state line. The Hutsonville Bridge was the first crossing north of Vincennes, and the last for another 40 miles. They were confident it was the one they would take.

"They turned east off Highway 1," Henry said. "Bridge ETA, 5 minutes."

"And the eastern army?"

"Just passed Linton, heading toward Dugger," Timothy said. "They have drone defenses up, so no aerial view, but we have eyes on them."

Their focus switched back to the southern force as it breached city limits and fast approached the next critical juncture, near the center of town.

"C'mon, turn, turn, turn..."

After the bombing, a team built as natural a barrier as they could with a felled tree and debris at the strategic point on Trencher Street where the column had come to a stop.

The diversion worked. The army rerouted a block east onto what remained of the courthouse square.

Enemy armor filed into the square and circled the courthouse ruins until the block filled entirely. They realized too late that the outlet streets were all blocked by rubble that had been purposely bulldozed into place.

One hundred resistance fighters crouched behind rooftop parapets on all sides. Another sixty hid by second-story windows with rifles and RPGs in hand.

* * *

Robby arrived at the western outpost right in time for the

show. The enemy rolled through the river town of Hutsonville and stopped short of crossing the Wabash into Indiana. Soldiers were gathered around the gas station where Robby's dad used to buy beer on Sundays, and years later, he went to buy legalized marijuana.

"What's the hold up? Are they checking under the bridge?"

The charges were not particularly well hidden.

Cooper received word over the radio from the scouts on the other side of the river.

"Two men are walking it," Cooper said. He switched his channel. "Kent, be ready to bail us out. They are snooping around."

The two soldiers concluded their cursory walk without so much as leaning over the edge. The column proceeded onto the bridge.

Cooper set his radio aside and grabbed the detonation device. Robby snuck to the end of the tree patch where a tank hid beneath brush and limb, pre-aimed at the foot of the bridge a thousand yards ahead.

The first vehicle peeked over the crest of the bridge.

"Hold...hold..." Henry watched the drone feed, waiting for a simple equation to work itself out – half the army on one side, half on the other. "...three...two...one... detonate!"

Cooper pressed the button. Brownish-gray clouds shot from beneath each side of the bridge, over the river. The vehicles mid-bridge vanished. The sound of the explosion reached the tree line a half-second later.

"Go! Go! Go! They're split!" Henry called.

Robby ducked inside the tank from the commander hatch. The crew inside took aim at the lead vehicle at the foot of the bridge and fired a direct hit.

The other ambush party was perpendicular to the road, parallel to the levee, and much closer. They took out the next in line. Men fired rifles from prone positions. Each tank fired the next round as quickly as possible.

Four friendly drones streaked overhead and launched a salvo of missiles, taking care of the back half of the column stuck in Illinois.

What remained of the waylaid forces finally activated their drone interference defenses, taking air superiority out of play. They showed other signs of recovery. Tanks fanned out into the fields into formation and men darted about the wreckage.

Robby's tank fired a third round blindly at the black cloud of smoke, center column. If their position wasn't pinpointed before, it was now.

"Hey!" Cooper yelled as he banged on the side of the tank. "Time to go!"

"We've got them! Let's finish them off!" Robby said.

"Not the plan. Get out, now!"

The other ambush party backed off. Men fled over the levee and retreated to boats to escape north on the river. The tank was abandoned. The crew exhausted their capabilities. They had only trained for two days.

Robby's crew wasn't any more knowledgeable, but it still took Cooper and a lot of angry voices over the radio to get them to follow orders. They finally got out and ran to the back side of the tree patch and jumped into their getaway trucks.

Before they even peeled out onto the road, the abandoned tank was hit.

They floored it through Graysville and headed toward Sherman – where another skirmish was about to pop off.

Cal peered over the parapet of the old Newsstand building on the courthouse square. The enemy was getting antsy. Word of the ambush to the west had reached their ranks.

"What the hell is taking you guys so long?" Cal said on the radio.

"Be advised, our drones are out of commission," Marcus said. "You guys have the go-ahead."

Cal thanked him off-air, sarcastically. He nodded to his trusted partner, Luke.

Luke mounted a rocket launcher on his shoulder, as did others on the other three sides of the square. Guerilla warfare 101 – aim for the first vehicle in a column, and the last.

Luke took a deep breath, stood, and took steady aim for the front. A soldier shouted from below just before he pulled the trigger. The rocket streaked like a bolt of lightning and blew up a tan Humvee. A rapid succession of rocket explosions followed.

Friendly tanks pulled forward from hiding spots off neighboring city blocks and fired into the square, adding to the devastation.

The remaining fighters leapt up from their rooftop positions and fired down at the trapped forces. Fish in a barrel.

They scored massive damage in mere seconds. The enemy maneuvered to recover and fight back. An enemy tank on the northside fired a round at the building just right of Cal and Luke. The whole façade collapsed, killing everyone inside. Three men tumbled down to the street from the rooftop.

A tank on the southside barreled into a storefront and

backed out, destabilizing an already unstable structure. Heavy machine gun fire was exchanged in every direction. Groups broke off and barreled through barricades and engaged the peripheral tanks or fled down city streets. Enemy soldiers broke into storefronts to take the fight into close quarters.

There were casualties on both sides, but the home team took a decisive lead.

Then, the Apache arrived.

Hellfire missiles destroyed the entire southside of the square in the blink of an eye. The attack helicopter then strafed the north with a 30mm chain gun, mowing down all but a handful of the rooftop fighters.

Cal and Luke frantically reloaded the rocket launcher as the Apache circled back. When Luke fired, it veered and released a shower of evasion flares, adding another colorful spectacle to the battle. The rocket exploded harmlessly.

"Everybody off the rooftops!" Cal yelled into the radio.

His orders were generally followed, but a few stubborn kids on the opposite side stuck around for one more go at it. They fired their rockets simultaneously, one of which clipped the tail rotor, sending the aircraft into a wild tailspin. It crashed through the roof of a gymnasium a block away.

Cal and Luke looked at each other in awe.

"Damn kids think this is a video game," Cal said.

The rooftop fighters fled to the backs of the buildings and scaled fire escape ladders down to the alleys. The snipers in the windows retreated similarly. The element of surprise had worn off and the rule was to not get greedy. The enemy had regained footing, and more helicopters were approaching. It was time to leave.

* * *

There was a *rah-rah* moment in the War Room after the initial successes, but only for a second. Marcus interrupted.

"Who the hell let Robby out of the bunker?"

The room got quiet and innocent people avoided eye contact.

"You know Robby..." Henry said.

"Well...get him back before he gets himself killed."

"How? *Saving Private Ryan* style? You know he won't listen."

Marcus glared at Henry and picked up a radio. "Robby, what's your status?"

"We're about to park at this church and take off on foot toward the square. What's up?"

"We need you back at the bunker, ASAP."

"More than the guys downtown? We heard the courthouse got bombed. I want to see it."

Henry and Timothy wanted Robby safely in the bunker, too, but his obstinance was too predictable. They stifled their laughter.

"Melonie is in labor," Marcus said. "It was going to be a surprise."

"Oh, shit. Okay. On my way."

Marcus tossed the radio at Henry and smirked.

"Well played," Henry said.

Marcus returned to commander mode. The looming army to the east was bigger and would not be so easily surprised. The terrain was entirely different than a river bridgehead or small-town urban warfare. It was mostly open fields on old coal mining land, patches of woods, stripper pit lakes, and not many houses – all the reasons he chose to build the bunker where he did.

Chapter Fifty-Five

What remained of the enemy contingent at the Hutsonville Bridge attempted to reunite with their comrades in downtown Sherman. They were picked apart before they could even reach the McDonald's on U.S. 41.

Fighting in Sherman intensified and spread, street-by-street. At every turn, someone was there to take a shot, and then vanish. Enemy soldiers yelled in foreign languages. The panic was palpable.

Additional Apache helicopters posed the greatest threat. Their sensors sniffed out pockets of fighters and rained fire on their positions.

But ultimately, too many good guys had too many rocket launchers and RPGs. Another two Apache were downed, causing the others to abandon the airspace.

The last cluster of enemy forces attempted to break out the way they came. They didn't make it past the railroad tracks south of town.

Smaller skirmishes continued, but the bulk of the force was defeated.

Robby sprinted into the bunker infirmary and found Melonie lying in a half-reclined bed. Dr. Nora stood by her side.

"Is this really happening?"

Melonie shared a glance with Dr. Nora. It wasn't *really* happening, but it was what it took to get Robby off the battlefield. A messenger ran the idea to her and Dr. Nora, straight from Marcus.

She smiled and nodded meekly before poorly faking a contraction.

"It started a couple hours ago. I think this is it."

"It might take some time, but the baby is coming," Dr. Nora said.

He went from holding her hand, to tapping his foot rapidly, to getting up and looking out of the window in under four minutes.

"Promise me you're not going back up there," Melonie said.

"Of course, babe. I'm just curious about the latest news on the fighting."

Outside, a group of men jogged across the bunker proper into the train tunnel.

"I should check in with Henry and Marcus, let them know I'm back."

"That's fine. Just get back soon."

He kissed her on the head before bolting. As soon as he left the room, Dr. Nora and Melonie burst out laughing.

"Want to get up and walk around before he gets back?"

Melonie shifted her protruding belly and set her feet on the ground and took a few steps. "I was faking a minute ago, but I actually have started having a few cramps…"

Her water broke and splashed at her feet. She froze in place.

"Oh – um, this is *really* happening now."

Dr. Nora covered her mouth. "Let's have you lay back down. I'll run and get the delivery nurses. I'm just a heart surgeon."

* * *

Kent left the drone operations to the Russian team. They couldn't fly over the eastern army due to the interference, so there wasn't much left they could do in general.

He had an idea that he could not get out of his mind. It was a hectic time to experiment, but he thought Azoulay's AI could unlock a powerful weapon they had in their arsenal but hadn't figured out how to use.

He was working with Akili as if she were a person. Asking questions, giving tasks and feedback, all verbally.

Timothy's curiosity was piqued.

"What do you have cooking over there?"

"Want to head up top and find out? Could be big."

Marcus was caught up in minute details on the map while Genie fed him updates. Marcus nodded yes through Kent's request to leave, but didn't listen to a word.

They drove a half mile off the bunker site on pavement before turning down a rough gravel road. On the other side of dense woods, they came to a hilltop clearing where the HIMARS truck was positioned.

It was loaded with M26 short range cluster munition rockets. Three six-rocket pods were stacked to the side for reload. They only needed to figure out how to launch them.

"Let's see what she can do," Kent said as they climbed into the cab. "These things usually have satellite support, which we sort of have. I doubt we can home in on targets, but I bet we can target a spot on the map."

Kent plugged the laptop in.

"Akili, can you access the weapons system of this HIMARS vehicle?"

"*One moment...Yes, I can, and I have.*"

Timothy and Kent looked at each other in disbelief.

"Okay, can you integrate with the Trencher Satellite network's global positioning system, and use it to aim the rockets?"

"*This might take a moment... Integration is complete. I only need a coordinating piece of data tied to a location.*"

"I got it," Timothy said. "Akili, pull up every Trencher battery unit in the town of Dugger, Indiana."

Akili pulled a data file and exported it into a spreadsheet.

"Akili, can you overlay this onto a map?" Kent said.

"*Absolutely, here you go.*"

Akili took four seconds to compute the request and produce the map. There were 42 Trencher battery units spread around the town.

Timothy grabbed the radio. "Marcus, we have something."

Marcus relayed the army's location from the scout reports. The forces had convened in a school parking lot, near the start of the main road leading to the bunker. They were starting to move.

"Let us know when our guys are out of the way."

Marcus ordered the scouts to fall back, and that they had 5 minutes to do so. He cut it close by telling Kent and

287

Timothy that they were clear to fire two minutes after.

They put on noise cancelling headsets and told the other men outside to do the same, and to get back. Timothy let Kent do the honors.

Akili dialed in the coordinates of the high school, taken off the Trencher battery unit tied to the school. She instructed Timothy to flip an analog switch to arm the rockets, and flip another to fire. He followed her instructions, and they heard and felt the missiles firing.

The rockets screamed from the pods and trailed smoke high into the sky. They jumped out of the truck and watched the 10-mile trajectory, and the distant flashes at the end.

Reports started to come in. The rockets destroyed the high school and the exact area they aimed for, but only caught the tail end of the army, a fuel truck and a handful of armored vehicles. It wasn't nothing, but they missed the bulk of the force by a minute.

"Have the men reload and relocate," Marcus said. "Get back to the bunker. God only knows what they are about to throw at us."

Chapter Fifty-Six

The forces from Texas were all but defeated after the occurrence at Hutsonville Bridge and the courthouse ambush. Timothy and Kent's HIMARS launch mostly missed, but it sent a message.

As the remaining eastern force crept forward, another major movement was detected – in the skies.

"We've got inbound aircraft!" Cami reported.

Henry called out a warning. Men at the site crowded into the fortified elevator dome. Those who couldn't fit returned to the trenches and prayed. Fighters further afield took cover where they could.

The bombers flew low and slow, dropping thousands of bombs over the nine miles between the ground army and the bunker. Fallow fields, woods, and barren coal lands were bombed at random, but concentrated along and between three county roads, though careful not to hit the actual roads.

The scouts and resistance fighters that couldn't retreat from the roadsides ended up being the safest.

Kent and Timothy were still a quarter mile from the bunker. They ditched their vehicle and took cover in the woods.

Laser-guided missiles destroyed tanks and armored vehicles, no matter how hidden they were. Most of the fighters had distanced themselves, but there were dozens of casualties and literal tons of assets lost.

The greatest blow came from the disarray, shock, and awe. Men were forced out of position and ambush points were abandoned or destroyed.

The bunker site itself only received a pittance of bombs, and Kent and Timothy were safely further out. When the ominous rumblings ceased, they made their way back to their vehicle. Once they hit the blacktop road and got out of the woods, they looked southeast in time to see one more bomber high in the sky.

It looked as though it was dropping a black cloud of dust, or ash.

As the particles fell, they started to swarm like a flock of birds. As the debris fell further, it spread into a pattern. By the time they were a few hundred feet above the ground, they were uniformly spread, creating a grid of black dots in the sky.

"What the hell is that?" Timothy said.

"Samaras bombs – each about the size of a hawk," Kent said. "They have the blast radius of a grenade and can stay airborne for an hour. They dive at whatever is beneath them without a friendly signature."

* * *

The enemy divided into three columns on three parallel roads leading west toward the bunker. They rolled forward under the protection of the deadly sky grid.

Before the grid fully took shape, the squadron out of

West Lafayette, led by Cooper, took action to slow the center column.

They pulled a train of dirt-filled railcars over the crossing near Cass. There was no surer way to create a traffic jam in rural Indiana.

Unfortunately, the sky grid formed over them before they could leave.

They received word over the radio what the objects were and what to do if one dove on their position. The advice was to dive and roll and hope for the best.

The lead enemy tank came to a halt fifty yards out from the blocked crossing. It would only be a matter of time before the center railcar was blasted away. The connectors were unlikely to draw fire, at least initially. Men with RPGs hid inside.

At Cooper's command, they stood and fired at the front of the column, scoring direct hits on the tank and the Humvee that had pulled beside it. Black smoke and fire poured from the truck.

They did not wait for the response. They climbed out on the opposite side and fled the scene on four-wheelers. They had a house in Cass staked out, 200 yards away.

Killer drones started to fall out of the formation and dive at the speeding ATVs.

They swerved and evaded the explosives as best they could, but the last of them took a hit. Both men were badly injured and left on the road. Going back would have gotten them all killed.

Cooper called into the bunker. The railcar blockade worked, but it was only a matter of time before the column rolled into Cass. He didn't like their position, yet moving out in the open was also extremely dangerous.

Timothy interjected. "Cooper, we have the HIMARS

reloaded. Get your men out of those houses and make a run for it. I only need one of you to let us know when the enemy rolls over those railroad tracks."

"Copy. Stand by."

Cooper ordered his men to make a run for their ATVs, dive-drones be damned. He volunteered to stay back.

It didn't take long for the explosive drones to swoop down on his fleeing men like angry birds. Luckily, he didn't see any connect while he watched.

In the other direction, the blockade was blasted away. The lead tank nudged a railcar down the tracks to clear a path.

Cooper made the call. "Fire away at Cass. I'm getting the hell out of here."

He sprinted out of the house and took his ATV onto the road. The ominous grid was shifting to accommodate for the drones that had departed out of the formation. He gunned it and dodged his first bomb sixty yards later.

They dove with greater frequency the further he got. They landed in front, behind, and all sides. He flew off-road into a field so he could vary his movements more randomly. His gut told him his luck wouldn't last much longer. He had to find cover.

He gunned it toward a tree line. A bomb exploded right before the edge, sending him careening into the brush. He miraculously avoided the first line of trees, but hit a fallen log hidden in the undergrowth soon after.

He flew through the narrow tree line and splashed into a pond on the other side. It wasn't until he was underwater that he felt just how much shrapnel was lodged in his body.

He resurfaced and looked skyward. A black dot released from the grid and caught his eye. He dove as deep as he could. The drone exploded on the surface.

He made it to shore and crawled to cover without triggering another attack. A roar sounded from above. All he saw were streaks of thick smoke.

The HIMARS rockets exploded spectacularly, wiping Cass off the map – and every enemy combatant in it.

* * *

The second HIMARS attack would be the last. Apaches tracked the trails of smoke and made quick work of the vehicle before it could relocate. The men operating it escaped, but the weapon was lost.

It wasn't all bad – a ragtag group of fighters took one of the choppers down.

Timothy and Kent were stuck on the fringes of the battlefield. From their vantage point, they could see the samaras bombs slowly descending. Many started to fall with no apparent target – a sign that the whole thing was about to come crashing down. It would be one hellacious hailstorm, but they would regain their mobility if they made it through. They called in their observations and told everyone to hunker down a little bit longer.

The other columns continued to advance. Two creek bridges were blown on County Road 575, but they were shallow, and the land flat enough that the enemy continued through, approaching only three miles out from the bunker. The other column took fire from the dense foliage, but never really slowed down.

The trenches around the bunker site were going to come into play.

Chapter Fifty-Seven

The sky grid finally fell – all at once – with each drone expending its last bit of energy to avoid its own forces upon impact. Of the good guys, nine unlucky men were injured, and one was killed, adding to the eighteen injuries and six deaths attributed to the dive drones prior.

Robby paced the War Room, beside himself for not being in on the action. Being on the verge of becoming a father added to his anxiousness.

"If you don't get back to Melonie, I'll have you handcuffed to her hospital bed," Marcus said. "Get out!"

"We should be up there fighting – not letting everyone else do the work."

"Someone's got to see the big picture."

Robby left the as Kent and Timothy returned. They made a sprint back to the bunker after the dive drones fell. Marcus pulled them aside.

"I want our drones searching further east, behind the army. Betancourt must be somewhere in that direction. Look for a camp, his aircraft, pockets of interference – anything. If we hold this army off and get to him, we end this whole thing."

Kent and Timothy went to the corner where the Russian drone pilots were stationed. They were already on it. Henry returned to fielding reports as Genie posted them to the real-time dashboard.

"I need updates, people," Marcus said. "Where are they?"

"They are converging about a mile out at the chokepoint," Henry said. "Is it time?"

Marcus gave Henry a thumbs up.

"Blow up the road," Henry said over the radio. "I repeat, blow up the road."

* * *

At the last chokepoint between the enemy and the bunker site, men scrambled into position.

A stripper pit lake ran along the road, elevated slightly above it. The other side had dense woods up to the road. It was their last best place to delay the incoming army and do real damage.

Leftover dynamite from the bunker's construction was brought above ground and dedicated to the chokepoint. The ordinance was planted on the outer earthen banks of the lake and inside the rusted drainage pipe beneath the road.

The enemy columns converged with what little remained of the decimated central column. They all barreled forward to close the final mile.

The armor slowed, as if skeptical of the reprieve from constant ambush. When the tentative lead tank hit the road above the dynamite-packed drainage pipe, the detonation was set off.

The tank disappeared in a cloud of dust and tumbled

into the blast crater along with the next two vehicles.

A second later, the earthen bank along the stripper pit blew up in a rapid cascade, unleashing the waters.

A wave washed over the road. Soldiers on foot were washed into the field on the opposite side of the road, some as far as seventy yards out. From there, they were easy targets for the men in the tree stands.

Resistance fighters came out from cover and fired at the drenched column. Rocket-propelled grenades were launched, and small arms fire filled the air.

Flanks were set in motion. It was a start, but it was to be determined how long they could hold up before they had to fall back to the trenches.

* * *

Early reports were favorable, but there simply wasn't enough firepower, or water, for a total rout. The enemy was bogged down but fighting back.

Marcus wanted an update from the drone team regarding their other pursuit.

"Any signs of Betancourt?"

"Nothing yet," Kent said. "We're a couple towns out and haven't come across anything yet."

Big Pigg's voice blared through the intercom in the room, requesting a word with "The Boss."

"What do you have, Pigg? We're busy here."

"Got this kid calling in from Linton. Says there's an army and a spaceship-looking thing over there."

Marcus, Henry, and Timothy's eyes lit up.

Timothy switched the channel over and took the receiver.

"Timothy here. Is that you, Cameron?"

296

"Hey, Tim! Yes, it's Cam. I thought you guys would want to know that there is a bunch of military vehicles in the Linton City Park."

"Great catch. We heard there was something that looked like a spacecraft?"

"I've never seen anything like it. I know there used to be air taxis in the big cities, but this is way more high-tech. It flew over to the hospital to charge its battery at the helipad."

"Alright, Cam. Keep an eye on them, but also keep out of sight. We are going to send men that way."

"I don't know how we missed it," Kent said. "We flew right over it."

"Betancourt must have stealth tech the rest don't have," Marcus said.

Taveon and Ellis, who were leading the 200-man army that was sent east through the train tunnel, had already surfaced at the Quarry and worked their way west to Bloomfield. They were only twenty minutes from Linton. Marcus sent updated orders.

He then grabbed a jacket, put a radio in his pocket, and shut Timothy's laptop.

"What are you doing?" Timothy said.

"They can handle the bunker defenses. You, me, and Henry are taking the backroads to Linton."

Chapter Fifty-Eight

Robby ran out of the infirmary when he saw Marcus, Henry, and Timothy jogging across the bunker proper.

"Where the hell are you guys going?"

"Linton," Marcus said. "Betancourt's aircraft was spotted. Our flank army is closing in."

"Wish I could be there."

"How is Melonie? Is she starting to dilate?" Timothy asked.

Robby looked confused. "I didn't notice anything with her eyes, but she is having more contractions. What happened to having to stay back to command?"

"Our people know what to do here," Marcus said. "If we get Betancourt, it puts an end to it all."

Robby shook his head and laughed in disbelief that he was going to miss the action.

"Go get the bastard."

* * *

Henry took the backroads away from and around the frontlines before hitting State Road 59. They met

Cameron at a house on the edge of Linton.

He sported a less-scraggly mustache and had put on some healthy weight since the last time they saw him. He filled them in on the latest whereabouts of the enemy.

"They are still at the park, but half went to the hospital to guard that aircraft. Have you guys seen it? Looks futuristic."

"Yes, and our first priority is to destroy it," Marcus said. "Rather, our guys coming from the east will."

"We want to create a distraction," Timothy said. "Divide their attention, so they don't see them coming."

"Like, blow something up?"

Timothy nodded. "We brought explosives. Is there anything close but not too close that we can draw their attention to?"

Cameron thought for a moment. "We could blow up a mobile home next to the park."

* * *

Cameron led them on a trail behind a bowling alley and an empty public pool on the north end of the park. Betancourt's soldiers were gathered in the distance, their armored vehicles parked near a commemorative tank from a forgotten war.

They strung dynamite along a row of five mobile homes at the north end of the manor. Near, but far enough away to get a running start to safety. Cameron wanted to check inside the last trailer before they blew it to smithereens. It was his childhood home.

He made a quick pass and stepped out empty handed. From the cinderblock front step, he looked to his right and locked eyes with a soldier assigned to patrol the perimeter of the park.

Marcus, Timothy, and Henry were also in plain view, but fiddling with the last dynamite stick.

Marcus was the first to look up and notice Cameron frozen, and then the frozen soldier. He pulled out his handgun and fired wildly toward the soldier, sending him scampering off behind a dilapidated trailer.

They fled to the tree line and laid down in the weeds. Marcus took out his radio.

"Taveon, Ellis – move out! Hit the troops at the hospital with everything you've got. Do not let that aircraft take off."

"Hear you loud and clear, Mr. Trencher. We're rolling out," Taveon answered.

Marcus took the detonation device out of his bag but paused.

"If we wait, we might catch a few in the blast."

"Not worth it," Timothy said. "We need to draw them over now and get out to the hospital."

"Fine."

Marcus pressed the detonation button without a countdown. Five mobile homes exploded at once, sending fire and aluminum debris sky-high. Henry and Timothy cursed at him for the lack of warning.

"You guys are crazy!" Cameron said. "C'mon! The hospital is this way."

Cameron led them along a field and through a patch of woods. They emerged in a small neighborhood bordering the hospital. The nearest house had a view of the grounds, so they broke in and set up camp.

From the back living room window, they could see Betancourt's ship. His men were preparing for takeoff.

There was a sudden commotion amongst the enemy

soldiers as they pointed eastward, yelled orders, and ran to positions.

Taveon and Ellis's fleet of fifty white pickup trucks came in hot. They barreled through two armored vehicles on the main road and flooded into an open lot adjacent to the helipad. Men hung out of the windows and fired assault rifles before they even came to a stop.

Betancourt himself finally made an appearance. Bodyguards escorted him from the hospital to the helipad. He ducked into the aircraft.

A wild RPG round blasted the third story of the hospital. Another hit an armored vehicle in front of the aircraft. The hail of bullets was so thick, Henry didn't feel safe watching from the window 150 yards away.

"C'mon, guys, the aircraft!" Marcus said.

The highly trained enemy began to fight back with cohesion. A soldier got on a mounted gun and sprayed the field of trucks. Another errant rocket flew over the battlefield. The advantage of the ambush had leveled out.

The brigade from the park arrived and decimated the left flank. Taveon and Ellis's army still had numerical superiority, but it was suddenly halved. They were fighting valiantly, but without the weaponry or training of Betancourt's forces.

The air started to kick up around the aircraft.

"He's about to get away!" Marcus said.

Marcus grabbed Timothy's rifle and made a move to the door. Henry and Timothy stopped him.

"You're not going to take it down with a rifle," Timothy said.

The aircraft lifted off. Marcus seethed as he watched it climb ten, twenty, thirty feet in the air. It slowly rotated toward Taveon and Ellis's army. None of them wanted to witness what it was about to unleash.

Just before the barrage, a rocket slammed into the left side of the craft. It listed, lost thrust, and then slammed into the hospital parking lot, skidding twenty yards in their direction.

"Back in business!" Henry said.

They crowded back around the window. The chaos behind enemy lines was difficult to comprehend. Their own friendlies were further in the distance, technically firing towards them.

The tide slowly began to turn in their favor. A dozen enemy soldiers were pinned down. Others fled into the hospital. The man on the mounted gun was now slumped over, dead. Another armored vehicle took an RPG. The brigade from the park was pushed back after their initial charge.

Marcus never took his eye off the downed aircraft. There were explosions and action to see around it, but they were there for one man.

Finally, Betancourt abandoned ship. Four bodyguards accompanied him at first, but he waved three of them off and sent them to fight.

Betancourt and his lone guard started to run away from the fighting – directly toward their position. They jumped the fence into the backyard of the house they were hiding in.

"That's him, right?" Henry said.

"It is," Marcus said, grabbing Timothy's rifle again.

Timothy took out a handgun, Henry and Cameron clicked the safety off their rifles.

They moved quickly and quietly out to the driveway to cut them off. They listened for footsteps in the overgrown yard between the houses.

Betancourt and his bodyguard rounded the corner.

"Stop right there!" Marcus yelled.

The soldier reflexively aimed at them. They all fired, and at least two of them hit center mass. If the man wasn't dead before he hit the ground, he was soon after. Betancourt dove away and put his hands up.

"On your knees!"

He did so, slowly, as if annoyed that his slacks were now wet. He brushed away the grass stuck to his jacket and finally looked up and recognized who held his life in their hands.

"I see you've decided to come up from your bunker."

"Call your men off," Marcus said. "Tell them to cease fire, and I'll tell mine to do the same."

Cameron clipped the radio off the dead soldier and handed it to Betancourt.

The smugness faded from Betancourt's face, replaced with the incredulous scowl.

"You pathetic, backwoods simpletons really think you can—"

Marcus slammed the butt of his rifle into Betancourt's nose. He writhed in the grass as blood poured from the gash.

"It's a bullet in your kneecap next. Call your men off, *now!*"

He put the radio to his mouth while in a fetal position. "Cease fire. This is Betancourt. I order you to cease fire."

"Tell them to drop their weapons. Call off the forces at the bunker."

"Lay down your arms, immediately. Cease fire at the bunker. This is over."

Marcus looked back and nodded to Henry.

"Cease fire! Cease fire! We got Betancourt. The

enemy has been ordered to cease fire. I repeat, cease fire!"

The fighting around them quickly died down. They dragged Betancourt to his feet and held him against the side of the house until they saw their own men securing the grounds.

They marched him through a fence gate and past his downed aircraft. His disarmed men could not believe their eyes.

Taveon and Ellis ran over to meet them.

"This the evil motherfucker that's been killing people all over the world?" Ellis said.

"My father in Europe knows where we are. He will wipe this place off the map."

"Tell your European daddy to come on over. We'll whoop his ass, too," Taveon said. He turned to Marcus. "What do you want us to do with these other guys?"

"Disarm them, and try not to kill any more, unless they run," Marcus said. "Keep them in line until we get some buses here to transfer them to the prison in Carlisle. Except this one – he is coming with us."

Chapter Fifty-Nine

They returned to a procession of jubilant resistance fighters. A great many bunker civilians joined, many seeing the surface for the first time since they were forced underground. Demoralized prisoners of war were being marched up the road as they entered the gate.

Betancourt was pushed through the crowd by Ellis and his men. Had anyone known who he was, it would have been impossible. He looked straight ahead with his chin high, maintaining all he had left – arrogance.

Timothy retrieved the bullhorn from a trench soldier and delivered it to Marcus.

"I think they want to hear from you."

Marcus climbed the same mound of dirt as he did before the battle. The first thing he did was ask for a moment of silence for the ones they had lost. Thousands bowed their heads as a solemn silence swept over the war-torn grounds.

"We may never know how many lives were saved today thanks to your bravery and sacrifice, but I'd venture a guess in the tens of millions. Maybe billions. This battle in little old Sherman County, Indiana, will go down in history.

"We will stay vigilant. It is too early to know if more fighting is to come, but it is not too early to start rebuilding. It is crucial that we secure food, shelter, medicine, and establish communication and security.

"For those of you who traveled here from across the state and beyond, you are free to return home, or you are welcome to stay. Keep in touch and we shall rebuild a peaceful and prosperous society together.

"All I ask is that you stick around a little while longer – because tonight, we celebrate!"

The crowd roared and fired their guns into the air.

* * *

Marcus, Timothy, and Henry scrubbed down in a corner of the quarantine room. The rest of the chamber had become a triage center.

The area outside of the infirmary, beneath the windows of Marcus's suite, was also occupied by the wounded. Cooper smiled with a tinge of madness and saluted them as they passed. He was shirtless and dotted with shrapnel.

Marcus and Timothy stopped by every injured man and woman to show gratitude.

Henry found Mariya among the nurses and doctors. He didn't want to interfere, or disregard those who nearly made the ultimate sacrifice, but he wanted her to see that he was okay.

When she did, she leapt into his arms.

"It's over," he said. "I'm safe. We're safe now."

After a long embrace, she wiped away her tears and looked out at the injured men and women.

"There are about fifty with severe injuries and at least a dozen more that haven't been moved down yet. We still don't know how many deaths."

"It's horrible that it came to this."

They watched Becky and other nurses apply bandages and make their rounds. Dr. Nora was in the infirmary performing surgeries on the most critically wounded.

"I'm guessing they moved Melonie out since she was faking the baby thing?"

Mariya frowned. "Faking? She had the baby an hour ago. But yes, they moved her to an apartment on the other side to make room."

"Huh, I thought Marcus made the whole thing up to get Robby to stay. Please tell me he stayed..."

"Go see him...Room 715! We'll catch up later."

She got on her toes to give him a kiss before rejoining Becky, who was tending to a dive drone victim. Henry pulled Marcus and Timothy aside and told them that Melonie gave birth. They were equally confused.

They made the trek to the other side. A midwife slipped out of the room carrying a stack of towels. She whispered, "Mom is doing great."

Melonie was sitting upright with the newborn in her arms. She gave them a kind, exhausted smile. Robby was by her side, too enamored to notice their entry.

"Congratulations, mom and dad," Marcus said.

Robby grinned ear-to-ear but spoke quietly. "Hey guys, come meet my daughter, Annie."

"Daughter? You certainly deserve that," Henry said. "I kid...You're going to be an awesome girl dad."

"I wanted a girl all along. The boy talk was all reverse psychology."

Robby delicately took Annie from Melonie's arms. He talked about her eyes and hair and how mightily she cried when she came into the world. He bragged that the nurses said she was in perfect health. She had already fed and taken a nap.

Marcus let his mind drift to Daylin. All the talk about rebuilding society was for the crowd. He cared more about reuniting with his son. Seeing Robby and Melonie and Annie only made the feeling stronger.

The midwife returned to the room to check on Melonie.

"We better let you two get back to parenting," Marcus said.

"Oh, I almost forgot – did you guys get him?"

Marcus smiled. "We got him."

* * *

They took the elevator down to the cells where Betancourt was under close supervision to prevent self-harm and keep would-be assassins at bay.

He was stripped of his expensive attire and given standard issue bunker clothes, which was close enough to prison garb.

A chair was set outside the cell, which Marcus took.

"I want you to know that you will not make it out of here alive," Marcus said. "But if you want the remainder of your life to be less miserable, you will cooperate."

Betancourt said nothing.

"First, you will reveal your organization's remaining assets and plans. We've got a world to rebuild. Second, you will meet daily with my friend Henry who will record your side of the story. Think of him as your biographer."

Betancourt shook his head, seething. "My father..."

"Ah, yes, your father. If you cooperate, we will set up a call. I can't wait to hear what he offers for your exchange. Maybe he won't offer anything."

"I saved this planet, no matter how you record it for your skewed revision of history!" Betancourt said, rising to hit feet. "How soon you all forget the chaos and decay and *rot* that was our world before my family, my organization, ripped the band-aid off so we could start to *actually* fix the problems! You, of all people, a billionaire... they would have had your head on a stake by the end of the decade! The stupid, useless, consumer masses... You despised them as much as I!

"The planet has already begun to heal. Humanity will evolve leaps and bounds after this cleansing, even if you cut it short a few billion. Write down what you wish. But mark my words, I will be the hero in your story – not you."

* * *

They gathered in the War Room for debriefing. They thanked Genie and Kent for their long hours and told them to go enjoy the evening.

"All that stuff I said up top, we will get to it eventually," Marcus said. "I once saw a cheesy poster that said, '*Think globally, act locally*,' and that is what we should do. Get food production in order, rebuild housing in town, broaden our network. I can't stomach the thought right now, but we should start thinking about government.

"But, like I said, that will have to wait. I need to see my son. When I get back, I promise you'll get my best effort to contribute to the rebuild – lead it if I must."

309

"We could all take a little time to ourselves," Henry said. "What about you, Timothy?"

"The girls want to spread their mother's ashes closer to home. I'm aware of the risks, but they can't grow up in a bunker.

"Also, the controls for the other grids require manual uploads at each regional headquarters. So, yeah, we will take a grand tour and get them up and running."

"Should be one hell of a road trip."

"What about you?"

Henry played with the ring in his pocket.

"I hope you don't mind sticking around a little while longer, at least until Marcus gets back. I'm planning something I want you all to be a part of."

* * *

Henry and Mariya walked the gardens, hand in hand. It was quiet, with only the peaceful sound of the waterfall echoing off the walls. Almost everyone was up top where the victory celebration was underway.

Henry stopped at the obelisk to dial up a starlit sky.

"Don't you want to celebrate with everyone?" Mariya said. "We can see the real stars up there, you know."

"In a minute. I just want to be with you right now."

They meandered toward the gazebo. He hoped it wasn't too obvious he was leading her there.

"Remember our romantic dinner date? I still can't believe everyone pulled all those strings for us."

"It was special. Even though Robby started playing that raunchy Madonna song halfway through."

He laughed. "I wanted to impress you so bad. I was already in love with you."

"I was already there, too. Truly, madly, deeply."

Her musical reference brought a smile to his face. It had become their song. It was almost too perfect that she mentioned it.

He turned his head and threw a sly nod to a hidden co-conspirator. A moment later, Savage Garden's "Truly, Madly, Deeply," started to play from the garden speakers.

Mariya leaned away and gave him a look. *What are you up to?*

He got down on one knee.

"Mariya, I've fallen more in love with you every day. I want to spend the rest of my life with you. Will you marry me?"

She let go and covered her mouth, and then said, "Yes, yes!"

He put the ring on her finger, and they kissed.

Cheers erupted from the bunker proper. The whole gang was there – Marcus, Timothy and his daughters, Steve and Mercedes, Brad and Becky, Brittney, Kent, Genie, Dr. Nora and Baby Ben, his parents – even Robby, and Melonie in a wheelchair.

The newly engaged couple embraced their friends and family.

"I heard what you said about my musical selection," Robby said, with a tablet in hand. "I guess now is a good time to throw on that Madonna song you like so much."

Henry chased Robby as the intro to Madonna's "Erotica" played. Robby ran halfway to the elevator before giving up.

Marcus took a step toward the exit. "Are we all ready to go? It's a true southern Indiana party up there – open field, pick-up trucks, country music, and booze."

They made their way to the elevator. Robby stayed off

the platform with Melonie.

"We better get back to the baby," Robby said. "Anyways, I swore off partying in fields after that time in high school when the cops showed, and I hid in a ditch full of poison ivy. Y'all behave!"

They emerged up top to cheers from those who noticed. Marcus and Timothy quickly found a tailgate to sit on and observe the festivities while the others mingled with the crowd. Brittney delivered shots of bourbon and made them take them before she ran off with Kent. Genie, Steve, and Mercedes cut it up with rednecks. Timothy's daughters played with friends. Tom Petty sang about those Indiana boys on those Indiana nights.

"What a crazy, crazy life," Timothy said.

"It's been interesting, that's for sure," Marcus said. "Aren't you glad that professor made us lab partners at Rose-Hulman?"

"For the record, that guy was still an asshole, and I was dropping out either way, but I certainly became a much wealthier dropout." They clinked their plastic cups. "Finding a lifelong friend wasn't bad either."

Fireworks exploded in the distance, eliciting *oohs* and *aahs*. Henry and Mariya slow danced in the muddy field with a dozen other couples while Timothy's daughters ran between them with sparklers. Thousands were laughing and smiling and living life to the fullest.

They would never get back what they once had, not even close. They lost people they would never get back, but that was always going to happen. It was all okay. Being alive had to be good enough, and it was.

Epilogue

The winter following the victory over Betancourt and his armies came and went in peace. It was a normal winter, too, with no subarctic temperatures. Mike Azoulay's heroics in Cuba had damaged the geoengineering apparatus beyond repair. There would be no more mini-ice ages around the globe, killing untold millions.

The drone virus did permanent damage. A year on, and they had yet to see any in the skies that were not their own. It was still too early to declare total victory, but there were no indications that Betancourt's network was still operating in North America.

The list of collaborators that Azoulay released set off a worldwide manhunt. Gangs of angry, highly motivated men raided private bunkers and private islands. There were still plenty who were out of reach, but their days were numbered.

Refugees from the east trickled into Indiana. They claimed that communication was established with resistance movements in Europe, and that some remnants of the organization were still committing genocide in the Old World. But their drone networks were also infected, and without the solar shades and chemical clouds, they could not kill on the scale envisioned. The tide had turned, globally.

Domestically, there were constant rumors of a reforming federal government, but never any evidence. There was, however, a constant candidate put forth.

He was a world-renowned genius before the collapse. He led the defeat of the global conspirators that brought it about. He controlled most of the national power grid and already had an army willing to fight on his behalf. Was there anyone left who could do any better?

* * *

The prisoners of war captured after the battle were sentenced to death. They would go down in history with the Nazis who worked concentration camps and filled trenches with bodies on the eastern front.

Before they were executed, Henry and his team of historians recorded every detail that they would put forth. Most were Russian and Eastern European. The Russian friends from Crane helped translate. To the best of their ability, they recorded every stop they made across the U.S., and what atrocities they committed.

One army started in the northwest and travelled south through California, killing indiscriminately along the way. They eventually headed east, hitting Phoenix and Tucson and every town between before a prolonged tour of Texas.

The other army started in New England and worked down the Atlantic Coast. They supplemented the drone efforts in the most densely populated parts of the country where the most survivors were likely to still be on the surface.

The middle of the country was the last priority. The harsh geoengineered winter and the drone fleets were expected to do the bulk of the work, and did, until a handful of troublemakers in Indiana found a way to fight back.

Betancourt's execution date was stayed indefinitely. He was a bargaining chip they had to hold on to, in case his mysterious father was in fact still out there leading the global holocaust. A year on, and there was no effort to establish communication and negotiate for his freedom. He was forgotten.

Henry got him to talk during their interviews, eventually. The historical record would be invaluable to humanity moving forward. At least, he hoped.

Betancourt was forced to do field labor in the spring. Summer came and went, and there was still no word from his father. No army came to his rescue. They talked about scheduling the execution, but they were in no hurry.

* * *

Every few months, another region would pop up in the Trencher grid control system. It was their way of knowing where Timothy was in the world – Omaha, Denver, Sacramento, Seattle – and that he and his daughters were alive and well.

Timothy installed the blood key override controls at each regional headquarters, just as they had done in the Midwest. He waved overdue payments and lifted restrictions, letting power course through the grids. A year later, most of the Trencher network across the former United States was functioning at some capacity.

Each activation came with a message detailing his travels. People were still out there – some thriving and friendly, others desperate and dangerous. His role as the Johnny Appleseed of Electricity got them out of more than one dicey situation.

He documented what he saw across the post-apocalyptic landscape, but also included personal notes. Spreading his wife Shelley's ashes in Iowa brought great closure to him and his daughters.

He sent separate messages to Dr. Nora Weinstein. It was a long-distance relationship, but only until he made his way back east.

* * *

Shortly after the victory, and before Timothy departed westward, Henry and Mariya tied the knot.

The ceremony was a glorious outdoors-on-the-surface event. Kent officiated, Marcus was the best man, and Timothy and Robby were groomsmen. Melonie, Mercedes, and Brittney were bridesmaids, with Mercedes getting the nod as the maid of honor. Brad and Becky miraculously came up with the ingredients for a tiered wedding cake. Timothy's daughters served as flower girls and dropped real flower petals.

Mercedes caught the garter and told Steve he better get out there and loot a jewelry store for a ring.

It wouldn't be long before Robby and Melonie got around to a proper wedding, and the same was rumored for the odd couple, Brittney and Kent.

Henry and Mariya celebrated their one-year anniversary by finally taking a honeymoon. It was only a few hours away to the rustic ruins of French Lick, but they made the most of it.

They stayed within the growing safe zone spreading from Sherman County. A reasonable level of law and order was established on the main roads and in the towns in between.

Neither wanted to venture too far. They had a baby on the way.

They were not alone. There was something of a baby boom. The people of Sherman and much of central and southern Indiana had security, food, shelter, medical care, and growing optimism. They had hope.

* * *

Robby played a role in coordinating farming efforts that spring and summer alongside the farmer near Bloomfield that had saved his life. He also helped with the reconstruction efforts in Sherman. The challenge of rebuilding with limited and recycled resources appealed to his artistic talents.

The majority of his time was devoted to raising his daughter Annie. Melonie was pregnant with their second child. They claimed land on the western half of the county like homesteaders. He had a thriving garden, art studio, several Jeeps, and a perfect family. They hosted dinners parties and attended others several nights a week.

He had never felt so grounded and connected. He had never been so happy.

* * *

Marcus spent a week in Tennessee following the victory, where he reunited with Daylin and Ashley. He didn't want

317

to push too hard for them to join him back in Sherman, but luckily, he didn't have to.

Ashley wanted to go. Her family was more of the once-or-twice-a-year-visit type, she said.

He liked Ashley but didn't know if he loved her. But he did know he could co-parent with her and worry about the rest as it came.

He put Daylin and family first, but soon returned to his de facto leadership role. People looked to him.

He focused on the basics – food, water, shelter, security, communication. They quickly rebuilt the town of Sherman. So many survivors flocked to the area that the population swelled to near pre-apocalypse levels.

He heard the talk of government...with him at the helm. He brushed it off. There was too much work to do locally, and regionally. It was foolish to focus on anything greater, he would say.

Privately, he let his mind work through the idea. Once he felt like he had a plan, perhaps he would socialize the thought more openly. He wanted to wait until Timothy returned before he spoke a word of it.

There was no denying that he believed in himself, and that he was as capable as anyone alive.

* * *

The bunker became a ghost town before the first snow, save for a crew of farmers who kept up with food production through the winter. By late summer, when the surface crops were ready for harvest and bountiful, there was no need for the bunker.

Henry, Robby, and Marcus got together to make one last walkthrough before locking it up. Marcus claimed he wanted help forming a maintenance checklist. Anything to not sound sentimental.

They watched the waterfall in the gardens ebb to a trickle after the water was shut off. The giant bulb in the obelisk that once projected stars was removed, leaving the dome above plain and ordinary. The café chairs were put up on the tables.

Priceless works of art were left on the walls. The swimming pool was drained for the first time since Robby drove a golf cart into it. Every turn brought about memories. Some happy, some painful.

They ventured to the other side where Timothy and his family suffered with a thousand others. They passed the mine and went to the bottom floor where the coal chutes led to the dormant power station. It felt haunted.

Marcus broke down in tears. Henry and Robby tried to stop him from visiting the makeshift crypt where the engineers who built the bunker were buried, but he insisted. It was his greatest regret.

They made a brief stop in the train tunnel. A wall was built at the end and a basic security system put in place in case someone wandered all that way underground. The train sat at the station, having been unused since transferring livestock from Speedway.

Every other bunker in the network was evacuated or abandoned – the Quarry in Bloomington, the Louisville Mega Caverns, the Speedway Warehouse bunker, Meridian Hospital, and the roundabout bunker beneath Carmel.

They made their way back toward the elevator, stopping one last time to gaze across the space.

"Can't say I'm going to miss it," Robby said. "But we had good company."

"I never would've made it without you guys," Henry said.

"I never would have *started* this without you guys," Marcus said. "It'll always be here. Let's pray we never need it again."

He lingered behind while Henry and Robby went to the elevator. He turned off the lights and stared into the darkness, listening to the silence where there was once life. He was overcome by grief. He should have saved more. He could have done more.

When he finally gathered himself, he shut the door behind him.

They rode the elevator back to the surface, and back to making the most of the rest of their lives.

Acknowledgements

My thanks for very generous help from:

Karen Noble, Jennifer Noble, Eric Dalen (editor, book 1), Elijah Hollis, Ben and Bethany Voight, and all the other friends, family, and acquaintances who read one or all the books in the series. Also, a special thanks to all the readers that took a chance on a total unknown. I hope you enjoyed the story.

About the Author

Shane Noble is originally from Sullivan, Indiana, and now resides in Louisville, Kentucky. He graduated from Bellarmine University and taught middle school for six years before moving on to the private sector where he does super-exciting technical writing.

Thank you for reading!

Best way to follow for future releases, for now, is the **Trencher's Bunker** *Facebook page or the* Shane Noble *Amazon author page.*

www.ingramcontent.com/pod-product-compliance
Lightning Source LLC
Chambersburg PA
CBHW020534020726
47494CB00006B/1764